For J

--

Jessica Gadziala

FOR A GOOD TIME, CALL...

DEDICATION:

To everyone who has learned to love their scars.

ONE

Fiona

"Oh, yeah baby, stick it in there. Right there. Like that. Mmhmm. Yes, baby. Fuck me harder," I was screaming into the phone. Loud, obnoxious, porn star groaning. I propped my legs up on the headboard, looking at my newly painted toenails. Hazard Pink. I reached upward, wiping at a line that had smudged onto my skin. "Fuck. Oh, fuck. Yes. Yes. Yes!"

I could hear his violent masturbation through the phone. The wet, squishing sound of his hand yanking on his mediocre penis. He was close. He was always easy. A little bit of heavy panting, some filthy talk, then just incoherent mewling and he was screaming out "Mommy" and coming all over his chest.

"Oh. Oh! I want to feel your hot cum inside me. Now, baby. Now!"

I hung up a minute later and held a pillow over my face, laughing. I tried not to judge. I really did. Everyone has their thing. There were the guys who couldn't get off unless you told them what a useless piece of shit they are, how their pencil dick was the most pathetic thing you've ever seen. Then there were the guys who needed you to slap yourself hard so they could imagine they were spanking you because you were such a naughty, naughty girl.

Then there were men like Bob; Bob with his mommy issues; Bob who Freud would have loved; Bob with the oedipal complex. Bob who secretly wanted to fuck his mother.

I tried not to judge.

But it was really hard to keep a straight face when someone was pulling furiously at their peter and cried out for their mother in a pained, little boy voice.

That shit was hilarious.

I got up and went to my small kitchen, walking straight to the coffee machine, the panda face toe separators making me arch my feet up awkwardly as I moved around, adding grounds and fresh water.

I spent almost no time in my kitchen, save for coffee refills when it was too early or too late to go out and get it from the closest coffee house. My oven wasn't even hooked up. My refrigerator had next to nothing in it but milk for my coffee and leftover Chinese takeout cartons.

Still, I had spent a lot of time decorating it. White cabinets, white walls, bamboo counter tops. It was clean, modern. I had a habit of needing things neat. I blamed the hell hole I grew up in.

I was never one of those girls- the girls in the pretty pink dresses with their perfectly french braided hair, skipping rope, making up back stories for their barbies. I wasn't the girl who was read bedtime stories about a snail who wanted to be a triathlete. I wasn't the girl who was told that she could be anything, anything at all that she wanted to be.

So after a few rounds of unsuccessful odd jobs... I became a phone sex operator.

"Your parents would be so proud," my grandmother sneered when I told her. To be fair, I only told her because I knew it would piss her off. I knew it would offend her sensibilities. I was the shame. Never mind the human garbage that was her son. I was the black sheep. I was the disgrace.

I took a work call at her dinner table that night, shoving my beer neck into my throat, gagging on it, as I gave the best fake blowjob performance I could muster. I guess it could be said that I have rather poor impulse control. But the look on her face had been priceless.

I took my coffee out onto my tiny little balcony in my long-sleeved t-shirt and pink undies. No one would see me from that high up. Not that I would care if they could. *Oh no! There's a woman in... panties!* People needed to get a grip. My bare legs were the least offensive thing about me.

It was getting cool. Fall was coming on with the smell of moldering leaves and musty dampness. I took a deep breath, greedy for the change. Hot August was never good to me, spending my days wiping sweat from my brow and hoping my makeup wasn't running. The whole thing made me irritable and short-tempered.

But September was finally releasing its hold on summer and letting Autumn have its reign. I could already feel myself relaxing, my body sinking into the turnover. I could take on the city streets again, walk aimlessly, spend too much money on clothes and shoes and makeup.

I glanced down at my legs, still pasty pale. I had always avoided the sun like the plague, partly because it was just stupid to crisp your skin for the sake of vanity and partly because my thigh tattoo was still healing. It was a black and gray tree, a huge ax sticking out of the trunk with the proverb, *"The ax forgets, but the tree remembers"*. I had been waiting a long time to get it done; a lifetime really. And now that it was there, I couldn't stop looking at it. It was probably partly why I never wanted to wear pants.

I leaned my forearms on the flimsy railing that better sense told me I needed to replace before it gave way under my weight one day.

Below, the city lived up to its promise. People were milling around in endless droves, men and women in suits, tourists with their cameras, the homeless with their cans or soap boxes. No one gave a good goddamn about anyone else. There were no pleasantries, no masks. Everyone was just a proud asshole. They were my kind of people. They were the reason I moved to the city in the first place.

Back when I was eighteen and I was still going strong.

I'd come a long way from those first days. I had shown up with a backpack in my arms full of clothes and what little money I had. Those days were full of clawing hunger and filth and cold and fear. Those days I didn't have a roof or food or safety. Those days that still somehow managed to be better than what I was running away from.

A sound at my right had me turning. It was a sound I recognized because it was the sound my sliding door made every day. Someone was opening the door to the balcony of the apartment next door. Which was impossible because it had been vacant for the past year and a half after the last tenant OD'd on the heroin he was always stabbing into his veins. After three days, the smell was foul enough to send me down to the super and bang on his door until he got his drunk ass up to check things out.

I didn't think they had ever even put an ad up for the vacancy.

But the door was opening and a man was stepping out onto the small space, five feet from me, invading my perfect little privacy.

He looked over at me. He wasn't supposed to fucking look at me. Those were the rules of the City.

But he was looking at me.

TWO

Fiona

He was tall and wide with shoulders like a linebacker and solid down the middle. His arms strained against the material of his black t-shirt. His arms, I noticed with a deep sense of appreciation, were covered in sleeves. Black and gray ink. He had on loose fitting bluejeans, the unmistakable rectangular bulge of a cigarette pack in his front pocket.

He had a strong square jaw that gave him deep cheekbone hollows. His hair, long enough to need to slick back or tuck behind his ears, was black as were the severe-looking eyebrows over his shockingly pale blue eyes. There wasn't a hint of laughter or smile lines. His lips didn't look like the kind that found amusement easily. In fact, he looked like he probably spent all of his time scowling. He was six-feet and three inches of intimidation.

Great, my new neighbor, the psychopath.

Not that I could expect any different in my neighborhood, in my building in particular. For all I knew, there was a meth lab one floor below just waiting to explode and take us all down with it.

That was the kind of place I had set up camp in, on purpose really. I could afford a better place. Phone sex operators actually make bank.

"Are you just going to stare at me all day, or are you going to introduce yourself?" he asked, his voice a deep, gravel sound.

If he wasn't supposed to look at me, he definitely wasn't supposed to speak to me. Neighbors didn't get to know one another. They didn't show up with a welcome pie. That was small town comfort stuff. This was the big, bad City.

And I sure as hell wasn't the girl next door.

"Neither," I said, turning my attention back to the street below. The yellow cabs were speeding by and slamming on their breaks. The lights changed and huge hoards of people crossed the intersections at the same time.

"You know if you're going to keep dressing down for me," he said and I fought the urge to glare at him, "I prefer thongs."

Then there was the double swoosh of the door opening and closing.

That fucker.

I sipped my coffee, fully aware that he was probably sneaking glances at my half-bare ass through his glass door, and not particularly caring. He could go ahead and stare at it. I had to spend endless hours running on the ancient treadmill in the makeshift exercise room the complex boasted of to keep my shit jiggling just the right amount, for nothing other than my own vanity.

So I had a new neighbor. It didn't matter all that much. I made it my business to mind my own goddamn business. I ducked my head if someone entered the hall at the same time that I did. I couldn't point anyone out in a lineup. But I knew things.

The couple across the hall consisted of a dominant wife and weak husband. The nagging that woman was capable of was impressive. The guy on the other side of me was a hermit and a good three-hundred and fifty pounds. He had groceries delivered and made meals to post on his pretentious foodie blog. The people below had three teenage boys who had knock-down, drag out fights daily.

In the end, it didn't matter that he was new. I would find out his thing soon enough: his drug habit, his drug dealing that brought all kinds of unsavory types around that I needed to be aware of, the pets, the psychotic banging on the walls. Whatever his deal was, I would find out sooner rather than later.

I went back into my apartment. My living room was a pale gray color with all white accents: white sofa, white coffee table, white cabinet I kept my television on. The brightness felt clean and safe, almost hospital-like in its sparseness. I had no use for knickknacks. I got my news and fashion fixes online. I kept my clothes clutter in the luxuriously large closet that I had sacrificed a few feet of my already small bedroom to. I didn't need that much space to sleep, but I did need space to hang my endless collection of dresses and jeans and shirts and shoes. Oh, the shoes. My room itself was painted with thick horizontal gray and white stripes, ten inches thick at each turn. I liked it to streamline from the living space and hall.

The inside of my closet, however, was painted a bright crayon yellow. Shoes were stored in their boxes on the floor, four boxes high underneath the massive closet system I had bought online. Bright colors spilled out of the drawers and down from the wire racks.

I reached in, grabbing a red off-shoulder crop top, a pair of black high waisted jeans, and a pair of patent leather heels that matched the shirt. Night would be coming on soon enough and I needed to be prepared.

The days were fine. The days I spent taking calls, cleaning, looking around online, watching TV. The days I kept busy. The nights were the hardest to get through alone in a small apartment with the memories making the walls close in tighter. The memories that could fill up a room and drown me in them.

I almost never stayed in. I was never 'not in the mood' to go out. It didn't matter if it was a Monday night. It didn't matter that I was always alone. It didn't matter. I needed to get out and in a City that never sleeps, there was always something to be found to do.

I put my clothes on the counter in the bathroom, which wasn't really a counter at all. I had had the typical square cabinet torn out and replaced with a long oval ornate antique table with scalloped edges that I had painstakingly painted white then distressed, then painted a pale robin's egg blue, then distressed again until the white was peeking through. I had a guy cut the hole for the sink and put the thing in place in front of an enormous floor to ceiling mirror. I put a small upholstered stool in front of it and used it like a vanity to do my makeup. The walls were the same robin's egg blue as the table.

I took pride in my apartment. I spent a lot of money getting it how I wanted it, even though no one saw it but me. Literally. No one else had stepped foot in it in the two years since I moved in. There was just something in taking a thing as ugly as a cramped New York City apartment and turning it into your own personal sanctuary that gave me the tinglies.

I grabbed a fluffy white towel, reached in to turn the water in the shower on, then stood in front of the mirror and started to slip my shirt off, then my panties. I had a certain kind of appeal. I was five foot seven with thick thighs and a small waist. My boobs would have been the envy of the girls I went to school with... had I gone to school, high and round, ample enough to fill out a blouse nicely without making me look like a cartoon character. My hair was long and blonde, falling in a beach-wavy mass toward my chest, just brushing my nipples. My face was round and soft with a small rosy mouth and big green eyes. My best feature was my skin. Pure and milky. Flawless naturally.

That was, if you could look past the scars.

My hand moved downward, touching the scars that cupped my breasts underneath. They were thick bands, very pink still, even after all the years, and smooth. Scars are so weirdly smooth to the touch. I reached downward toward the outer side of my thigh, the one without the tattoo, and stroked those scars. Those were different scars- a few dozen tiny little straight lines in various stages of healing. They were violent red reminders of why I needed to go out at night.

There were other scars, the worst scars. They were old and almost skin tone. *Almost.* They were scars that were too awful to let myself think about. They were scars I avoided looking at or allowing anyone else to see.

I sighed and climbed into the shower, letting the hot water wash away the growing sense of unease I was feeling. I would take an hour and put myself together, towel drying my hair, applying mascara and eyeliner, getting dressed. By then it would be late enough for me to hit the street and get something for dinner, grab some coffee, maybe find a band playing or an art exhibit or a poetry slam. I just needed something to take me away for a few hours before I had to change tactics and hit a bar.

Then I would shame walk home at 4 AM still half drunk on a Tuesday morning, ready to slip out of my clothes, scrub off my makeup, and fall into bed around five. Then I would sleep until eleven, get up, have some coffee and get ready for my lunch calls. My quickie guys.

The "I want you underneath my desk sucking my cock while I have a meeting" guys. The "I want to bend you over the fax machine and fuck your ass" guys. In other words, my upper-middle class, married, businessmen. Those guys paid my rent each month.

Then the day would be a mismatch of calls. I would do video calls for my executive clients. They were the stockbrokers, the judges, the CEOs. They were the callers who paid a pretty penny to have me tell them how I want to suck them off or fuck their brains out, or tell me to touch myself. And I would pretend to play ding-dong with my clit until they came neatly into a tissue. Those guys made my shopping obsession and endless nights out possible.

I slipped into my shoes that pinched my toes and were bound to keep me in constant pain all night. That was good in a twisted way. Pain was always a good distraction. I could sink into it, it could save me from downing the last few shots of the night. The walk home would be excruciating enough to block all the ghosts out.

I was halfway out my door when I heard his open. I looked down at my feet, clutching my keys in my fist as I quickly moved past him. I wasn't embarrassed. At least, I was never usually embarrassed about my nights out. No one paid much attention. Everyone needed their own kinds of salves for their wounds. It was a fact people in bad neighborhoods generally just accepted about each other. I wouldn't judge you for dropping acid to forget if you didn't judge me for drinking too much to forget.

But I felt embarrassment as I shuffled past him.

The sooner I found out his flaw, the better. He wouldn't be the random guy next door with the piercing eyes and great ink. He would be just another fucked up tenant I could feel normal around.

THREE

Fiona

I had put up with it for three days in a row, which was generous, especially for me, especially given how cranky it was making me and that it was costing me money because I was sleeping past noon.

The new guy started bang-bang-banging around six-thirty every morning. And I don't mean that kind of banging, the banging with the moans and the grunting. I could sleep through a fucking orgy on the other side of the wall. No, this was the sound of hammers on nails and wood and God-knew what else. I tried to let it go. I had done more than my fair amount of improvements since I moved in too, but I had the decency to do it in the middle of the damn day when no one was trying to sleep.

I tried burying my face in my pillow. I tried turning on the TV. I tried turning on music. I tried everything in my power to keep to myself, to not have to go over there.

But by the third morning, I was running on empty and no amount of coffee was going to make up for that kind of lack of sleep.

I crawled out of bed in my white silk pajama pants and matching tank top, throwing open my apartment door and storming next door. I was slamming on his door violently, making it shake in its jamb and one of the copper letters tilt out of place.

"Keep your panties on," I heard from inside, followed by some slamming and shuffling. The door pulled open without the sliding of a lock, which in any neighborhood was foolish; in ours it was downright asking for it. He pulled the door open, keeping a hand on the side of it and looking down at me. I saw his eyes dip down to my breasts, the nipples sticking shamelessly out of the thin, cool material. *Typical.* Then his eyes found mine. "What?"

What? *What?* That was what he was going to go with? Well, I was going to tell him what. "The fucking banging," I said, running a hand through my wild hair. He stood there dumbly, cocking an eyebrow as if he was going to need more than that. "It is six-forty-five in the morning." More eyebrow cocking. "I am trying to sleep," I added, hoping that would make the idiot get the point.

A smirk toyed at the edge of his lips. "It's not my fault you're a vampire," he said, shrugging a shoulder and slamming the door in my face.

I knew I shouldn't have been offended by rudeness. Hell, I was rude, especially with my neighbors. But I was pissed. How dare he? I wasn't going to let it go. I couldn't let it go. I was going to be too damn exhausted to go out that night and then all kinds of bad things were going to happen.

There was one perk to this guy though- an unlocked door. I grabbed the knob and swung it open, barreling into his apartment and grabbing all the hammers I could find off of his makeshift work station: a piece of plywood laid up on old metal saw horses as he looked down at the plans in front of him on that very table. He turned his head at me as I stole his tools, his face impassive.

I left as quickly as I had arrived, three hammers clutched to my chest as I went back into my apartment, locking all four locks, dumping his tools into my kitchen sink, and falling back into bed. I waited for it. A part of me was expecting him to have an extra hammer hidden somewhere and for him to continue his banging, only with more relish. But that didn't happen. I was met, instead, with the much easier to deal with sound of a hand saw. I actually found it almost soothing and I fell back to sleep easily, waking up feeling somewhat less zombie-like around twelve-fifteen, which wasn't so bad. I could still fit in a good three calls at lunch.

I got out of bed, put on the coffee, and grabbed my work phone in a bright pink case that boasted: *Phone sex is OFF THE HOOK!*

I had laughed when I put the special order in online, drunk at five o'clock on a Wednesday morning.

FOUR

Hunter

The girl next door had a lot of sex. I mean, *a lot of sex*. For whatever reason, it was mostly during the day, noon and on until around five when the groaning, moaning, and filthy talk stopped and I could hear her showering and her stereo turning on as she got dressed to go out. Again.

Every night.

I tried not to judge. To each his (or her) own. We all dealt with our shit in different ways. I buried myself in work and half-killed myself at the gym. I worked on my new apartment. She fucked nonstop and drank almost to oblivion every night of the week, coming in at four or five AM, her heels clicking loudly on the linoleum in the hallway.

Since I moved in three days ago, I couldn't stop thinking about her, and it wasn't her drinking habits, or her crazy high sex drive.

It was her eyes.

From that first day when I unlocked the apartment and saw her on her balcony in her panties drinking coffee, she had been invading my thoughts. When she had turned toward me with that delicate little face and big green eyes, I was done for. What man wasn't a sucker for a pair of emerald green eyes?

It didn't matter that she was rude and unsociable. Hell, I was rude and unsociable too. It was half of the appeal to the Godforsaken city, no one was going to ask me to take in their mail or water their plants. No one was going to care what I did with my time. If she were some middle aged woman or some fat guy, I probably would have just inclined my head at them whenever I caught them on the balcony or in the hall.

Her slow, unconcerned about being noticed inspection of me had forced me to engage her.

"Neither." That word had been stuck in my head ever since. Not just the word, the tone in which she said it, like she didn't give a damn about me or what I thought about her. I found that refreshing. It wasn't a common outlook for women, at least not in my experience.

I heard her stumble home that morning around five, still wearing the little black dress, tan fishnets, and thigh high boots. I could hear the boots hitting the floor as soon as she was inside her door, then some shuffling and silence. She was my new wake up call.

Maybe a part of me felt a little guilty for banging early in the morning. But for the first few days, there were no complaints. There was no banging on the wall, no telling me to pipe the eff down. Nothing. So I had just figured she was a deep sleeper.

When I walked over to see who was banging like mad on my door, she had been the last person I was expecting. She had looked mad as a fucking hornet in her white silk pajamas. Her hair looked like she had spent the last hour and a half being thrown around her bed instead of sleeping alone in it. Her eyes were small and red, almost pained looking.

A part of me maybe felt a little bad. Maybe. The other part of me was too into what I was working on to give a shit. It wasn't my problem that she was a heavy partier.

But, damn when she pushed that door open and stormed in, grabbing my hammers like a madwoman... it took everything I had not to bend her over on my makeshift worktable and make her scream all those filthy things she yelled at other guys during the day. A good, solid fuck that was what I was due for.

She was gone before I could even really shake the idea, slamming her front door for good measure. I could have been spiteful and gone into my toolbox and used one of my other hammers. I could have done that, but that would steal the fun of going over there sometime in the near future and getting my stuff back.

All in all, it had been a good move even if the neighborhood, building, and the apartment were several steps down from what I was used to. It was a more expensive city; a downgrade was to be expected. That being said, there was plenty of work to be done and I always liked a good home improvement project. The last place I'd lived, I had spent years getting it how I wanted it to be. I always liked the idea of fixing things up myself.

When I got my hammers back.

Her timing actually wasn't bad. I needed to shower and get to work anyway.

I grabbed my wallet and my two black and metal cases with my guns safely nestled inside and headed out the door. I would be missing the porn show in the next apartment that day, which was disappointing. That woman had some inventive dirty talk.

Sometimes it was downright hilarious.

She'd once whinnied like a horse in the throws of it all.

I had to walk into my bathroom to laugh my ass off in private.

FIVE

Fiona

I threw myself down on the chair at my tiny dining room table, resting my face in my hands. I hated new callers. Granted, new callers were good because you never knew who was going to be a regular and therefore a steady income, but that being said, learning a new guy's perversions was always a feat. Was I their girlfriend? Was I their streetwalker? Was I a kink? Did I need to be spanked and owned? Did I need to be the spanker and owner? Did he want me filthy or sweet?

"Yes," I murmured, hearing his frustrated grunting. "Yes, baby. Right there. Like that." I could hear his breath hitch and had the horrifying realization that he was crying. "You alright?"

There was sniffling on the other end. "I miss her so goddamn much," he cried.

So, apparently that day... I was the therapist.

It was amazing how many men called in for a quick spank and ended up bearing their souls. They needed to tell me about how their wives never let them fuck them anymore; how she lost her sex drive after the kids. Or how they felt like freaks because they get sexually aroused by cartoon characters. Some of my most regular clients called and had a quick jerkoff session and then wanted to talk to me for half an hour about how awful their last date went.

At seventy-five cents per minute, I was making an easy two-thousand a week. Money was especially good because I was independent and didn't have to cut anyone else in, so most of that money was going right into my pocket. Hell, I only worked part time.

"Can you send me a pair of your panties?" new guy asked after he was done crying.

"I'm sorry?" I asked, sitting up straighter.

"Panties. Can you send me a pair of your panties? Like... after you've worn them." No wonder his girlfriend had left him. She probably caught him digging through her dirty laundry and smelling her panties. Oh, the pantie sniffers. "I'll pay you for them."

"Of course you will."

"What will it cost? How do we do this?" he asked, sounding excited.

"Fifty bucks per pair," I told him, coming up with the number easily. I knew it was a thing. When your job is kink, you needed to keep informed of trends and rates. You could usually make a good seventy-five to a hundred for a pair of used panties.

Underneath it all, I had good business sense. Even if my business was non-traditional. I knew what I was doing and I was always ready to capitalize on new ideas. The pictures of my feet went for five dollars a pop, especially when I did different things with them: soaked them and got them nice and pruny, submerged them in honey, covered them in chocolate syrup and sprinkles. Foot fetish guys loved that.

So I was more than a little happy at the idea of a new business venture. I could get panties on the cheap. I could wear them for a day... maybe two, then send them out, charging fifty bucks plus shipping.

"Plus shipping," I added. "And we would handle it like we handle these calls. You log into my account but instead of my invoicing you for the time, you can just transfer the money each time you want a pair."

"Okay. And I'll... add a note with an address."

"Great, Tony," I said, already thinking about the shopping I would need to do, the updating I would have to do to my profiles, and informing of all my callers. "Yup. Uh huh. I know. It was really great. Tomorrow? How about... one PM? Great. Yes. Mmhmm. Bye."

I checked the time, knowing I would probably have at least one more call before the men went home to their families. I went to my closet, picking out an outfit. I grabbed a polka dot t-shirt dress, black tights, a black faux leather jacket, and a pair of chunky black heels.

"Hello?" I said into the phone, slipping my pants down my legs. "Hey... Danny," I said, rolling my eyes. "Nothing much. I am just taking my clothes off so I can take a shower. Mmhmm, Danny. I am a very, very dirty girl."

I reached into the shower and turned on the water. "Oh yeah. I am getting all wet for you. You like that?" I stepped under the stream, holding my upper body away from the water. "Yeah, my teetee is so wet for you." Literally, he made me call my vagina a "teetee". What kind of damage did these guy's parents do to them? It was no wonder they needed to call and talk to me. "Do you want to touch it and see? Yes, I'll stand still while you inspect it. Yes."

"That feels good, doesn't it, sweetie?" he asked, sounding husky.

Danny liked me virginal. Oh, the virgin fetish, always going strong. Every man wants to be the first, the only; maybe because they thought if the girl had no reference to compare him to, then they wouldn't know he was completely and utterly unsatisfying.

Danny wanted us both to be fifteen and first-time touching. He wanted me unsure, turned on, but fearful. It was a careful balance to be maintained.

I made a whimpering sound.

"It's okay that it feels good," he murmured. "I like how you feel. I want to feel you on the inside," he said and I knew he was closing his eyes, getting into it. "I am going to put my finger inside your teetee," he said.

I pause a second then let out another whimper. "Ouch," I say, discarding the knowledge that a finger probably wouldn't hurt when you're fifteen and had been sticking tampons up there every month for the past three years. Then, "Ohhh," sounding airy, surprised, elated at the new sensation. Phone sex operators had to know how to put on a show.

"You're ready for me," he said and I shook my head. Oh yeah, one finger in the heater for two seconds and she's ready for your cock. That was totally how it worked. "I am going to put my rod in you. And it's going to hurt. Just a little, I promise." But he didn't want me to sound like it only hurt a little. He wanted me to cry out like he stuck a fist up there. So I did, the sound echoing off the shower walls. "Ow ow ow ow! Danny?" I cried out, sounding confused.

"You're okay. The worst is over now." Ha. Fat chance. *Stupid guys.* "Oh, you're so hot and tight. Feel how your teetee is holding onto me so tight?"

Then it was all grunting as he got himself really going, imagining his fist was my tight little pussy and he was thrusting wildly into it. I made gasps at first, half pain, half surprise, then it quickly became moans, groans, begging. Then it was just a high-pitched, dramatic "Oh!" and I was finished. And his hands were all sticky.

"Oh, baby," he said, back to his normal adult voice. "You get better and better."

"Why thank you, darling," I cooed, always sweet and accommodating. "You know," I said, turning so the water ran down my cold back, "if you want the panties from today, I can arrange that."

There was a pause, his interest peaked. Hook, line, sinker. "They're pretty white panties aren't they?"

Sure they were. "Of course."

"Great... how do I get them?"

An hour later, and soon to be a hundred dollars richer, I walked out my door and headed into town. Cheap panties, I needed a lot of cheap panties in all different styles and colors: pretty white bikinis, maybe with a little bow for my virgin lovers, red, purple, hot pink thongs for the somewhat normal guys, lace ones, silk ones.

If I timed things right, I could get more than one ready each day. I could wear one pair downstairs to workout in. I could wear another pair out on the town at night. Maybe even a third pair for sleep. Who knew. I wasn't exactly sure how strong an odor they were going for. But if I got sweaty enough, and maybe got myself a little excited here and there... maybe that would do it. Who would pass up the opportunity to use their vibrator more often and call it business?

I got back to my apartment around seven-thirty, a huge bag of panties in my hand, a good thirty pairs. It would be enough to get me started, to see how things went, see if it was going to be worth it in the long run.

Each step up the walk, into the elevator, and across the hall, filled me with more and more dread. I never stopped home, not even to change shoes when my feet were bleeding. Not when it was dark out- dark in my apartment, dark in my head.

But I couldn't exactly go out to a bar with a bag full of unmentionables.

I unlocked my locks, flicked on the light and ignored the strangling sensation in my throat. It was fine. *I* was fine. I just needed to drop the bag in my room and head right back out.

I had just closed my closet when there was a banging on my door. It was loud, insistent, off the hinges banging.

My heart flew into my throat. That was such a corny, overused expression and I hated even thinking it, but that was exactly how it felt. It felt like my heart had pounded free of my rib cage and shot up into my esophagus. That was what dread felt like, the kind of dread that came from banging doors with monsters on the other side, the kind of dread that came from experience.

I backed up into my bedroom, my legs catching the end of my bed and sending me flying onto it. I was trapped. There was no other way out of the apartment. That was stupid. That was something that I had never considered before- the need for a fire escape. Stupid, stupid me.

"Open up, Sixteen," a vaguely familiar voice called. But it wasn't the voice I was afraid of, not the one that brought back the memories. It was the voice of my pain in the ass noisy neighbor. What the hell could he possibly want?

"Fuck off," I called, walking into the living room, watching the door like it might push inward at any moment. He was big enough to make that happen.

"Open up or I'll take it off its hinges," he said and I knew he meant it.

"With what tools?" I called back, thinking of the hammers still in my sink.

"Aw sugar, it's amazing what can be done with a screwdriver if you know what you're doing."

Oh, hell.

"Fine," I grumbled, sliding the locks, but leaving the chain on and pulling the door open just wide enough to see him through. "What do you want, Fourteen?"

"Well, here's the thing," he started, his light blue eyes watching me through the three inch gap, "some crazy bitch broke into my apartment and stole all my hammers."

Frustrated, I grabbed the chain and pulled it, mostly because I wanted to really see him when I put him in his place. "It's not breaking in if the door isn't even locked," I said, opening the door up fully.

"Think the law would see it that way?" he asked.

"I think the law would see your construction noise at six in the morning to be a complete violation of the noise ordnance," I countered.

"Nicely done," he said, nodding and I thought he was going to back off. But then his arm shot out and slammed into the door, pushing it, and therefore me, out of his way and stepping into my foyer.

"Get out," I practically growled at him. Out. He needed to get out. I never let anyone into my personal space. No one. Yet there he was, a huge mass of man that made the space feel cramped and claustrophobic. I needed him out. Out. Out. Out. Who did he think he was barging into my personal space? A little voice in the back of my mind whispered that maybe I shouldn't have barged into his first then. But I told that nosy bitch to stuff it.

"I want my stuff," he said, watching my hand as it went to my neck and stayed there, finding myself unable to really suck in a breath properly.

"Fine," I said. "They're in the kitchen sink. Just take them and go."

He nodded at me, walking into the kitchen and I heard the scraping as he pulled the hammers out of the sink. "You did a lot of work in here," he said, sounding impressed. "It came out nice," he added, coming back toward me. But he didn't turn and go for the door. He walked past me, bumping my shoulder and moving into my living room. "It's very... clean."

"Thank you," I said through gritted teeth. He needed to leave. My chest was feeling tight.

Then he was walking down my hall, reaching into the bathroom and turning the light on. "Wow, this is well done. I like the table. That's different."

At that point, I just stopped breathing. Literally. No air was coming in or going out. He walked into the hallway again, me following dumbly behind him. He reached for my bedroom door handle and I couldn't take it anymore. "No!" I yelled, pushing myself between him and the door, looking up at him, not caring if he saw the raw panic in my eyes. I just needed him out. Right then. He could not, absolutely could not go into my bedroom. "No," I said again, more needy, more pathetic, hating myself for it. "Please."

He looked down at me for a long minute, his blue eyes searching mine. In the end, he backed up a foot, nodding. "Okay," he said, turning and walking back toward the front door. "See you around..."

Ugh. An introduction? Really? Weren't we intimate enough for neighbors?

"Fiona," I gave in. The sooner he was out, the sooner I could curl up into a ball. It was too late to go out. I was too worked up for alcohol to take the feelings away.

He nodded. "Hunter," he said. He opened the door and stepped into the hall. "See you around, Fee," he said, closing the door.

I went behind him and fastened all my locks, then walked into the bathroom, stripping off my clothes. There was a strange anticipation in my belly, like turning, like your belly does on a fast spinning carnival ride. That was always how I felt *before*. I reached around underneath my table sink vanity, looking for the smooth feeling under my searching fingers. Finding it, my nails dug at the corners and ripped the tape away, the razor blade falling into my hand.

I sat down on the cold tile floor in my undies, pulling my thigh up across my tattooed leg, taking a deep breath and looking at my half-healed scratches. It would help. It always helped.

I just had to bleed it out then bleach all the evidence down the drain.

SIX

Fiona

The panties sold well. One week in, I was on back order. It turned out that two times a day with a little working out or vibrator action was good enough. I sealed them in plastic sandwich baggies with a big round sticker on front with a lipstick kiss on it. Different shades for different guys.

I couldn't have been happier with an extra few hundred dollars in my pocket each week. I literally wouldn't be able to spend that kind of money; no matter how lavishly I pampered myself; no matter how much money I dropped on booze. I would be socking a good amount away for a rainy day, maybe for some other career path some day. Maybe I could open my own sex toy store or something, something that was all mine.

I slipped into a bright neon green thong, a special request, and got dressed for my night. It was Saturday. I needed to dress to impress if I wanted to get into anywhere decent. Even knowing all the bouncers wasn't going to help if I showed up looking like crap.

I grabbed a galaxy printed mini skirt and a blue tank top with a huge metal zipper up the center. You could literally just reach out and unzip me and *hello ladies!* I slipped into a pair of bright pink heels that matched a smattering of stars on the skirt, tied my hair back, and headed for the door. I would be freezing, but no one wanted to carry a jacket to a club.

"You could come home with me baby," a guy said, his breath hot on my ear. He had asked to buy me a round three rounds ago. I refused. I always refused. I paid my own way. Most men expected more than a polite 'thank you' when they had to come out of pocket.

"Nope," I said, feeling the room start to swirl pleasantly. That was the good point in the night, the lightness, the twirling. The beginning of the night was fighting demons and trying to get to the perfect drunk. The whole night after was spent trying to maintain the right kind of high without crashing or overdoing it and ending up vomiting a few hundred bucks into the toilet.

I was good. All I wanted to do was dance, get lost in the music, get lost in the generalized heated energy, get lost in the throbbing sex of a room full of people trying to get laid. That was as close to actual sex as I ever got.

The guy was going to kill my buzz.

"You know you want to. You've been flirting with me all night."

He wasn't wrong. I flirted. I schmoozed. I got wrapped up in the nothingness of my own company. Since it meant nothing to me, it couldn't mean much to them. Such was my drunk logic. Sober me knew not to poke a sleeping bear, and that was exactly what a horny guy at a club was.

"Sorry," I said, pulling away from the hand that was trying to stroke my neck. "I'm not interested." I walked quickly toward the dance floor, getting myself lost in the crowd. He could find someone else: drunker, looser, more willing to do a different kind of shame walk home than I was.

I pushed into the center of the crowd, turning myself in slow circles, my hips moving suggestively around, my arms up in the air. Lost. God, how *good* it was to get lost. I left the floor for the occasional refill, only to get right back on. I stayed there until I felt the sweat trickle down my neck, until my feet started to hurt beyond the numbing effects of alcohol, until the place started clearing out, which was always around three AM. That was when the more decent people decided to head back home alone or with someone else, deciding they had had enough debauchery and liver punishment for one night.

I moved back to the bar, nodding at the bartender who poured me two shots and then handed me my tab which I paid, but sat and waited with my shots until I needed them, until the fog started to clear, then I threw one back. The DJ started packing his stuff up and the radio turned on, classic rock replacing the brain-throbbing house garbage. I watched as the bartender cleaned glasses and capped the bottles. I heard the last few souls exit and one of the bouncers came in and took a seat next to a waiting two fingers of whiskey.

He was a huge man, six and a half feet of muscle and fat that could break through a crowd like a human battering ram. He had dark brown skin and a huge diamond earring in one of his lobes, but the kindest eyes I had ever seen.

"Drunk Girl," he said, nodding his head at me.

"What's up, Guy?"

"You're gonna need a transplant at this rate. Switch to pot or pills, girl."

"I did the pot thing a few years ago," I admitted. Oh, the silly oblivion. Unfortunately, booze worked better. "And I'm not a pills kinda girl."

He nodded, holding his whiskey out and I clinked my shot to his glass and I threw back the gin, enjoying the quick burn. "Need me to walk you home? It's late," he added unnecessarily.

"Is it starting to get light yet?" I asked, feeling like the night had gone way too fast to be sunrise already.

"Another fifteen and you'll see the sun pop over the buildings," he said, knowing the deal. I was at this bar twice a week, every week. We had had this conversation at least fifty times before.

"Okay," I said, feeling more tired than I usually did. I hopped up off my stool. "I think I am heading out then," I said, walking past him and placing a hand on his shoulder, a rare show of physical contact for me, but he was always good to me. "Thanks for the offer, Guy, but I got it tonight. I'm only a block away."

"Be careful," he said, nodding. "Nothing but unsavory people out this late."

"Not half as unsavory as me," I promised, making my way to the door.

I pushed into the night, throwing my head back to look at the still-dark sky, enjoying the cool air on my overheated skin. I took a deep breath, the air smelling of stale cigarette smoke, pot, and vomit. It was a familiar, almost comforting combination. I turned and started my walk home, my keys poking out from between my fingers.

It was a quick walk, and I always enjoyed the quiet. In the city that never sleeps, the only time you can be even the slightest bit alone on the streets was between four and five AM. You could see the occasional cab or homeless person, maybe even a stupid teenager or two, but, all in all, it was a nice kind of solitude.

That was until you felt someone grab you from behind just as you are about to go into your building. That was until you needed help and there was none to be had.

I screeched, swinging out with my keyed fist, but a hand grabbed my wrist and pinned it above my head, crushing until my keys fell with a quiet clatter to the ground.

And then there he was, the guy from the bar, the one who wanted to take me home. I had shrugged him off as harmless. *Stupid, stupid girl.* I would never learn.

"You think you can get me all hot and bothered and then just up and leave me, you stupid little slut?" His breath smelled like vodka and cigarettes, up close it was overpowering and nauseating. "Do you have any idea who the fuck I am?" he demanded, his face close enough that I could feel his spit on my cheeks.

My free hand cocked as far back as the building behind my back would allow, swinging and slamming into his ribs. But it came out weak and only made him grunt and grab that arm too and slam it against the brick behind me. He shifted his hands, taking both my wrists in one of his. His other hand moved for a moment to my throat.

Panic for me was a strange thing. As someone who had struggled with severe anxiety issues pretty much since I was eight years old, it always had its own strange pattern, its own personal triggers: not having my place clean, having people in my space, nighttime in general. Specific things I knew I couldn't let happen.

But in that moment, with a genuine need to elicit a fight-or-flight reaction, my body felt oddly calm, almost numb. I could blame the booze, but in reality, I felt almost sober. My body just didn't want to send me the surge of adrenaline it needed. Stupid, confused body.

"I don't give a fuck who you are," I yelled, loud enough for the dog in the apartment behind me to start barking manically. I could smell fresh smoke and I wondered if anyone was close enough to hear me if I screamed.

But then his hand tightened around my throat and I couldn't

get a scream out if I tried. "You're such a bitch. You're lucky you're so damn pretty," he said, leaning closer and crushing his lips to mine.

If I thought the smell of vodka and cigarettes was bad, the taste of it was worse. I slammed my lips together, holding them firm and practically un-kissable, but he seemed undeterred as he pressed his mouth against mine hard enough to bruise. His fingers dug into my throat, making the breath get stuck there and my face feel foreign and tingly.

Just when I thought I might pass blissfully out, his hand slid lower, touching the bare skin above the top of my shirt. His fingers grabbed one of my breasts, squeezing painfully. "Stop!" I managed through my sore throat, my voice coming out hoarse.

"Shut up. You like it," he growled, his hand finding the zipper and pulling it down.

The cool air hit my bare skin as the zipper slid down, making my nipples harden as if agreeing with his argument. His hand was just starting to graze the bare swell of my breast and I finally felt the panic building. The panic which, completely unreasonably, was more about the ugly scars underneath my breasts than it was about the fact that I was going to get raped five feet from my front door. His finger was about to graze my nipple when he was pulled violently away from me and sent five feet backward, sprawling into the street.

Then there was my neighbor. Fourteen. Hunter. He was straddling the man across the middle, slamming his fists into the guy's face with a sort of savage ruthlessness that I didn't want to see, but also couldn't look away from. Blood was everywhere... covering the guy's face, on the street, on Hunter's hands and shirt. Everywhere. It was impossibly bright and dark at the same time, the rising sun making it look almost cinematic.

It seemed like he planned on bashing his face in until he killed him and judging from the murderous look on his face, I was sure he was completely capable of doing just that. Then just as suddenly as it started, it stopped. Hunter sat back on his heels, breathing hard as he looked down at the guy for a long minute. He stood slowly, reaching down and grabbing the guy, dragging him out of the road and leaving him on the sidewalk.

He turned back to me, grabbing his cell phone out of his pocket and holding it up. I had a second of confusion before a bright light flashed and I realized he had taken a picture of me. Just in case, I figured, some cops came looking.

"Cover up, Sixteen," he said casually.

I wanted to, I really did. I glanced down to where the center of my chest was exposed. If you looked closely enough, you could see the very edges of the scars. I wanted to hide them, but my arms stayed heavy at my sides. My eyes went to his, blank. I felt so weirdly blank.

He exhaled a breath, moving a step closer and reaching for the two ends of the fabric, quickly putting the zipper into place and pulling it up. "Come on, Fee," he said, holding an arm out, gesturing toward the door. "Fee," he said, snapping a few times loudly next to my ear. "Snap out of it. I need to get you inside."

I watched him like through a window, like a television show, like he wasn't actually speaking to me, his words sounding far away and fuzzy. He stooped down, grabbing my keys off the sidewalk and holding them in his hand as he slowly started to reach out for me.

The fact that I didn't flinch away from him like he was made of fire was a testament to how zoned out I was in that moment. One of his arms slipped under my knees and the other around my back, picking me up off the ground and holding me against his chest. I felt the jostling of my body as he went up the stairs, the dropping sensation of the elevator as we got on the floor, then how he struggled to hold me and figure out my complicated locks.

He carried me into my apartment, depositing me on the cold

bathroom floor and turning to wash the blood off his hands in the sink. I watched as he scrubbed, looking down at his hands as he did so, his face impassive.

I felt hot. That was the only thing that broke through my comfortable little numbness: I was so unbearably hot. I lowered myself down on the floor, turning onto my side away from him and curling slightly up into the cool feeling.

The water turned off and I heard him turn and move closer, getting down on his knees behind me. I hadn't noticed my skirt had bunched up until I felt his fingertips whisper across the still stinging cuts on my thigh. "Oh, Fee," he said, sounding unbearably sad for someone so big and mean.

I closed my eyes against the knowledge that he was looking at my self-inflicted scars and wounds. I couldn't process that right then. I couldn't deal with that shame on top of everything else. I took a few deep breaths, feeling the pulling sensation of sleep and surrendering to it.

SEVEN

Fiona

I woke up on the bathroom floor, which wasn't completely unheard of, though it had been a really long time since that happened. The weird thing was the fuzziness in my brain, like I was hungover. I didn't *get* hungover. You wouldn't be able to drink the way I drank if you woke up with a blinding headache, feeling dried out every morning.

I pushed myself off the tile, sitting up and looking around with my sleepy eyes.

My throat hurt, a strange mix of pain and burning. I brought my hand up, noticing the bruise around my wrist and feeling a second of horror before the memory came back. Had I been so drunk that I had passed out? Then been... assaulted in some way? I glanced down at my shirt and had the blindingly bright image of his hands pulling the zipper down.

Then it all came flooding back, making me feel an awful cocktail of anger, fear, regret, and shame that made me dizzy. I crawled across the floor to the padded stool in front of my sink, pulling myself up onto it and looking at myself in the mirror.

It wasn't pretty.

My hair, as per usual, even without a bed to roll around in, was a mess. It had fought the confines of my hair tie and there were wavy strands falling around my face. My lips looked swollen with a hint of purple beneath the pink, easy enough to cover up with a little lipstick. My throat was red and purple and blue, a rainbow band completely across the front, tapering off to visible fingerprints at one end. My eyes looked bloodshot. I turned on the tap, washing my hands, pretending to ignore the blue bands around my wrists, then scrubbing at my face. I furiously brushed my teeth to try to get the taste of him out.

I stood up, noticing I was barefoot and completely at a loss for how that might have happened. I needed a clock and some coffee. How much time had I actually lost?

The smell of fresh coffee hit me as soon as I stepped into the hallway and I instinctively retreated a foot back into the bathroom before taking a deep breath and realizing that Fourteen must not have left.

Hunter. I probably should have started thinking of him by his name since he saved me from pretty definite rape only a few hours before, then brought me back to my apartment when I was in some kind of PTSD daze, where he had laid me on the floor and... oh fuck. He'd seen the self-injury scars. Great. That was just great. Now I was going to get his damn sympathy. I didn't need that shit. Little did he know, my digging blades into my skin was a hell of a lot less traumatic than what drove me to do it in the first place.

Oh well. I was going to have to face him sooner or later. It would be good to just rip the bandage off and get on with my day. I would just take a cab home in the future when I came home in the morning. No biggie. Future crises averted.

I took a deep breath and headed into the hallway, not caring about my crazy hair and smudged eye makeup. I wasn't trying to impress my neighbor. Besides, I needed to face him so I could kick him out and get showered.

He was in my kitchen, sitting on top of my counter, drinking coffee out of one of my mugs and reading a newspaper that was definitely not mine. "Just make yourself at home," I grumbled, reaching for a coffee cup and filling it.

"I picked up some bagels," he said, gesturing toward the brown bag on the counter. "I didn't know what kind you liked so I picked up a variety."

I felt my eyebrows draw together. He... went out and bought me bagels? Why the hell would he do that? "Why?"

"They're not free. I want payment in sex," he said, looking over when I didn't laugh. His brows drew lower over his eyes like he couldn't understand why I was asking why he did something like buy a virtual stranger an assortment of bagels.

I reached in the bag, searching around. Maybe it said something about the company I kept that such a small act of kindness like picking up breakfast after a somewhat traumatic event was shocking. And since I only kept my own company... it said something about *me*, about how messed up I was. I dug out an egg bagel, all plump and yellow. "Thank you," I said, the words sounding clumsy on my tongue.

He nodded. "There's cream cheese and butter in those little containers," he said, gesturing to the throw away condiment containers on the counter. I bowed my head as I cut open the bagel and spread butter on it. He watched me the whole time, his head turned toward the side looking at me, no doubt, like I didn't make sense. I knew I didn't. "You alright?" he asked after I had chewed a small bite.

I shrugged a shoulder, non-committal, unwilling to admit I was just pushing that morning's events into the vault with all the others. They were just more things to drown at the bottom of a bottle; just more things to spend my life running away from facing.

"I've had better mornings," I said, picking up my coffee.

"That's it?" he asked, looking almost angry. "Four hours ago, you were minutes away from being raped out front of your house and you've... had better mornings?" At my blank look, he hopped down off the counter, walking over to me and grabbing the coffee cup out of my hands and putting it on the counter behind me. He reached out, his hand lining up over the bruises on my throat, hovering away from my skin for a moment, I guessed to see if he would find a reaction. When he didn't, he pressed against the sore marks. "Seriously? This means nothing to you?"

Oh, please. It would be nice if the worst thing that ever happened to me was a hand pressing into my throat. But I assumed for most women... that was horrifying enough. "You won't hurt me," I said instead, looking up into his light eyes.

"Why would you say that? I busted a guy's face in last night right in front of you. You have no idea what I am capable of."

I reached up, watching my own hand like it wasn't attached to me because I couldn't possibly be doing what I was doing. I rested my hand over his on my neck. It was just a whisper of a touch, but a touch nonetheless. "You might be capable of a lot of things," I said, looking back up into his eyes, "but not this."

I saw him take a breath, slow, steadying. His hand softened on my skin, brushing over the bruises before falling. My own hand fell down at my side. "No. Never that," he agreed, taking a step back. He shook his head, as if clearing it of some nagging thought. "So you're fine?"

"I'm fine," I agreed.

He exhaled a breath through his nose, short, almost like a snort but without the noise. "You're all kinds of fucked up, Sixteen," he said, grabbing his paper and heading out of the room. I heard the door close before I exhaled.

All kinds of fucked up. He had no idea.

But that didn't mean I couldn't at least... try to be a

somewhat decent human being toward him, especially since he had been nothing but nice to me so far. Not everyone needed to be kept at a distance.

I showered, took my calls, packed up some panties, and ran out the door around five. I would miss out on a few calls, but I needed to get back home and then back out before it got dark. That night especially.

I walked into the store feeling oddly self-conscious, which was stupid. Among the shitstorm of awfulness of my childhood, I did get an education on manners, whether anyone who met me would believe it or not. My grandmother had sat me down and pounded the rules of decent society into me, as ironic as that was at the time.

I remembered the lesson on new neighbors: You should always go over and introduce yourself, bring a baked good, but only if you made something really well, really memorable. My grandmother said this, knowing I knew damn well that she had never baked a thing in her whole life. There were servants for tasks like that. But her housekeeper made the best peach cobbler this side of the Mason-Dixon line.

If you were not culinary inclined, she would say with a very pointed look at me and my mother, then you should bring a plant. That way, any time they had to water it, they thought of you. That was so ridiculous even to my nine year old ears that I had to bite my tongue to keep from smart mouthing her.

I picked out the manliest pot I could find, a white skull, and picked out a three-pronged cactus plant to be put in it. The girl at the counter was actually willing to transplant it for me and I took it feeling foolish.

Would it really be that hard to do a nice thing? Was I so messed up that I had to feel like an insecure child when I stepped just slightly out of my comfort zone?

In the end, it didn't matter how I felt. Plant in hand, I walked past the dried bloodstains still on the road and sidewalk, into my building, then up to my floor.

I stopped out front of fourteen, taking a deep breath, before reaching up and knocking on the door.

EIGHT

Hunter

The damn couple across the hall was what woke me up, arguing at four in the morning like maniacs. I got up with a sigh, heading out onto the balcony for a cigarette. That was when I saw her walking down the street, drunk again, but able to keep a straight line.

The guy came out of nowhere, slamming her against the wall and out of my view. I should have reacted then. With her active sex life, though, I just figured it was one of her guys surprising her with some quick, rough, outdoor sex. I couldn't judge them for that. It sounded like a good time.

Then I heard her yell, loud enough for the dogs in the building to stir. "I don't give a fuck who you are." Then I was running, through my apartment, into the elevator that was too damn slow in that kind of situation, then out onto the sidewalk.

"Shut up. You like it," the guy had said, reaching and groping her breasts.

I lost my shit.

I had been so good for so long, keeping myself calm, keeping myself out of situations that could trigger the all-consuming rage that could pop up, that I had trouble reining it in once it started. In that moment, any control I may have had slipped away as I barreled toward the guy, grabbing the back of his neck and hauling him into the street.

I spared Sixteen the barest of glances to make sure she wasn't hurt, and then I went apeshit on the guy, straddling his middle and banging my hands into his face. I forgot how good it felt. God, how fucking good it felt- to feel your hands smash into soft flesh, to hear the bones underneath snapping. There wasn't a high like that in the world. At least, not for me, not for someone with my history.

I was out of breath before the alarm started ringing in my head- loud, shocking. I sat back on my heels, looking down at the torn flesh, the swollen eye sockets and lips, the mess of a mangled face I had created. I couldn't say I hated the sight.

I dragged him back onto the sidewalk with the full realization of what I had done and the repercussions there could be if I got caught. I pulled out my phone and snapped a picture of Sixteen: her eyes huge and scared, the marks already forming on her neck, the bruised and fat lips, the open blouse. It would be proof enough that he got what the fuck was coming to him if trouble did come knocking.

I slipped my phone into my pocket, trying to keep my eyes on her face. When she wouldn't, or couldn't, cover herself, I let my eyes drop for the shortest possible amount of time while I zipped her up. Then I had to pick her up and carry her up to her apartment. It was strange to see a woman like her, a woman who seemed so badass and untouchable, be so completely vulnerable.

I carried her into her bathroom and set her on the floor, turning to wash the blood off my hands like I had done countless times before. I watched it lighten and swirl around the sink before going down the drain.

I heard her moving and turned, watching as she rolled onto her side, curling up into herself. Her skirt hitched up and her full left thigh became visible. I knelt down on the floor behind her, reaching out. Unable to stop myself from touching them- the dozens of red, pink, and white marks from a careless blade and self-loathing hand. I knew she had issues, but *damn*.

It took more than most people realized to sink a blade into your own skin. The sensation of animalistic self-preservation was hard to overcome. You had to really need the rush of relief to be able to make yourself do it. Sixteen had some demons. And instead of facing them, she was burying them in all the sex, in the alcohol, in the splitting of her own flesh. She was spending her life punishing herself.

She fell asleep quickly on the floor and I didn't want her to wake up in her bed, confused, and freaked out at how she got there, so I left her on the floor. I took off her shoes before going into my apartment to change into something less bloodstained before coming right back.

Because, on top of everything else, she shouldn't wake up alone, not after that kind of night. I slipped out around eight to grab some food after getting a look inside her refrigerator. I came back, ate a bagel, made a pot of coffee, and read the paper, sure she would wake up sometime around ten or eleven.

But she came out a few minutes later, looking exactly as awful as I thought she would. Her hair was falling out of its band, her eye makeup was smudged out toward her hairline, her throat and wrists were bruised painfully.

"I've had better mornings."

I wanted to throttle her. I really did. I had never met someone so incredibly frustrating in my whole life and I had met a bunch of pain in the ass people. So I went up to her, trying to get a reaction, trying to show her that what had happened to her was all kinds of wrong. But she looked up at me with those huge green eyes and told me I wouldn't hurt her. And offuckingcourse I wouldn't hurt her, but that wasn't the point.

She shouldn't have been fine. Of all the things she should have been: shocked, angry, horrified, hurt, sad, vulnerable, vengeful... "fine" was not one of them.

But, perhaps even more than she was fucked up, she was stubborn. Pushing at her wasn't going to get me anywhere except maybe locked out behind one of those huge walls she had around her. And I preferred the opportunity to be able to at least speak to her again. I didn't know why. Maybe it was just the mystery she had about her. Maybe I just wanted to figure her out.

Or maybe I just needed to go out and get laid. It wasn't like me to obsess about some chick living next door. It was probably all of the loud, kinky sex she had that was making me get all worked up about her.

There was a knocking on my door sometime after six that night- light, hesitant knocking, so I knew it wasn't the hellcat next door. No one from my past knew where I was so I grabbed a hammer off the table and went to the door.

Then there she was, in a pair of blue skinny jeans and a tight golden sweater, holding a potted cactus out at me and looking completely petrified. "Sixteen," I said as way of greeting, inclining my head at her.

She looked down at her feet for a second which were stuck into a pair of brown leather boots with four inch heels. I didn't know how the hell she was able to wear all of the ankle-breaking shoes I always saw her in all the damn time. "I... I ... ah..." Was she stammering? Seriously? The chick with the chip on her shoulder and walls higher than Mount Everest was nervous? "Here," she said, pushing the cactus out until I took it. "It's a... 'welcome to the building and thanks for saving me from rape' gift."

"Wow, they have a whole section for that, huh?" I asked, trying to lighten the mood.

It worked a little. She snorted, shaking her head. "Look, I know I'm a bitch and I am really, really bad at the whole human interaction thing," she started, her green eyes looking even bigger with her hair pulled and braided down her back. She looked younger, almost soft. "But I do have manners. And you were good to me..."

"Hard for you to say that, huh?" I asked, watching the look of discomfort on her face. "Consider us even. You haven't been assaulted and I have... a... cactus."

She smiled then, a strange, self-deprecating kind of smile. "I figured you would think of me whenever you saw it."

Because she was prickly, I thought and laughed, the sound foreign to my own ears. When was the last time I had really laughed?

"That was pretty damn clever, Sixteen."

"I thought so," she said, shrugging. "Well... um... I just wanted to drop that off. I have to go..."

"Gotta get ready to go out and drink again," I supplied and I swear I saw a trace of embarrassment cross her face. "Tell you what," I started, not even sure what I was about to suggest until it was out of my mouth, "why don't you just... hang out with me tonight instead?"

She glanced worriedly out past me toward the balcony. "No. That won't work. You don't understand."

"Then help me understand," I suggested.

She ran a hand over her eyebrows, her shoulders slumping slightly. A part of me wanted to tell her never mind, to go do whatever it was she did at night just so she didn't keep looking as anxious as she did right then.

"I can't be home at night," she said before I could tell her she didn't have to tell me. "Like... when it's dark. I can't be home."

"Not even with company?" I asked, more than a little curious about why a grown woman was still, for all intents and purposes, afraid of the dark.

"I wouldn't know... I never have company," she rolled her eyes. "You were the first person to be in my house and only then because..."

"I barged in."

"Exactly."

"So what's the harm? I'll cook something. We'll watch a movie. Whatever. Give your liver a break. I mean... what's the worst that could happen if you're home at night..." I started and her eyes darted immediately downward. *Ashamed.* "Oh," I said, thinking about her cuts. So that was the deal. The nights she didn't go out, which, since I moved in, was one, those nights, she cut. "Well... whatever. I won't judge."

She looked up then, her eyes relieved, like I had offered her a life vest when she was drowning, like no one else had ever just blindly accepted her problems before. And I realized with a feeling of sympathy for her that no one probably ever had.

"Come here," I said, looking down at her, watching as she stepped past the doorway. I knew it was bad timing. I knew we shouldn't... but I couldn't fucking help it.

NINE

Fiona

He was going to kiss me. *Holy fucking hell.* He was actually going to... kiss me. I had to admit, of all the things I thought might happen when I knocked on his door: yelling and arguing came to mind. Making plans to hang out and getting kissed were certainly not on the list of possibilities.

He moved closer, closing the door behind me and slowly backing me up into it. There was a strange lightness in my stomach, a quick, insistent and undeniable fluttering. My neighbor was giving me freaking butterflies.

I felt the cool door behind my back, hard and unbending. I pressed against it, hoping it would shake me out of it, ground me. Because he was right in front of me, as close as he could get without touching me and his eyes looked heavy-lidded and I swear all I wanted to do was melt into him.

And that was fucking terrifying.

His hands went around me, landing on the door on either

side of my head. He leaned down toward me, making me tilt my head upward to keep my eyes on his. I found myself suddenly lost in them. His body moved slowly forward. His knees brushed mine, then his thighs, his pelvis, his stomach, chest. His boot-covered feet slid in between my heels, holding my legs slightly open.

His head dropped lower and I felt his breath warm on my cheek.

What was taking him so long? I could have sworn my entire body felt like it was standing on edge, like it was waiting for the contact, like it wouldn't survive if I didn't get it. How long had it been since I was kissed? Longer than I wanted to think about. Years? Probably.

The last time I remembered was in a bar the first week I moved into my apartment, some random hot guy who was more than willing to accommodate me after one too many drinks and sexy songs from the speakers. I had grabbed his face and pulled him down to me. I remember it being frustrating and lacking.

I took a deep breath, watching Hunter. He leaned in quickly, taking my lips into his. I swear white sparks went off at the contact. I heard myself whimper as he pressed hard, taking my lower lip between both of his and sucking. There was a bolt of desire from my belly and downward, making me want to clench my thighs together, but his feet were holding them apart. His teeth dug into my lower lip, moving slightly back and forth. My arms went out, grabbing the sides of his hips, as much contact as I felt like I could initiate.

He grunted, his tongue thrusting forward into my mouth. I felt my body shudder and his arms moved downward, encircling my back and trapping my arms to my sides. I was completely at his mercy and I realized with more than a small shot of fear, that I was completely comfortable with that.

Hunter pulled my body tight against his. I sighed into his mouth, pressing my tongue into his, getting lost in the sensations. I felt like I was floating and drowning at the same time, like I was fully submerged, but free.

That's what kissing Hunter felt like: freedom, after a life of being imprisoned.

His teeth grazed my lower lip then started planting soft, quick kisses over my lips, before they left me entirely. I whimpered and I could feel his laugh come out as air across the bridge of my nose. He rested his forehead against mine, still holding me against him. "So... pasta for dinner?" he asked, infuriatingly calm while I felt like my body was in utter chaos.

His arms slid downward then released me and he pulled the door open, moving me with it until I stepped out of the way. Was he kicking me out? It seemed like the sonofabitch was kicking me out. Then he was slowly closing the door and I was sure of it. I was getting kicked out. What the actual hell?

I walked back to my apartment, unlocking the door, closing it, then collapsing against it.

So... that just happened. I slowly slid down to the floor, pulling my legs to my chest and encircling them. I felt frustration laced through every fiber of my being. Every bit of me was craving something it knew I wouldn't give it. Horny was horny, but this felt like more. This felt stronger. This felt overpowering.

Maybe it was because I spent all my time denying the possibility of sex. My body got used to not having it. It wasn't even an issue anymore. I dealt with the physical frustration with the aid of my trusty vibrator.

But now I got a taste of what I had been missing out on, what I had denied myself, and my body was reacting with years worth of repressed need. My skin felt like it was humming with it. I pressed my thighs together for a second, a hand going to my lips. If there was ever a kiss to end the famine, that was the one. A huge feast of a kiss. That was great and all, but then I was kicked out... like some common whore. That was simply *unacceptable*. I heard his door slam shut and the elevator chime then stood up and made my way to my bedroom.

Good. I wanted him to leave.

I slipped out of my shoes and jeans, then reached in my nightstand.

Thank god for vibrators.

I lay down on the bed and twisted it on, closing my eyes and trying to get lost in the sensation, trying to ease the aching desire. But ten minutes later, I brought it into the bathroom, dropping it in the sink and running the water over it. My O was not going to make an appearance.

I blamed Hunter.

I went back to my closet and picked out a quick outfit: a plain tight black club dress, black tights, and a pair of polka dotted shoes. I wouldn't go back to the same club I was at the night before. It just didn't feel right. I would go back eventually; maybe in a week or two. Besides, I usually didn't do the same place two nights in a row anyway.

I pulled my hair out of its braid, grabbed my wallet, and went to the door.

"That's a little overdressed for pasta and movies, don't you think?" Hunter asked, standing in the open door holding a brown bag in his arm.

I thought it was canceled. I really did. I wouldn't have gone through the work of getting changed if I thought we were still on for the night.

"I didn't think we were still doing that."

"Why?" he asked as if genuinely perplexed as to why I would think that. So kissing your neighbors was totally normal for him then. Jackass.

Well, fine. I could play the *who can pretend to care less* game. And what's more... I would win. I had been playing this particular game my whole life.

"I heard you leave," I said, shrugging a shoulder.

"Yeah, to buy groceries, for dinner, remember?" he asked, holding up the bag. "Why don't you slip into something that doesn't look like you could work a corner in it and come back out to help me?"

I rolled my eyes, let him pass, closed the door, and slid all the locks. "I hope you can cook in the microwave. I don't have the stove hooked up," I informed him, making my way back toward my bedroom.

What outfit would make the absolute best barrier between me and him and my still throbbing desire? I slipped into a pair of tight jeans and an oversize gray long-sleeved t-shirt. I pulled my hair back again. I might not have been a cook, but I knew hair in the food was generally frowned upon.

When I walked back into the kitchen, he was already boiling water on the stove. Across my counter was an assortment of vegetables and herbs, a box of whole wheat pasta, a small carton of heavy cream, and a plastic container of Parmesan cheese.

"I hooked up your stove. I mean... you seriously have never even made mac and cheese in here in..."

"Two years," I supplied, walking over to the cherry tomatoes.

"Two years? You order takeout every night?"

"And morning. And sometimes afternoon. So what do I do?"

He glanced over his shoulder at me. "Slice those tomatoes in half."

"Oh, no," I said, sounding serious. He turned around, brows drawn down. "I don't think I can handle something that complicated. I might... chip a nail or something," I added, reaching in the drawer for a knife. "So what are you making?"

"*We*," he corrected, "are making fettuccine alfredo with tomatoes, broccoli, and mushrooms."

As little as a half an hour later, we were both sitting on my sofa in the living room, some random comedy he brought over in the DVD player, heaping plates of pasta on our laps. He had even brought drinks for us. Lemonade. Because we were eleven.

I had to admit, the food was probably the best I had had in months and it really hadn't taken all that much effort to prepare either. Maybe cooking was a habit I could pick up after all. Hunter finished his food in a flourish, then reached over and started stealing the tomatoes off my plate. "Not a fan, huh?" he asked, popping one in his mouth.

I scrunched up my nose. "They *look* like they'd be delicious. But then you see the insides and they're squishy and seedy and... no."

Hunter laughed, shaking his head. "So... how is this going so far? With the not going out thing?"

I glanced at the clock. It was barely eight. I had another eight hours to kill if I wanted to get through the night without more scars to feel embarrassed about. "So far so good." I glanced at the two other DVDs he had brought. "That isn't going to do it."

He shrugged a shoulder. "There are other things to kill the time," he said and I knew what the suggestion was. I also knew that I needed to nip it in the bud.

"What? Braid each others hair and play MASH?"

"Sure," he said, grinning a little. "I don't think I would end up in a mansion though." I knew I must have given him a look because he smiled. "I had a lot of female friends in grade school."

"Sure you did," I said, sending him a disbelieving look. "I think it was just you under the covers with a flashlight praying you ended up with Billy, not John."

He ignored everything I said. "Do you have any siblings?"

"Don't we know each other well enough for neighbors?" I asked instead, watching the TV. But he just patiently stared at me until I gave in. "A brother," I told him knowing there was venom in my tone.

"Sore spot?"

I snorted, reaching for my lemonade. "You'd have a hard time not finding a sore spot."

He looked down for a second, but came up with a devilish look in his eyes. "I think I found a spot earlier that wasn't sore."

Little did he know. I took a quick breath. "Hmm?" I asked. I needed to feign ignorance. Nothing happened. Nothing was going to happen.

One of his eyebrows raised and I knew he knew what game we were in the midst of. "What? Need a little refresher?" he asked, leaning forward.

"Wasn't that good the first time, Casanova," I said, reaching for both of our plates and walking into the kitchen. It was going to be a long night if we were going to keep being close and not touching. And we absolutely, positively would not be touching. I scraped the plates and walked to the sink wishing I had the foresight to turn down his offer of hanging out. I really couldn't see whatever was going on with us working out in the long run.

I mean... how many movies can you really sit still and watch in a row?

I heard him get up and walk to the bathroom. I exhaled the breath I had been holding until I remembered...

There was a loud, deep chuckle from behind the closed door and I brought my hands up to my face, touching my too-hot cheeks and closing my eyes against the knowledge of why he was laughing.

My vibrator was still in the sink where I left it.

Holy fuck.

After I just told him the first kiss wasn't good.

Way to go, Fiona. You totally just lost the game. And made a complete fool of yourself. Good job.

I heard the door creak open and quickly turned the water on in the sink, rinsing the plates off, ignoring his lingering presence in the doorway, silently praying to a God that I didn't believe in that he wouldn't bring it up.

Please, please let him have a little tact.

By the time I had washed and dried the dishes and carefully stacked them away, I felt enough time had passed that he wasn't going to say anything. It would fall flat after so long. So I turned back around, face calm, pretending I wasn't dying a little bit inside.

His face was blank for a excruciatingly long moment. Then he pulled his hand from behind his back and there in his hands, in all of its bright purple glory, was my vibrator.

If there was a devil, I wanted him to rip a hole in the Earth right that moment and drag me into hell. I would rather spend all of eternity having hot pokers stabbed into my eyes by Hitler than have to face the man in my kitchen with my vibrator in his hand.

He opened his mouth to say something and I knew it was my chance to try to save at least a little dignity. I just needed to speak first. "For you?" I asked, trying to sound calm, breezy. "I probably would suggest a cock ring. But if you're dead set on the vibrator thing, I think a less... thick one would probably be best. I believe the ass can be a rather painful place to stick things that size."

"So does this guy just... live in the sink?" he asked as if I hadn't even spoken, a habit I was finding incredibly infuriating. "Or maybe you were a little more impressed with our little kiss than you had let on."

Little? Little kiss? More like earth-shattering, knee-knocking kiss. But he wasn't going to know that. "Don't flatter yourself," I said, rolling my eyes.

His eyes darkened, the half-teasing smile slipping from his lips and setting them in a firm line. Somehow he was sexier when he wasn't smiling. Which wasn't right. "Come here," he said, his tone deep, firm.

No. Nope. No way in hell. I was not, was absolutely not going to walk over there. Except that, even as I was thinking that, my feet were carrying me over toward him. Just when I was within a foot of him, he turned and walked toward the living room, expecting me to follow behind like a little lost puppy. Which I wasn't going to do. I was a strong, independent, no bullshit woman. I wasn't going to do it.

Except I was; I was following him into my living room, onto the cushion next to him which he patted very much like you do for a fucking dog. But I sat right down, looking at the TV which was on the home screen of the movie, playing the same fifteen seconds over and over. It was the most annoying loop in creation.

He just sat there silently, my vibrator still in his hand like it was something as innocuous as a remote control instead of something I routinely pressed up against my naughty bits. Each second that passed made my body get more tense; my thoughts raced from here to there and back a hundred times.

"Hey Fee," he finally said, quiet, almost like a question.

I turned to face him automatically and found him a lot closer than I thought he was. His free hand snaked around to the back of my neck, massaging for a second before grabbing it and pulling me forward.

That kiss was different. It was slower, lighter, lingering. I felt the tension slip out of my shoulders as his lips whispered across mine, touching, retreating, then pressing again a little harder. I turned my body toward his and the hand at my neck pulled me closer until our chests were touching. I fisted my hands in the couch cushions, my lips begging for more than he was giving me.

He pressed his body forward, until I felt myself sinking backward against the fabric of the couch. His body followed mine, his hand slipping off my neck to brace his weight off of me. His head tilted and his lips moved slowly down toward my neck, touching my skin softly, making me arch up into him. My head fell back, giving him full access, my eyes closing. His hand grabbed at the collar of my shirt, pulling it to the side so he could kiss along my clavicle.

I nearly found my O right then and there, his lips pressed into the dip of my collarbone. I felt my hips thrust upward toward his, needing the relief like I had never needed anything before. A strange strangled whimper escaped my lips and he pulled upward, sitting back and off of me. His hand went toward my crotch, reaching for the zipper.

I nearly flew off the couch- like someone had dropped a bomb, like there was another person in my head screaming out "NO!" as loud as their lungs could allow. He couldn't unzip my jeans. If he unzipped my jeans, he would reach in. If he reached in, he would feel them: the scars. And if I was particularly unlucky, he would see what they spelled out.

If my life had taught me anything, it was that I was very, very unlucky.

My hand slammed down on his, but my words caught in my throat. Caught somewhere between mortification and desire, my voice and brain, and body couldn't decide what to say.

His eyes went to mine, heavy with desire for a moment before he registered the panic. "No?" he asked, watching my face. I shook my head emphatically side to side. "Okay," he said, leaning forward again, taking my lips, slowly, patiently stoking my desire to a point where it pushed past the worry.

Then I felt it. His other hand had moved, sliding my vibrator up my leg and placing it between my thighs. It just sat there for a minute, making my body tense in anticipation, making me feel suspended in a indescribable nothingness for a second. He lifted his head from mine, his blue eyes opening slowly as he quickly flicked my vibrator on.

My legs shot out, one of them slamming into his hip in the process. My arms reached out, grabbing the front of his shirt and holding on like my life depended on it.

Where was this feeling earlier?

But if I were being honest, it had never felt like that when I had taken care of myself before. Maybe it was his presence that was making my thighs shake and my back arch up off the couch. Maybe it was Hunter that made me feel like the only thing that existed in the world were the sensations he was giving to me.

I moaned and it was nothing like the moaning I did for work. It was nothing like the exaggerated, screaming sounds of ecstasy I faked for the callers. This was a hushed, desperate sound.

"Does that feel good, sugar?" he asked, his own voice a husky timbre.

"Yes," I cried out, twisting my hands into his shirt. God, I was close already.

"How about this?" he asked, starting to move the vibrator in circles.

My thighs clamped around his waist, my fingers dug into his skin beneath his shirt. I guess it was the change in tempo, but all that was coming out of me was strangled noises.

"Come for me, baby," he urged. "Just let go."

And, with that, I did. A fast, frantic throbbing deep inside had me crying out loudly, springing up and burying my face in his neck as my body shuddered. He kept working the vibrator in circles, drawing every last second out of the already completely overwhelming orgasm.

I kept my face buried in his skin, breathing in his sawdust and soap smell, blinking furiously at the tears I noticed had found their way to my eyes. The vibrator shut off and I struggled to slow my breathing.

"Well," he said, taking a deep breath, "that killed twenty minutes."

I shot backward, my eyes wide. When I saw the smirk on his face, I broke off into a fit of giggles. Literally. School girl giggles. I wasn't a giggly kind of girl. But there I was on my couch in my living room, a hulking man above me, a vibrator still pressed into my thigh, and I was curling onto my side with a hand over my mouth, laughing.

"Now all we have to do is do that... twenty or so more times and we will be seeing the sun," he added, moving up off me and onto his side of the couch.

If we did that twenty more times, I would see the face of the God I didn't believe in. I pushed myself back into a seated position, my legs feeling heavy and wobbly as I placed them on the floor in front of me. Hunter silently got up and slipped another movie into the player, placed the vibrator in the middle of the coffee table as if that was a totally normal place for it, then he settled back in.

A few hours later, I felt my eyes getting intolerably heavy. Checking the clock, I noticed it was barely past two in the morning. That wasn't possible. There was no way I was so bone deep tired at two in the morning. I pulled my legs up on the couch, turning slightly to the side so my face could rest against the back cushion. No, I couldn't be tired, but I was. My eyes fought against the heaviness for a long time and I felt my head falling forward, then jerked it back, trying to stay awake. I needed to stay awake. Just a few more hours. I could make it a few more hours.

My head fell forward again and I pulled it back, my eyes finding Hunter's on my face. "It's okay," he said quietly, his eyes looking a little heavy too. "I'll stay, Fee. Until the sun comes up, I'll stay. You can sleep."

I believed him.

And then I slept.

TEN

Fiona

I woke up alone. I blinked at the sun shining brightly through my balcony doors, moving to a sitting position. I glanced at the clock with a sense of utter disbelief. It was after seven in the morning. I had slept through the darkest part of the night. I sat there for a moment, half expecting to hear Hunter shuffling around, to smell coffee brewing or breakfast cooking. But there was nothing.

He was gone.

Taking a deep breath, I stood up, cringing at all the aches in strange places from sleeping on the couch. I made my way to the kitchen and made coffee and headed back toward my bedroom. That's when I heard him. He wasn't in my apartment, but in his own, steadily hammering as loudly as he pleased.

I stared at the wall between us, smiling a little, but only because he couldn't see me. He couldn't know there was a feeling of victory in me, a feeling of relaxation. It was the closest to at-ease I could ever remember feeling. I had let him touch me and I hadn't felt like I was going to melt into a pool of anxiety. I had touched him without a fear that he would ask for more. Then I had slept. I had friggen slept. In my own apartment. At night.

That moment was as close to happiness I might have ever felt.

I showered, packaged panties, and started taking calls in my ridiculous criss-cross black panties and a black wifebeater.

"I've been a very bad girl," I teased into the phone, lying on my bed and staring at the ceiling. "Yes, sir," I agreed.

"I am going to take off these ropes and you are not going to go anywhere. Because I own you now," he growled at me. "Say it."

"You own me now," I repeated.

"Good girl. Now take off your panties and lay over my lap."

"Yes sir," I agreed, grabbing the wooden ruler off of my nightstand. It would give the closest possible sound to hands on flesh I could manage.

"I am going to hit you four times and you are going to tell me each time that I own you. Understood?"

"Yes, sir," I said, switching the phone onto speaker. Dominants were the easiest to please. Well, in the realm of phone sex that is. It was all agreeing and 'yes sirs'. A few bright red marks on my skin for a day or two. All in all, it was easy work. I didn't have to think of dirtier and dirtier things to say; he told me what to say.

"One," he instructed and I slapped the ruler against my thigh, starting slow to create a build up, perhaps enjoying the smarting a bit more than was normal.

"You own me," I said, sure, confident.

"Two."

Harder. It was making me a little hotter than I expected. I pushed my thighs together against the rush of wetness. "You own me," I said again, sounding more breathy.

"Three," he instructed, his voice strained. He was close. I had to make the next two count.

I took a deep breath and swung. My hips thrust upward and my breath caught. "You own me." That time, my voice was barely more than a whisper.

"Four," he said through clenched teeth and I knew the second the ruler landed he was going to come.

I cocked the ruler back further, slamming it down with a whimper. "You own me," I strangled out, too caught up in my own feelings for a work call.

I heard his breath catch and then exhale in a harsh whoosh, followed by some shuffling. "Be a good girl and send me those panties," he said after a minute, still demanding, still dom. He wasn't a part time dominant. This man was the real deal. I was just one of his subs when his real subs weren't within reach.

"Yes, sir," I said, hanging up.

There was silence in the wall between us and I shifted, turning so my feet were on the headboard, turning so I could stare at the wall, as if I could see through it. I wanted to see him bent over his work, his biceps twitching with each swing of his arm. But instead, I was imagining it was me laying there, my ass in the air and getting the spanking I had been pretending to get a moment ago.

My hand slid down my body, touching the material of my panties and finding my clit quickly. It was all his fault. It was his fault that I was feeling so insatiable. Normally a good session with myself would last me at least a day or two.

I grabbed the ruler from where I had dropped it after the call. Each time I heard the hammer land, I swung while working slow circles over my clit. I closed my eyes, sinking into the sensations, sinking into the fantasy. Before long I was moaning which wasn't something I usually did while alone. A few small whimpers, some heavy breathing, but never out and out moaning. But this time it came from somewhere deep inside as I built slowly up toward my orgasm.

On the other end of the wall, the hammer stopped and my ruler dropped, forgotten, to the mattress. My hand went to my breast, teasing over the nipple as I arched up off the bed. An image of Hunter above me, naked, looking down at my bare skin like there was nothing wrong with it as his hand reached between my legs flashed into my mind... and then I came, hard, crying out as I rolled to my side, still stroking my clit until I was completely spent.

I lay there for a long time after, curled up into myself, staring at my wall. In a matter of two days, so much had changed. They were small things by most peoples' standards, but huge for me, life changing for me. Things that I had learned to accept as basic facts of my life had changed. I could have someone in my apartment without a holy heart attack. I could spend a night in my apartment without cutting myself. I could be touched. I could maybe have some sort of friendship with someone.

They were big deals.

I climbed out of my bed, changing into a suitable outfit for a Sunday. I decided on a burnt orange tight tunic dress, brown tights, and low brown heels. Sunday was the day I called my grandmother. Sunday was the worst day of the week. I swear she could tell what I was wearing through the phone- whether I had on too much lipstick, if my skirt was too short.

I didn't stay home at all after noon on Sundays. I wore low heels and comfortable clothing because I knew I would be out and about for the better part of sixteen hours. I wouldn't be in any kind of shape to be home with a house full of sharp instruments.

I grabbed a huge oversize, heavy brown cardigan sweater, my wallet, and my extra cell phone and left my apartment . I didn't take the calls at home. I felt like they would taint my perfect little sanctuary with their awfulness.

I walked down the street, grabbing a coffee, and located the ugliest back alley I could find. That was the kind of place for this kind of call. It was a call that I made every week because I had been blackmailed into it two years before. If I didn't make the call every Sunday, on time, no matter what... she would give him my address.

And then my very carefully constructed life would fall to pieces.

I paid the homeless guy who lived between the two restaurants twenty bucks to get lost and come back in exactly twenty minutes screaming like a bloody lunatic. I always needed an escape. We didn't have an agreement on how long I had to listen to her, but I could never bring myself to hang up without an excuse.

That was how weak a voice from my past made me.

I inspected an egg crate in the back and sat down on it, dialing the number. I set my coffee on the ground, bringing my hand to my mouth as if it could block the sickness I felt rising in my throat.

"May God be with you," she answered the phone, her voice sharp and I swear I could feel it reverberate through every cell in my body.

"And also with you," I mumbled, moving my hand from my mouth to my eyes.

"Fiona Mary," she said, sounding surprised though I knew she had been expecting me. Of course she was. She didn't really give me any kind of choice. "How are you on this fine Sunday?"

Dying. Literally just dying slowly. "Fine, Grandma. How are you?"

"Swell. Just swell. I just got back from service with John and Isaiah." *Also known as your father and brother. In case you forgot.* That was the tone she used, like I was the bad guy. "How was your service?"

Yeah. Right. "I don't go to church, Gram," I said, my voice strained. Because I wasn't thinking about her and religion. I was thinking about my father and brother. I was wondering if they were still at her house, if they were listening in. The thought made the bile rise up far enough for me to almost choke on it.

"'For God so loved the world, that he gave us his only begotten Son, that whosoever believeth in him shall not perish, but have everlasting life.'"

"I know I am not going to Heaven, Gram." And I didn't want to be there if those three got in anyway. What kind of God would allow that?

"It's never too late to fix that," she said, no hope in her voice. I was doomed for hell and she knew it. There was no saving me. But she was a good, faithful woman; she had to at least pretend to try to help me find my way to the so-called light.

"How is the weather there?" I asked, changing subjects. If I didn't steer the conversation, it would go places I couldn't deal with.

"It's beautiful here. The foliage is lovely. Unfortunately the whole town is putting up those Godforsaken Halloween decorations."

I definitely didn't want to get her started on Halloween. "And how are the ladies in your book club?"

"Wonderful. We are working on organizing a bonfire for those lustful romance novels they are always filling the shelves with at the library."

"That's great, Gram," I said, my voice hollow. She was in a good mood. Maybe the call wouldn't be as bad as I had been expecting. I think a part of me was certain that because a few good things happened to me, something big and ugly needed to follow. That seemed to be the usual pattern.

"And how is work, Fiona Mary?"

Work. Ha. How gratifying would it be to tell her I had masturbated after taking a phone call from a man who jerked off while he listened to me slap myself? But that wasn't an option anymore. I was screwed ever since that one fake BJ at her dinner table.

Since then, I had racked my brain to think of a job she would think was respectable enough. I couldn't work at a bank because greed was a sin (never mind that she had more money than God). I couldn't wait tables because I wasn't allowed to work on Sundays (never mind that she frequently went out to eat on Sundays and made people work to feed her). Eventually, I had decided that I worked as a receptionist at a dentist's office. A doctor's office was too risque, too many chances of seeing or hearing about something that would be damaging to my soul. But there was nothing even remotely sexy about teeth. So I worked with teeth.

"Things get busy now that the kids are back in school. Lots of check-ups," I said, taking a deep breath.

"Well that's good. An ounce of prevention is worth a pound of cure. Especially with the teeth God gave you. You only get one set so you better take good care of them."

"Right," I agreed. Seven minutes down. Thirteen more. I could do it. I could get through it. You could tolerate anything for thirteen minutes.

"And are there any suitable young gentlemen in your life?"

This was a trick question that I had screwed up answering at least four times in the past. The trick was knowing that my grandmother did, in fact, want me to have a young, respectable gentlemen in my life. Because I was too old to be unmarried. Because sin was just waiting for susceptible women like me, the devil and his orgies just waiting for me to fall victim to my lust. So I needed to get married. Right away. I needed to be a virgin in a white dress in a big church. And then I needed to lie like a dead fish on the wedding night and let my husband screw me with his half-erect penis and come inside me so I could get pregnant quickly.

But... I couldn't be dating him for too long. We couldn't go out alone. We couldn't be alone. And he had to have a job that she would find acceptable. And he had to be a good, God-fearing virgin himself.

So far, I have dated three of these such men. But it always ended because...

One went into the ministry (HA that had been a fun lie).

One had given into sin and I had to break up with him.

And the last one went on missionary work in Africa.

I was half-tempted to tell her that my sweet little missionary died of ebola and I was grieving. She would like that. It was good to have heartbreak in your life. Something about strengthening your faith or some nonsense like that.

"No not right now, Gram," I said instead, tapping my head on the brick to the side of my head. "I haven't been going out and socializing much."

"Idle hands are the devil's workshop," she warned.

"I know, Grams."

"Hold on one moment, Fiona Mary."

It was always my full name. Because Fiona was not an acceptable name. Fiona was the name my mother had given me because my father refused to be in the delivery room, because men were not supposed to be involved with such an unclean act. And my mother, my poor, poor mother, had found her spine long enough to scribble a non-biblical name on my birth certificate. I couldn't even imagine what the repercussions were from that event. Because my name was supposed to be Mary. I was supposed to be named after the virgin mother.

Little did they know, I would end up being a lot more like Mary the whore than Mary the virgin.

But, for some reason, they never insisted it get changed: my father and grandmother. Which I had always found odd. They had the power. My mother was nothing but an ant under their shoes. But they had left me with my first name, calling me Fiona Mary every time they spoke to me, or about me, instead.

Hell, maybe they blamed my awful name for the reason I turned out so badly; so ungodly. Normally they would blame my mother like they always used to. But she was long dead; so it had to be the name.

"Fiona Mary, are you still there?"

"Yes, ma'am," I said, looking up at the small slice of sky above my head.

"Good," there was a strange fuzzy sound, like you used to get when cellphones first became a thing, when there was static on bad connections.

"Fiona Mary," a different voice said, deeper, masculine. Familiar. So fucking familiar. It was the voice I still heard in my head in dark moments. It was the voice that still broke into my dreams. "Fiona Mary, this is your father."

No shit, Sherlock. As if I could ever forget. No matter how much I drank, how many slices I carved into my skin... I could never forget.

"Grandmother," I said instead, my voice with an edge to it.

"Don't you dare hang up, Fiona Mary," she warned with a voice I knew wasn't one for bluffing.

I probably shouldn't have been surprised. It was really more shocking that this was the first time she pulled this stunt. Knowing I was at her complete mercy, knowing what power she had, knowing how easily this would wreck me. She really was one vindictive, monstrous bitch when she wanted to be.

"Fiona Mary," she said, her voice checking if I was defying her.

"I'm here," I said, a croak of a voice.

I turned on my egg crate, letting the side of my face touch the wall then starting to bang it against the bricks silently.

"Go on, John," she encouraged my father as I felt the side of my face between my eyebrow and my hairline break open on a sharp piece of mortar between the bricks.

"Fiona Mary," he said again, his voice taking on the edge I remember. "You need to stop all this foolishness and sin and come back home. Your grandmother told me about your little stunt at her house and I am appalled at your behavior. I did not raise a girl to grow up and become one of Satan's playthings. Spreading your legs for every horned creature that comes your way. Letting them penetrate you. And sodomize you. You whore. You evil little whore..."

I felt the blood trickle down the side of my face, dripping onto my dress. At the end of the alley, I saw the homeless man standing there watching me, his eyes sad. You knew you were a pathetic, worthless piece of shit when someone with no home was taking pity on you. Noticing me noticing him, he screamed like I had asked. Five minutes too early, and five too late.

"Fiona Mary... what is wrong? Fiona Mary!" my grandmother yelled.

"I have to go," I said, numbly. "I have to go. I'll talk to you next Sunday." As soon as I finished speaking, I hurled the phone at the ground, watching its pieces shatter and spread across the alley.

I was rocking. Back and forth. My arms were wrapped around my middle like they could hold me together. But it was too late; I was pieces across the floor for years. I saw something on the ground catch the light, shining, pulling my attention. It was a long, jagged piece of glass. Green, like it had at one time been a beer bottle. I reached out for it without thinking, bringing it quickly toward me and rolling up one of my sleeves.

It was perched above the faded bruises on my wrists, just barely touching my skin. I needed it. I needed it like smokers needed cigarettes; like addicts needed their fix. I needed it like I needed air in my lungs. Because I couldn't fucking feel like this. Not after so long. Not after getting away. Not after creating my own little life. I needed to feel better. I needed the cuts and the rush of adrenaline and endorphins my body would release. I needed to feel better.

I pushed the tip into my skin when I felt a hand touch my

arm, shocking me enough to not pull away. I looked up into the deep brown eyes of my homeless man. I saw the knowledge there, the pain, the acceptance of it. "Don't," he said, his voice coaxing. "Don't," he said again when I just blankly stared up at him. He reached for the glass, taking it out of my hand and tossing it toward a far corner. He sighed as he heard it shatter against the ground. It was a sound almost like relief, like he actually gave a damn if I cut myself to pieces. "It's not worth it," he said, shrugging. "Whatever it is. It isn't worth it."

It was. It so, so was. His voice alone, his words alone were enough to send me spiraling into a darkness I had been denying for years. I was a cowering child again. I was useless. Oh my God, how I believed in how useless I was. Every time he said it, I fell for it. I believed it somewhere in my marrow. It was a part of me, my uselessness.

I released a strangled breath, bringing the palms of my hands to my eyes and pushing painfully, keeping the tears away. Because I wouldn't cry. I wouldn't ever cry. Not over this. Not over them. Over him. Never. I sucked air into my lungs, greedy for the tightness to release, and stood up. "Want to get drunk?" I asked him, waiting for the pause. There was always a pause. But he would agree. Why the hell would he refuse?

"Alright," he said.

We walked in silence to the closest bar, a rundown shithole of a place that didn't even have a back bar. I ordered endless shots of vodka.

I drank until my body couldn't take it anymore, then ran to the bathroom and let it all come back out. When I walked back into the bar, my homeless man, my little savior, my drinking buddy was gone. I shrugged, feeling too shitty to care, and started drinking again.

I was obliterated. I walked home a stumbling, pathetic, numb mess. I dropped my keys four times trying to unlock my door when I heard Fourteen's open. "What the fuck, Sixteen?" he asked, sounding as groggy as he looked. He took one look at my face and shook his head. "Jesus, Fee," he said, reaching for my keys and unlocking my door himself.

Up close, he smelled like comfort: like sawdust and soap, like him. And I smelled like cheap vodka and old cigarettes and vomit. "Thanks," I managed, feeling my high sink toward a low at a pitch that made me unsteady.

"What the..." he said, his hand reaching out toward my face. "What is this?" he asked, touching the skin next to my eye.

"Bar fight," I managed, sinking into my apartment. "You should see the other guy." Then I slammed the door and locked it, because I couldn't take his niceness. I didn't deserve it.

ELEVEN

Fiona

The banging woke me up. It wasn't the hammering I had come to expect, but banging on my door. I didn't have to ask to know who it was. While the night before was a blissfully fuzzy mess, I did remember running into him in the hall. And judging by the blood all over my pillowcase, he was going to want to know what happened to me.

Just give up dude. Accept that I am some kind of fall down, pass out alcoholic. A hopeless case.

"Give me a minute, Fourteen," I yelled, going to my closet as I stripped out of my clothes from the night before which smelled awful. Like... frat house awful. I pulled on an old white t-shirt and a pair of bright pink shorts, threw a mint in my mouth, and made my way to the door. "What?" I said as a way of greeting, the pounding in my head from the fight my face had had with that alley wall was making me beyond grumpy. Not to mention that his idea of a reasonable hour was eight in the morning.

"What? Where the fuck were you raised with manners like that?" he asked, pushing inside my apartment, a tray of coffee with a bottle of aspirin in one of the cup holders in his hand.

I cringed at the mention of my family. That was a sore, sore spot at that moment. "You're only allowed in because you brought coffee," I grumbled, following him toward my kitchen. What was with him and the thinking he owned the joint thing?

He rolled his eyes, watching as I took one of the coffees and shaking two aspirin into his palm and holding it out toward me. "You got to have a headache. I don't think I have ever seen someone that shitfaced and still walking before," he said as I took the pills.

"In heels nonetheless," I added.

"What the hell happened to your face?" he asked, trying to peek at the cut but I turned my head away.

"It hit a wall." A few dozen times. With no help from anyone else.

His breath hissed out of his mouth as he moved across the room to me, grabbing my chin and holding my face still as he looked. "This probably needs stitches," he said, his face looking impassive, like he had seen nasty cuts a million times. "You're lucky it's not infected."

"I poured some vodka on it," I shrugged, having a vague memory of someone laughing as I dropped a shot down the side of my face.

"It still needs to be cleaned up. Maybe if you don't want to go to the hospital, put some glue on it."

"I know the drill," I said, thinking of my own brushes with cutting too deep in my leg. When I had the horrifying realization that I might have to go to the hospital and answer questions; or get a psych evaluation. Glue and I were good friends.

There was a long silence that had me looking down at my coffee cup. "What is up with the self-destruct spiral, Fee?" he asked, his voice softer than I had ever heard it before.

"Why do you care?" I shot back. He didn't. No one really cared. They just felt like they were entitled to the intimate details of your life. *Spell out your pain so I can make a map of it. I want to know there are people more fucked up than me so I can feel better about myself.*

"I don't know," he said, tucking his dark hair behind his ear. "I just do."

I ignored the warm feeling inside, the ping of hope that someone might actually give a damn, that someone would notice if I just gave up this fight after all. "Don't," I said, the word coming out sadder than I intended. I didn't want him to care. He couldn't care. I wasn't the kind of person you should let yourself care about. I would only let you down.

"Too late," he shrugged.

"Why? Because we kissed? Because you got me off with a vibrator?" I rolled my eyes. I shrugged it off. Men hated that shit. Them with their silly fragile egos. "Get over yourself."

"This isn't about me," he said instead, not sounding the least bit insulted. "But if I'm not mistaken," he said, looking cocky, "I heard you yesterday morning calling out my name while you got off."

Oh, the fucker. Jesus. Was I really that loud? I didn't even remember calling out his name. But seeing as I was thinking about him, that was entirely possible. "Do you have a point? Being on someone's highlight reel isn't a big deal. I had a pizza delivery guy end up on mine for a month straight." Nope. Not true at all. But I certainly made it sound like it was.

"What's your damage, Sixteen?" he asked, shaking his head.

"What?" I asked, not sure if that was an insult or an actual question.

"I don't know," he said. "We all got it, but with the booze and the bad decisions..."

"Maybe I'm just stupid," I suggested, finishing my coffee and dropping the cup in the garbage. I needed to put some space between us. The air in the small kitchen felt thick and stifling. I walked into the hall and then the bathroom.

"You're not stupid," he said, following me. "You're just... coping. I was just curious as to what you're trying to cope with."

"What makes you think you're entitled to know that?" I asked, reaching into the medicine cabinet and pulling down the witch hazel and glue. He watched my reflection in the mirror as I wet a swab and dabbed at all the dried blood, trying to get it as clean as possible before I put the glue on. I pretended to not notice his gaze.

"I'm not saying I'm entitled to know," he said reaching for the glue as I tried to watch in the mirror and glue at the same time. His hand pushed my hair out of my eyes and held my face still. "I'm saying that I'm here. And I want to listen if you want to talk."

I closed my eyes as I felt him push my skin together and wipe glue on the seam. God, how I wanted to tell him. A part of me felt like it would ease the burden. To no longer keep it so secret. But the other part knew I would never be looked at the same way again. "I'm not in a talking mood," I said quietly as he let go of my face and stepped away.

"Okay," he said, shrugging a shoulder, "but it's an open invitation. That's going to scar. Maybe an inch or so but it should heal neat."

"What's one more scar?" I mumbled to myself, but judging by the look of pain on his face, he heard me. Which was only made worse by the knowledge that he had seen my thigh.

"What do you say you go get cleaned up and I'll take you out to breakfast?"

I could. I mean my job didn't exactly demand that I answer every call. Hell, I didn't answer to anyone but myself. But I knew I shouldn't. We were already too close for comfort and I couldn't risk whatever careful balance I was keeping with my new found social skills and my normal hermitage.

"Or I can just whip up a quick omelet and let you get back to your day," he said, sensing my hesitance.

"Alright," I said and before I could change my mind, he was walking out of the bathroom and closing the door behind him.

I grabbed a towel and planned to take a quick shower, but as soon as the water hit my skin, I knew I was in for a while. I needed the water scalding and I needed to scrub and re-scrub yesterday away. My father's words always felt like they left a coating on my skin, like I was covered in them, like they would sink in and become a part of me if I didn't wash them away. Also, not to mention the alcohol and the vomit and dried blood and God only knew what else I had all over me that I needed to wash down the drain.

By the time I finished, my bathroom was a cloud of steam. I dried myself off and realized with panic that I had neglected to actually bring any clothes with me into the bathroom. I wrapped the towel tight around me, holding the knot for good measure and snuck toward the door.

He was probably just busy in the kitchen whipping up some kind of awesome concoction. If I made a run for it, he wouldn't even see me. I pulled the door open and darted out, running right into a giant wall of man.

I yelped, trying to spring away, but his hands landed hard on my shoulders, holding me still. "Sorry I ah..."

"Forgot to grab clothes?" he asked, his voice sounding amused.

I was way too close and way too naked. This couldn't be happening. No f'n way.

"You're... you're supposed to be making me food," I stammered.

"Yeah, I got all the food out on the counter and everything and then I heard that water and I couldn't stop thinking about you in there... one room away from me... all naked and soapy."

"I'm not naked or soapy anymore," I said, not able to look above his chest. If I looked up, I might have given in; I might have just let it happen. And that... well that couldn't happen.

"Not soapy, no," he said, his hand dropping lower and touching the top of the towel. "But you're just one... tug," he said, grabbing the edge and holding it, "from naked."

I slowly pulled air in through my nose, trying to pull some self-control in with it. But words failed me once again and my hand went up to cover his, holding it still.

"Look at me, Fee." My eyes went up slowly, looking at his shirt, then his throat, his chin, lips, nose. Then finally, eyes. They were impossibly blue, almost see through. "There you are," he said, his other hand sliding up the side of my face, his thumb stroking across my cheek. I felt my mouth fall slightly open, watching him, stuck in that moment. "Kiss me," he said and I felt the demand settle in my belly.

And then I was going up on my tiptoes and pressing against his chest. His hand slipped from the towel and slid around my back, settling between my shoulder blades. My hand moved up his chest, touching the stubble on his cheek, sneaking back into his hair and pulling him downward.

One kiss. It wouldn't hurt.

Even as I told myself, I knew it was a lie. Because kissing Hunter was like stepping into the sunlight after being in a cave for a year. It was blinding. It was warm. And, most of all, it was comforting.

His lips met mine with a fierce kind of passion, reckless and needy. My teeth bit into his bottom lip, digging in and pulling. It wasn't tentative. We had already done our exploring. I just wanted more. I wanted everything. My tongue slipped into his mouth, stroking his as my hand grabbed the back of his neck, pulling him closer. My other hand dropped from the towel, wrapping around his shoulders.

His arms slid down my back, one wrapping hard around my hips, the other around my ass, pulling me closer. My breasts were pressed against his chest, painful but it felt good. I could feel his hardness pressing at me through his jeans, pushing into my belly, reminding me of things I forgot I wanted.

God, how I wanted.

I sighed against his mouth. His hands moved, reaching down and grabbing my ass, pulling me up and off my feet, crushing my heat against his erection. My head fell back on a gasp and his face moved downward and sunk into my skin. First his lips. Then his teeth.

He put my feet back on the ground, one of his hands moving between us, grabbing my breast through the towel, squeezing. His thumb rubbed at my already hardened nipple for a second before grabbing it between two fingers and pinching. Hard enough to make my eyes fly open and a half-groan, half-cry escape my lips.

"It's so sexy how fucking hot you get so easy," he growled, pushing me back against the wall. He grabbed my arms, pinning them above my head then continuing his assault on the sensitive skin on my neck. One of my hands moved down his back, slipping under his shirt and touching the hard muscles of his back. "So sweet," he said, running his tongue over my earlobe.

His hand touched my thigh, resting at the outside of my tattoo then stroking the soft skin on the inside of my knee in small circles. Then they were moving slowly upward. His fingers brushed the hem of the towel that just barely covered my crotch.

No. Yes, oh God yes. But no.

I wrenched my hands from his hold, slamming them against his chest and shoving him. Off-guard, he flew back a step, stumbling slightly. I clutched at my towel, my hands shaking. Across from me, Hunter leaned against the wall, raking a hand down his face. "What the fuck, Fee?" he asked, his voice a harsh whisper.

I sighed, looking down at my feet. I was frustrated, unbearably frustrated. And I was angry. At myself and also at the monster who made me how I was. And I was sad. I was sad for all the things I could never have. But above all... "I'm sorry," I said, knowing it meant nothing. But it was everything.

"I don't get it," he said, his eyes piercing into me. "The walls are fucking thin, Sixteen." At my blank look, he let out a short humorless laugh. "I hear you, Fee. Everyday. With all your men." He rushed across the hall, pushing up against me, leaning down in my face. Intimidating. He was really intimidating when he was angry.

And then I understood. He thought I was a slut. He thought I was easy. And yet I was toying with him. I was teasing him. "Hunter..." I said, trying to sound reasonable.

"No, don't," he said, slamming a hand against the wall.

That was the Hunter from that Tuesday morning. He was my dark savior. He was savage beast who pummeled a man's face in. He was not my Hunter; the one who cooked me dinner and gave me the safety to sleep through a night; or the one who glued me back together.

This was a rabid pitbull straining against his leash. I wondered fleetingly who would win as I saw him close his eyes and take a long, steadying breath.

We stayed that way for a long time, him still and silent, me apt and fascinated. A muscle ticked in his jaw. His fist clenched and unclenched at his side. Then his eyes slowly opened.

The leash won. He pushed off the wall, taking a step back. "Your omelet is in the microwave," he said and turned and walked out of my apartment.

He walked out of my life. Because I didn't think I would ever see him again, not after that, not after letting me see him lose his cool like that.

I walked to the kitchen, finding a omelet with cheese,

mushrooms, and spinach, and sitting down to eat it.

He had showed me some of his damage and he was ashamed of that. Little did he know, I wasn't someone who could judge. So what if he had anger issues? I had ripping myself open issues, and alcohol issues, and daddy issues, and brother issues, and grandmother issues. I was the Long Island Iced Tea of damage: everything but iced tea included.

Honestly, I was happy to see the flaws in him. It was hard to not feel like a sad sack of awfulness next to someone who had proved himself to be nothing but pretty damn perfect: a good cook, a concerned citizen, a fair friend, and so ridiculously good looking on top of it all. It was too much.

I liked the screwed up Hunter better.

It was a shame I wasn't going to be seeing him again.

TWELVE

Fiona

My bathroom floor and I have had an on and off again relationship for a long time. He was the keeper of my nastiest secrets. He was my cool, comforting companion on nights when I found myself stuck at home.

I hadn't heard from Hunter in a week. Another Sunday. Another private alley. Another call to my grandmother.

"You really should listen to your father," she told me, her voice accusatory. "He is a great man. He understands the scripture. He's just trying to guide you."

"Yes, Grams."

YesGrams.YesGrams.YesGrams.

I had a bag of groceries at my feet and a half-assed idea to pick up cooking. So I had to go home. And once I was home, I wasn't going anywhere.

I heard nothing from his side of the wall. There was no hammering or sawing at six in the morning. There was no talking, no TV, no nothing. I had a rush of panic at the idea that maybe he had left, moved on. But I saw the pile of cigarette butts in his ashtray on the balcony get higher everyday. He was still around. He just didn't want to give me any excuse to go to his apartment. Which was for the best; or at least that was what I kept reminding myself- five, ten times a day. It was for the best. Things could go back to how they used to be. Me, myself, and I. Drunken stumbling me. Solitude.

You gotta protect the world from you, Fiona. No one deserves to have to deal with you.

My internal monologue had taken a turn toward the negative lately. True, my head had never been a happy place to be, but suddenly it was becoming a landmine-filled field of self-loathing. I could hear his tone slipping into my subconscious; my father's. Because that's how good he was. One phone call and I was different.

I made myself spaghetti which came out too tough and the sauce too watery, deciding that maybe cooking wasn't a science but a skill; one I obviously did not possess. But I ate it and drank a bottle of wine. Wine. Which was weird for me. I bought it thinking it would keep me from going out and drowning in a bottle of something harder. I didn't keep liquor in my apartment. That was just asking to become a day drinker, a full-blown alcoholic.

I got a tingling sensation once I finished the bottle, a nice warm feeling. But it didn't last. My mood soured and the alcohol latched onto the negative internal dialog like a life preserver. And I was spiraling downward.

So there I was with my good old bathroom floor, in hot pink undies and a black and white striped bandeau crop top... looking every bit the mess I felt like. I had a pile of clean gauze next to me with some witch hazel and the glue. Just in case.

I had always heard that the first cut was the hardest. It was something I never agreed with. The first cut is full of promises. It brought with it the rush of good feelings and the shock at seeing the skin open and weep. For me, the first cut was the easiest. Every cut after felt like I was chasing a pipe dream. It was like trying to get drunker or higher when you knew it wasn't possible. There was always a cap. But those who are really dedicated keep trying anyway.

I was really dedicated to self-destruction.

The razor blade touched my skin and I slipped into the mindset. It had to be a different mindset, because no one in their normal, everyday brain would cut themselves open. It was a strange limbo of a feeling that I could get drunk on some nights.

This was one of those nights.

Twenty minutes later, my hands were shaking as I pressed witch hazel soaked gauze against the cuts. I didn't get my rush, no matter how many times I tried, no matter how hard I pushed. I felt all the more despondent, dropping the gauze and curling up on my side.

I couldn't cry. That was what I wanted to do right then: just let it out, purge the feelings in something other than blood for a change. But he could have the blood. He couldn't have the tears. I lay there for a long time, staring at the legs of my bathroom table, watching as they slipped in and out of focus, the wine making me tired as I came down.

Before I could think to fight it, I was falling asleep.

--

And I was six years old again. Our house was a shack in the

woods behind my grandmother's house. Estate. My grandmother's house really could be called an estate. But my father had slipped in between the pages of his Bible sometime in his late teens and shunned the idea of material wealth. He slept in the backyard for months as he cut down trees and nailed together the house I would eventually grow up in.

There was a small living/ dining area right inside the front door with a fireplace. It was the only place I had ever seen my mother cook food. We didn't have a stove or microwave. There were no luxuries.

The bathroom was an outhouse twenty yards from our front door. My brother and I had a small eight by eight room, split down the middle with a curtain. We weren't supposed to see each other dress or change, not even as small children. Sins of the flesh or something like that. My parents had a similar sized room, their bed pushed up against my wall.

I used to hear them at night, my father reciting scripture to my mother. "The husband should give to his wife her conjugal rights, and likewise the wife her husband. For the wife does not have authority over her own body, but the husband does."

And then there would be the sound of the bed slamming up against my wall, my father panting then grunting. He would fall asleep shortly after and I would hear my mother crying through the wall.

I couldn't remember her as anything but cowering. Her shoulders seemed permanently pulled upward by her ears, her face always trained on the floor. When I was little, I remembered saying how I thought she was pretty with her long blonde hair. My father had stormed across the floor, grabbing my chubby little six year old face and yelling about my sins.

The next day I came out for prayer to see my mother's hair sheared off, her scalp underneath ripped up and bloody.

I never spoke of my mother in front of my father again. And

my mother tensed anytime I opened my mouth when she was in the room.

My brother and I didn't go to school. There was too much sin and not enough God; not even in the Catholic schools. My father took my brother out with him, hunting and fishing and doing things I didn't want to know about. My mother would wait for them to leave and rush over to me, grabbing me and pulling me down on the dirt floor and drawing letters with a stick. She taught me to read against my father's wishes. After every session, she would grab my hands and tell me to look at her and in a shaking voice remind me how important it was that my father never found out about our lessons.

He never did.

The early years weren't that bad overall. I was fed. I had enough blankets to ward off the winter chill. I had it better than other kids in the world. The beatings always came out of the blue after offending some ideal of my father's. He would pull me outside and break a switch off of a tree, pull up my dress and hit me with the switch until I cried hard enough to wet myself. Then I would be left there, out in the heat or the freezing cold to think about my sins; to repent to God... overnight.

My mother would come to me in the morning, pressing compresses to my cuts and murmuring about the tempers of men. She would tell me to hold onto the anger, wrap it up like a baby to my chest and never let it go. Because if I let it go, he won. He owned me.

What she didn't tell me was that he had owned me from the day I was born; just like he had owned her from the day they had married. And as a little girl, I couldn't understand. I didn't grasp the point she was trying to make: If I didn't hold onto the anger, I would accept my beatings. I wouldn't stop to think about how unjust the punishments were for the crimes. I wouldn't wonder why my brother wasn't bloodied and left outside overnight. I wouldn't see my father for the monster he was.

I remembered my tenth year well. I started to share the household responsibilities with my mother. My father would ramble on with constant, unrelenting scripture quotes about the sins of the flesh, the weakness of women. I didn't understand at the time that my father was hinting at something I didn't yet know about: my upcoming blossoming; my womanhood.

Isaiah was twelve, all arms and legs and eyes that spent too much time on me and my mother. At the time I didn't understand that look. That look that, as an adult woman, you know is only one thing. You know that look and you know when that look is more than a look.

Isaiah pulled the curtain between our room open when he heard me come in for bed, standing there and staring at me while I changed. I wasn't much then, a sapling still. My breasts were just tiny buds that would still be mistaken for a boy's. But I wasn't a boy. And he stared. I would crawl into bed and pull the covers up over my head. I would hear him pull the curtain, his mattress give way under his weight.

Then he would be panting and grunting. Panting and grunting on one side of the room, from my brother. Panting and grunting on the other side of the wall, from my father. And a part of me was starting to understand that it wasn't right. Whatever was causing those noises... was not something I should have been allowed to be near. It wasn't something I should know about.

It was something that made my mother cry.

My father came in one night while I was changing, my back turned to Isaiah. Then he was screaming. Not at Isaiah, but at me. He was screaming words that were so angry and jumbled I didn't even understand them. He grabbed my wrist, pulling me out of the room in all of my nakedness, through the house, outside.

He threw me down on the ground, six inches deep in new snow. I remembered that feeling like it was yesterday: the stinging, burning, stabbing sensation raking over every nerve ending where the cold touched my skin. I remembered crying out, trying to stand. But he pushed me down, grabbing a branch from a tree and pummeling my back to raw strips of flesh. Then he dropped down on the ground next to me, reaching into his back pocket. He threw me over onto my back, letting the snow seep into the open wounds. Then I saw what he was holding- the moon flashing off of the blade in the dark. His hunting knife.

My screams were like that of a dying animal. Because that was what I felt like. I felt like I was being skinned, like I was being sliced for Sunday dinner.

Then, like a madwoman, my mother was running out of the house in her bare feet screaming, "Fire!"

--

"Fee, wake up," I heard through the screaming, the screaming I could never forget, the choking on your own spit screaming, the praying for a blissful end to it all kind of screaming. "Fee... fuck... wake up!" There was a sharp pain across my face and my eyes shot open, but not comprehending. I was still ten, in the snow, being mutilated by my father. I felt a hand on my knee and I shot out, fists colliding with flesh. "Fee, snap out of it," the voice said, grabbing the sides of my face and shaking my head once.

Then just like that, my dream faded, pulling backward like a fog. And there was Hunter, kneeling next to me, his light eyes looking downright frantic.

"Jesus, Fee," he said, letting my face go and sitting back on his ankles.

"How are you here?" I asked, feeling a little more lightheaded than I should.

"How?" he asked, his brows drawing together. "I broke your door down."

"What?" I asked, confused. "Why?"

He looked at my face. "You were screaming. I mean... blood-curdling screaming. I thought someone was in here trying to kill you. I kicked your door in." I nodded, feeling more than a little embarrassed and, what's worse, like I owed him an explanation. I pushed up on my elbows and his hand shot to my shoulder. "Slow. You've lost a lot of blood, baby."

My eyes widened, going to my thigh, feeling like I was choking on my self-consciousness. My thigh looked worse than I remembered through the haze that allowed me to do the damage in the first place. The cuts were deeper and he was right. There was drying blood on my leg, all the way down to my knee and a frighteningly large puddle on the tile floor next to me.

I reached out for the clean gauze, but his hands stopped me. "Fee," he said, my name like a question. "Talk to me."

"I had a bad dream," I said dumbly and he shook his head.

"How about this then?" he asked, gesturing toward my leg.

"It doesn't matter."

"To me it does," he countered.

"Why? Because I woke you up?"

"Because you scared the piss out of me tonight," he admitted. "I heard the screaming then I came in here and saw all the blood..."

"Don't worry," I said, sitting up, "no murderers here. You can go."

"I'm not going anywhere," he said, snatching the bottle of witch hazel out of my hand. "I'll do it," he said, squirting it over my skin then blotting at the blood until my skin was clean. "Do you want me to glue these?"

"No," I said, watching him minister to me, carefully, like he was afraid to hurt me. Which was something completely new for me coming from a man. I watched as he rose and dug around for triple antibiotic, coming back and smoothing it over the cuts. "I'm not a slut," I heard myself saying, quietly.

But he heard me and his head shot up to my face. "I never said you were," he said, his brows drawing together.

"It's just... last week..."

"Fee forget about that."

Was he just trying to placate me? Poor little screwed up Fiona who needed coddling so she didn't hurt herself. I couldn't let that be his opinion of me.

"I'm not a slut," I said again, my voice a little stronger. "I'm a phone sex operator."

His mouth had been open as if he was going to cut me off, then his eyes went wide for a second before a smile started tugging at his lips. "Wait. What?"

"I'm a phone sex operator." At his blank look, I shrugged. "You know... guys call me and I dirty talk them and..."

"I know what a phone sex operator is," he said, rolling his eyes. He sat there for a minute, lost in his own thoughts, looking entirely too amused. "That explains a lot actually," he said finally. "So the, ah, horse noises..."

I laughed, bringing a hand up to my face. "Oh my God... that guy."

He smiled with me for a moment before his face went serious. "So that other morning," he started, his eyes bearing into mine. "with the spanking..."

"A dom," I supplied.

"After," he said and I felt my face heat with the memory. "After you hung up with him." There was a long silence as if he expected me to say something. But I couldn't. "You were thinking about me. About me doing those things the guy had talked about."

"Maybe," I said, not able to look up at him any longer.

"When you were touching yourself," he said, reaching out and tilting my chin up so I faced him again.

"Yeah," I admitted.

"I heard you," he said. "Through the wall, I heard you moaning. I stopped working to listen." Which should have been creepy, but it wasn't. "I was stroking my cock listening to you." Jesus Christ that was hot. The image flew into my head and I pushed my thighs together to try to ease the chaos there. "Then when I heard you call out my name when you came..." he trailed off, shaking his head like he couldn't find the right words.

There was a pregnant silence between us then, both of us lost in thought. Him probably about my work, about me masturbating to the idea of him while he listened. I kept thinking about our failed attempts to get closer, to be intimate. I wondered if I should tell him, just bite the bullet and get it over with.

"Hey," he said, breaking through my swirling thoughts, "whatever put that look on your face... stop thinking about it."

"Hunter..."

"No," he said, shaking his head and getting to his feet. He reached a hand down toward me and I took it. "You don't owe me an explanation. I'm assuming there is some issue with actual, real life sex for you, right?"

"Yeah." He had no idea. He wouldn't want me if he knew.

"Okay," he said, still holding my hand though I was on my feet. It felt good. I don't ever remember having someone hold my hand. It was no wonder new couples always did it. It felt like comfort, like stability. "So now I know," he said. "It's not a big deal," he added, leaning forward and planting a kiss on my forehead.

He was lying. I knew that. I knew it was a big deal. Sex was always a big deal. When you were having it, it was a big deal. And when you weren't having it, it was a big deal. "Okay," I said, not believing him, but without the energy for a fight either.

"Why don't we get you to the kitchen and get some food in you to counteract that blood loss? And I'll go try to fix your door."

I sat in my kitchen nibbling on the cold, chewy spaghetti while he worked. I was glad for the distance. I needed to think. I needed to get my guards back up.

It had been a long time since I had that dream. And even when I did have it, it was usually as a third party, like I was looking on at the scene. But that night, I had been inside my little body. I heard all the swirling thoughts. I felt the cold. I felt the pain. I felt the screams bursting from my mouth. It had felt as real as it had thirteen years ago. It was like reliving it.

Under my breasts and under my panties, my scars felt raw and painful. They felt fresh and burning. I half expected to see bright red, bloody messes when I changed later instead of the pinky-white weirdly smooth skin I knew was there.

The clock on my stove told me it was just after one in the morning. Though to be fair, I didn't think any worse damage could come of the next three hours than had come in the past three. It was going to be one of those nights that I flicked around the TV endlessly, wincing whenever I moved my leg or something brushed across my cuts. But it was only a few hours and then I could sleep. Then things could go back to usual.

Or, as usual as my life could be.

"Alright," Hunter said, walking back into the room, a little sweaty from whatever he had been doing. "I put some boards up over the split. It's not perfect, but it will hold until I can replace..."

"You don't have to..."

"I broke it," he cut in, "I fix it."

"Okay," I conceded because better sense told me that there was no use arguing with him. "I'm... sorry I woke you up," I said when the silence stretched awkward.

"Hey nothing like a little mild heart failure to keep you young," he said, giving me a smile that I could only describe as flirtatious. "So... you alright?" he asked, watching my face. "I could stay..."

"I'm fine," I said automatically. It was knee-jerk. I was always fine. As if reading my thoughts, his brow lifted. "No seriously," I added, waving a hand. "I'm alright. I'm gonna watch a movie, wait for the sun to rise, then get some rest."

"Alright," he said, pushing off the doorway and moving toward me. His hands cradled my face and pulled it slowly up toward him as his face lowered. But his lips didn't press down on mine. They hovered above mine for a long time before pressing down, a whisper of a touch that lasted no longer than two seconds before pulling away. I felt myself waver slightly, horrifyingly, on my feet when he stepped back.

"See you around, Sixteen," he said, giving me an odd look.

"See ya, Fourteen," I called as the door slammed.

Alone, I curled up on my bed, wrapping my blankets tight around me like they could keep all the bad away. I lay awake thinking about nothing and everything: my father, my mother, my brother, my burning thigh. But mostly, Hunter.

Because, damn it all to hell, I was pretty sure I was falling for him. Just a little. And maybe it was just all the pent up sexual frustration. But a part of me knew it was more than that, that it was deeper. Maybe my frozen little heart was thawing a bit.

THIRTEEN

Fiona

My phone woke me up. My work phone with its absurd seventies porn theme song. *Bow-chicka-wow-wooow*. I fumbled blearily out of bed, looking for it on my nightstand where I usually left it. But as the sleep cleared from my brain, I realized it was coming from the living room. I stumbled around, looking at my door with its makeshift patching and noticed my phone on the tiny table I kept my mail and keys and wallet on. Which was weird. Because I would never put it there.

I reached for it, noticing the time with a squint. Most of my callers knew not to call before eleven. And it was barely after ten. I hit the call button. "It's a little early, darlin'," I said, sounding chipper if maybe a little tired. Every man was *darlin'* or *honey* or *love*. Every man was a sweet, sweet nothing.

"I thought you might make an exception for me," a familiar voice said.

You've heard that knocking over with a feather expression.

Well, you could have knocked me the fuck over with a feather as I realized who was calling on my work line, on my phone sex line. That's why my phone was out of place. He had moved it the night before, probably after going in it and figuring out my number.

I brought a hand up to cover my eyes, not acknowledging the big, silly grin that was on my face. Oh, Hunter.

"You there, Sixteen?" he asked after a moment, sounding perfectly at ease, like it was totally a normal thing he was doing.

"Yep," I said, shaking my head.

"Why don't you walk back to your bedroom," he suggested and my feet were moving.

"Okay," I said, looking at my bed like it was foreign.

"And get into bed," he suggested, his voice sounding almost amused.

"Okay," I said, settling my head back on my pillows. I swear I could feel his presence behind me. Through the wall, but only six inches away.

"What are you wearing?"

"You know what I'm wearing," I said, laughing.

"How would I know that? I'm Dan... from... Vermont. I've never seen you before in my life."

I snorted, smiling at my ceiling. "Right," I said. "Well, I have on huge baggy, ratty sweatpants and a housecoat."

"Come on, Sixteen," he groaned.

"Fine. I'm wearing pink panties and a black and white crop top."

"That doesn't match at all," he teased.

"Well, I wasn't expecting your call, honey. I didn't get a chance to dress down for you," I cooed in my usual tone I saved for callers. "Thongs, isn't it?" I asked, knowing it was.

There was a low, deep chuckle. "Yup. And I want a pair. I noticed that was a new service. Green thong. To match those gorgeous eyes."

Oh like hell. No fucking way was he getting a pair of my panties. "You don't seem like a pantie sniffer," I said.

"I'm not," he agreed. "I was just seeing if I could get a rise out of you. You're very professional," he said and it sounded like a compliment.

Little did he know, I was a swirling mess of anxiety inside. That was new for me. I never felt nervous on a call, not even my first call. I had stood in front of a bathroom mirror for days before, saying dirty words at my reflection, trying to get used to them. *Cock. Pussy. Cunt. Balls. Clit. Snatch. Dick.* I would lace the words together, trying to come up with the filthiest thing I could say. I was just trying to ease any possible discomfort or shock at what might come from a caller. I wanted to be prepared for anything.

Except my sexy as hell neighbor calling me from the other side of my wall. There was no way to prepare for that.

"Sixteen?" he asked.

"I'm here," I said, shaking my head. When was he going to give it up? This had gone on for long enough.

"Take off your shirt," he said quietly.

What? No. Oh, hell to the no. We were not actually going to have phone sex. Through the wall. That was... that was crazy.

"Hunter..." I said, my voice heavy with warning.

"Fee," he said, sounding reasonable. "Sex is an issue. I get it. I'm not going to press it," he said and there was a strange fluttering in my chest that I was trying like hell to ignore. "But phone sex isn't an issue. So let's give it a try, okay?"

No. Nonono. "Okay," I said, sounding shy and realizing that was exactly how I felt. Shy.

"So take off your shirt," he said, his voice again dropping low, sensual. I felt the desire settle deep in my belly, a heavy pressure.

"Okay," I said, sitting up and pulling it over my head.

"Lay back down, baby," he said and I took a deep breath and

followed my instructions. "Run your hand up your stomach slowly, up and over your breast, brushing it but not stopping. Then down the other side."

I closed my eyes, thinking of his hand as I touched my skin which felt alert, like it was at attention, like it was reaching out for the contact.

"Now put your hand around your breast, teasing the point with your fingers."

I heard a whimper escape my lips and cringed. "What are you doing?" I asked, trying to cover my unusual insecurity.

"I am taking my pants off," he said and, as if proving his point, I heard him stumble back and hit the wall. I smiled at the ceiling. At least I wasn't the only one who was slightly out of their comfort zone. "Now I am taking my cock out of my boxers," he said.

Oh, holy hell. I felt the desire shoot down between my legs. Electric. That was what desire felt like- a hot bolt of something you couldn't quite understand.

I could picture him, sitting on the floor, his back against the wall where my bed was, a hand reaching into his boxers and pulling out his hard cock. Stroking it once before settling at the base, patient, waiting to hear me writhing and crying out before he let himself stroke it right.

"You know how hard I get just thinking about you, Fee?" he asked, his voice husky. "It doesn't matter how much I come. I can't get the need for you out of my system."

I made a strange noise, something like a whine. I was needy as I worked my fingers over my nipple. My breasts felt oddly heavy. My nipples were almost painful they were so hard.

"I know you think about me," he said, "when you're alone. I know you think about my fingers in that tight pussy... my tongue playing at your clit. My cock buried deep inside of you." I pressed my thighs tighter together, hoping to ease the ache. It was actually painful. "Tell me you think about me."

"I think about you," I admitted, my voice an airy whisper.

"The other day... when you were touching yourself," he said, "what were you thinking of me doing?"

My hand slipped from my breast, going to my eyes and covering them. "I was thinking of you spanking me," I admitted, barely audibly.

"That's sexy baby," he said, his tone reassuring, like he sensed my discomfort. "And then?"

That was how I was going to die: lying on my bed on my phone sex line, telling my neighbor about how I rubbed my clit while thinking about him. That seemed like a fitting end to my strange life.

"And then fucking me," I finished, squeezing my eyes shut.

How the hell did women do this with their boyfriends or husbands? How could you get over the awkwardness? With strangers it was different. It was all talk. I wasn't actually touching myself. It was one-sided. Hot for them, empty for me. This was foreign territory and I didn't speak the language and I was in desperate need of a map.

"I would like to do that one day," he admitted, because it was true. I couldn't blame him for that. Of course he would want to have sex with me one day. That was normal. But he didn't say he was going to. He said he would *like* to. That distinction made a world of difference for me. "Move your hand down to your inner thighs, baby," he said and my hand moved as I let my legs fall open. "Run your fingers up and down that soft skin, not far enough up that you can brush your clit. Not yet," he warned and I was stroking. I was thinking of his big hands there instead of mine.

"I like this," I admitted, feeling silly.

"I like it too, sweetheart," he said, sounding breathless. "Now move your fingers between your legs, over your panties. Let me hear you touch yourself," he cooed.

I nearly shot up off the bed. I was too hot, too beside myself with need. The slightest touch felt overwhelming. I clamped my lips shut to keep myself from crying out, a muffled noise escaping.

"Don't fight it. I want to hear, baby. You sound so sexy when you touch yourself. Stroke your clit for me."

I was lost in that moment, working my fingers over my sensitive point. I heard Hunter's breath in my ear. Hours, days, weeks could have passed. I was outside of the world. I was fully immersed in myself and him.

"Slip out of your panties, Fee," he said, his voice sounding rough, "then touch yourself again without the barrier. Are you wet for me?"

"Yes." Oh, was I ever.

"Good. Do you want to feel me inside, baby?"

"Please," I groaned, biting into my lip to try to hold onto at least the smallest thread of self control.

"My fingers or my cock?" he asked, sounding about as turned on as I was.

Both. Either. Something. Everything. "Your cock," I decided, my thighs tensing for my next instruction.

"Thank God," he said at last.

"Are you going to..."

"Yeah, baby," he said. "I am going to think about your tight, wet pussy grabbing my cock and pulling it deep inside." If I didn't get to touch myself, I was going to explode. I was going to turn into a ball of flames and burn out hard and fast. I was going to be scorch marks and dust on my bed sheets. "Are you ready, Fee?"

"Yes." Yes. Yes. Yes.

"Do you want it soft or hard?" he asked.

"Hard." I wanted him inside me rough enough to fucking break the bed, to break through the goddamn wall, to fall through the floor.

"Good. Take two fingers," he said, pausing, waiting for me to get ready, "and when I said 'now' I want to to shove those fingers all the way into your pussy. Okay?"

"Okay," I said, my fingers poised at my entrance. Waiting. And waiting. He was stubbornly silent on the other end of the phone for long enough to have my hips gyrating off the bed, abandoning all pretense of not being a ball of need.

"Now," he finally said and I pushed my fingers deep inside, feeling my insides grab at me as I thought about his cock. On the other end of the phone, Hunter let out a harsh gasp as he started to stroke his cock. "Don't stop, baby. Think of me fucking you hard and fast. Don't stop."

I didn't need any more encouragement than that. My whole body felt like it was focused on the clawing need inside me, the rush toward oblivion, the desire to get there as quickly as possible. My legs pulled together and my hips thrust upward, the palm of my hand rubbing against my clit as I pushed my fingers harder and faster. I was loud. I was so loud that he didn't even need the phone to hear me, but I kept it to my ear, needing to hear his breathing. "Are you getting close?" he asked.

"Yes," I answered. So close. "Are you?"

As if answering my question, I heard his head slam into the wall. "Fuck baby. I need to hear you come for me. Come for me, Fee. Now baby."

My fingers plunged forward once more, my hand pressing against my sensitive clit and I was falling, falling over the cliff as fireworks went off somewhere deep inside me. "Hunter!" I cried out, loud. Loud enough to wake the neighbors three floors below.

"Oh, fuck, Fee," he strangled out and his breath caught. "Fuck," he ground out as he came. It was the sexiest thing I think I had ever heard.

I lay there for a long time, curling up by the headboard, wanting to be closer to him. I wanted him there right then, wrapped up with me, encircled around me. But I couldn't have that; so I needed to settle for what I did have. The sound of his breathing on the other end of the phone was getting slower, steadier. I bunched up a pillow and laid my head across it, my hand touching the headboard as if the wall wasn't there.

"That was a lot hotter than I expected," he said suddenly in my ear. I smiled, turning my face into the pillow. That was the closest to real intimacy I had ever had with a person. It felt natural. Right. But at the same time, scary and awkward. "Fee?"

"I'm here."

"It's not usually like that, is it?" he asked after a minute.

That was cryptic. But I knew what he meant. And a million times... no. It was never like that. "No," I said. "Haven't you ever..."

"Called a phone sex line?" he asked, sounding amused.

"No," I answered quickly. "No. I meant... had phone sex."

"Nope," he said, surprising me.

"You're really good at it."

"Aw made ya feel good, did I?" he asked and I could swear I heard the smirk through the phone.

"Don't tease," I said, rolling my eyes. "I'm serious."

"I'm serious too. You cried out my name loud enough for the entire east coast to hear you."

"Hunter..." I warned.

"Yeah," he said, laughing, "like that. But higher. More breathy. And a lot louder."

"Oh my God, shut up!" I said, rolling onto my back, smiling at the ceiling.

That was the appeal to people, to the opposite sex: to please each other and then lay there afterward and tease and joke with each other.

"Just being honest," he said, trying to sound innocent.

"You're not exactly quiet when you come either," I said, rolling my eyes and he chuckled. "But seriously... you give good phone," I said, slipping out of the dreamy romantic feel of the aftermath, slipping a little more back into myself. "Want a job?"

"Listening to dudes jacking off..."

"I'm sure there are plenty of bored housewives who would like to hear you as they tap the clit their husbands have never been able to find in all the years of their marriage."

"Baby, I could never make horse noises and slap myself with..."

"A ruler," I supplied.

"A ruler," he laughed. "Yeah... no."

"But that's men," I said, shrugging. "Women aren't usually like that. They like the dirty talk and the sweet words. They want the fantasy."

"And men?"

"Men want the kink. The dirty secret wish that they're afraid to tell their spouses about."

"That's actually kind of sad," Hunter said and I could hear him getting up and moving around his apartment.

"You wouldn't believe how many calls pretty much start with an orgasm and end with sobbing. Either they feel guilty or they feel ashamed of how filthy their minds are."

"What's your favorite kind of call?"

"I don't know," I said, moving to hang my feet off the side of the bed. "I guess the doms. It's nice to not have to do all the talking."

"And your least favorite?"

"The guys who like being humiliated," I said, deciding it was the most honest answer I could think of. Though the animal guys were a buzzkill too.

"Why's that?"

"I dunno... how many times can you tell someone their pencil dick is pathetic, you know?"

"Are those the guys who usually end up crying?"

"No, actually... you'd be surprised. The submissive men, in

real life, are usually very powerful people. Judges. CEOs. That kind of thing. The doms are generally the weak little milksops you find working behind the counter at the computer repair stores."

"Well yeah," Hunter agreed, "they cant get laid if they don't command it."

"What are you doing?" I asked hearing a clicking.

"Oh," he said, sounding surprised, "you know what? You would probably like this. Why don't you get dressed," he suggested, "and in real clothes. Not in one of those skimpy club dresses you like."

"Hey," I grumbled, walking over to my closet.

"Not that those aren't hot," he conceded, "but put on something less... binding. Then get that pretty little ass over here."

He hung up and I looked dumbly down at my phone. According to the counter, we were on the phone for the better part of an hour. I pulled on a loose white t-shirt and a pair of gray leggings. They would definitely classify as binding, but he was just going to have to deal. Most of my wardrobe was tight.

Blame the floor-length sack dresses I had to wear until I was eighteen.

I felt nervous as I dressed, a fluid sensation in my belly. I walked into the bathroom, brushing my teeth and scrubbing my face. I pulled my hair into a braid. Then undid it. Then tied it up in a messy knot and decided that that was going to have to do. I put on a coat of mascara and some chapstick, slipped into the only pair of flats I owned, and checked my reflection.

There was a difference. Around my eyes. Around my mouth. There was less of a downturn to my lips. My eyes were less squinted. I looked younger than I usually did.

Maybe even, dare I say it? Happy. I looked almost, just barely, happy.

I knew that was dangerous. I had never even been close to happy, but I knew it was a shaky ground to stand on. Especially when the happiness was tied to another person. Because, well, I wasn't exactly a prize and soon enough Hunter would see that. He would see that and he would move on to someone with less damage. And I would be left to find the ground giving way underneath me.

I would be all the more miserable once I got a taste of happiness and had it ripped away.

But that was a problem for future Fiona to deal with. Right then, there, in that moment, I was going to let myself feel the happy. I wasn't going to sabotage it. I was going to suck out all the joy I could. I was going to let it sink into my own bones. I was going to hope it was enough to sustain me through the famine.

And the famine would come.

But for right then, I was going to be happy and go see what my gorgeous neighbor with the best phone sex voice in the history of all mankind had in store for me.

FOURTEEN

Hunter

I heard her knocking on my door half an hour later. I was glad for a little time alone. As much as I didn't want to admit it, I was a little more affected by that damn call than I had expected to be. I thought it was just a clever way to get her more comfortable with me so maybe we could move forward with a more physical relationship.

I didn't know what her problem was with sex, but judging by the way she shoved me away, it wasn't small. The way she had nonchalantly blown off being attacked outside of our building had given me the awful idea that maybe that was it. Maybe she was raped. Not wanting sex would be a normal response to that. As would wanting control... especially over men. Which, in turn, also explained the phone sex business.

As horrible as it was to think that was what happened, it made the most sense, especially since she definitely had a healthy sex drive.

And she liked being talked dirty to. Jesus Christ, that

moaning...

I shook my head, cleaning off my new dining table, feeling myself start to get hard again at the memory.

I never considered myself a phone sex kind of guy. That seemed to be for pervs and losers; or husbands and wives when one of them was out of town. It didn't seem like something a guy who could definitely go out and find a girl to take home would do. But with Fiona, it had been less awkward than I had expected. Actually, it felt like the most natural thing in the world.

She was different with me than she was with her other guys, her usual callers. With them she was loud, obnoxiously loud and filthy. Holy fuck did she have a dirty mouth. But with me she had seemed shy and uncertain. Maybe because she wasn't wearing her work mask; she wasn't pretending to be anyone. She was just herself. And while I would certainly like to get her to use that filthy mouth with me sometime, I wanted it to be her, not phone sex operator Fiona.

I walked around putting things away. I was still working on a lot of projects, but my apartment was a lot different from the last time she had seen it. The walls had been painted a warm burnt orange color. I had made a small round black dining room set, black coffee table, and bought a black leather couch. It was a bit... man cave-y, but I liked it. It felt homey. Her cactus was sitting in the center of the coffee table.

I walked down the hall, going into my bedroom. I hadn't gotten to that room yet. The walls were bare, an ugly faded white. My bed took up most of the floor space, a giant king sized bed in a child's sized room. But a man needed a good bed. I went into my small closet and grabbed a gray t-shirt.

Then I heard her door close. I walked out toward the living room, expecting her knock. But there was nothing for a long time and I could just picture her outside the door, arm raised, trying to get the courage to knock. It was at least a full minute before she finally did.

"Hey, Dan," she said when I opened the door, smiling a little. "You know... Vermont looks a lot like New York."

"Fucking overpopulation," I said, looking down at her, impossibly sexy in a t-shirt and leggings. How was that possible?

"Soo..." she said after the silence dragged on for a minute, "are you inviting me in..."

I moved out of the doorway and she walked in, looking around. "You did a lot of work already," she said, running her hand over the dining room table. "Did you make this?"

"Yeah," I said, feeling the smallest twinge of insecurity which was completely ridiculous.

"Wow," she said, looking around, her eyes falling on the cactus and a small smile toyed at her lips. "I really like this color. It's... cozy." She turned to me, her big green eyes finding mine. "Is this what you wanted to show me?"

"No," I said, shaking my head and moving toward the hallway closet. I reached in, grabbing the two metal cases and bringing them to where she was standing next to my dining room table.

"What's in there?" she asked, eying the boxes.

"My guns," I said.

"Your... guns?" she asked, taking a small step backward, her eyes going wide.

"Oh," I said, smiling. It was easy to forget sometimes that the word meant something else. "Not those kinds of guns," I said, clicking open the cases and pulling the trays out. "Tattoo guns," I clarified.

"You're a tattoo artist?" she asked, sounding surprised and pleased at the same time. I had seen one tattoo on her: the one on her thigh. The tree with the ax and quote. It had been well done. She had obviously done her research and picked a good artist.

"Yep," I said, holding out my arms. "I obviously have an

appreciation for ink."

"I noticed," she said, her eyes looking down to inspect the pictures. "How long have you been doing it?"

"I started when I was eighteen, but I didn't start doing it as a career until maybe a year or two ago. And even then, very part time. I had other work to do."

"Are you working at a place here, or just... like... going to people's houses?"

"I have a place I work at part time. I'll occasionally do private sessions. Parties even, but not as often."

"Can I see some of your work?" she asked, looking down at the gun with a look I recognized. It was the look of someone who wanted another tattoo.

I nodded, going back to the closet and dragging out my black portfolio and handing it to her. She pulled out a chair and sat down, opening the book and looking down at the pages. "You do a lot of color," she said, running her hand over a picture of flowers: daisies and lilacs.

"I do black and gray too. But the color really pops. Sometimes black and gray can look really muddy. Especially over time."

"Did you go to art school?" she asked, not looking up.

I smiled, rocking back on my heels. "Do I look like someone who went to art school?" I asked and she laughed.

"I guess not. But you're really good at drawing."

"Just something I was always good at I guess." I totally didn't spend hours pouring over drawing manuals when I was a kid. I didn't go through a sketchpad a week trying to perfect the same images over and over. I was not a pain in the ass perfectionist about my craft. Nope. Not me.

"Alright, stick it in me," she said, a sly smile on her face.

I felt my mouth fall open slightly. "What?" I asked.

"Get your mind out of the gutter, Fourteen," she teased,

pointing to the tattoo gun.

"Oh," I said, shaking my head. Of course she meant the needle. "Hey, with a mouth like yours, you can't blame me for thinking you meant something more..."

"Lascivious?" she supplied.

"Exactly. So... where am I sticking it?" I asked, my voice low and sexual.

She giggled. She actually giggled. The hardass chick who lived next door and ran a phone sex business actually giggled. "I was thinking the back of my neck," she said, shrugging.

"Okay," I said, walking up behind her and lifting her hair out of the way. "What do you want to get?"

"Surprise me," she said.

I dropped her hair, moving to squat down next to her. "Don't you know better than to give a tattoo artist free rein? You could end up with my name tattooed across your face."

She gave me a small smile. "I trust you," she said and the certainty in her voice nearly made me fall on my ass. She trusted me. If only she knew how stupid that was. "I don't know... give me something that you think... fits me."

"You're sure?" I asked, already knowing what I wanted to do, knowing it was her to a T, but worried slightly that she might find it offensive.

"Positive," she said, grabbing her hair and tying it up higher on her head.

"I can do color?"

"I'm sorry," she said, leaning forward and resting her head on her hands on the tabletop. "I am a canvas. I don't talk."

I got up to my feet, smiling as I pulled out my guns and inks. I shaved the back of her neck then grabbed a felt tip marker, drawing an outline on her skin. "How do you sit?" I asked, hoping she wasn't a squirmer.

"Like a rock," she said, sounding almost sleepy. "I have a

pretty high pain tolerance."

No shit. With the marks she carved into herself, I doubted a few needle pricks would bother her. An image of the night before flashed into my mind and I squinted about it. I was trying not to think about it.

About those God-awful, painful screams that woke me out of a dead sleep and had me running before I was even awake, had me slamming through her front door and charging through her apartment, only to find her in a puddle of blood on her bathroom floor. There was a razor blade on the ground next to her antiseptic supplies.

And she was asleep. She wasn't screaming about the pain she carved into herself. She was screaming about some other pain... pain that was likely the reason she cut into herself in the first place. To forget. To cope.

She had barely even flinched when I had cleaned her up. She would sit pretty for me. "Alright," I said, stepping back and setting up a spread next to her on the table. "Ready?" I asked, turning the machine on and feeling the comforting buzzing in my hand.

"Ready," she agreed, shifting slightly to give me the best access, her forehead on her hands.

I worked with painstaking precision. I wanted it to be absolutely perfect.

In the end, I stepped back, wiping away the extra dye and blood and surveyed the finished result.

It was a heart locket tattoo. Special. Like her. I made the heart fucking beautiful. It was pink and feminine with intricate black and gray filigree around the edges and the antique key hole in the center. Then I wrapped the whole thing with a chain. And then I put a pretty bow sitting on the top of the heart to the left.

To me, that was Fiona. She was beautiful. Perfect, really. But she had locks, and walls, and chain link fences to keep anyone from finding out how amazing she was.

"Don't hate me," I said, reaching into my box for a spare mirror.

She sat up slowly, rolling the tension out of her shoulders. "I'm sure it's great," she said again with certainty. "Come on, I want to see." She reached out and tugged at the hem of my shirt as she turned to walk down toward the bathroom.

I followed her, turning on the light. "Alright," I said, "turn around." She did and I handed her the mirror. "Check it out."

She lifted the mirror, backing up against the bathroom counter to get as close to the big mirror as possible. "Oh," she said, her eyes going wide, her mouth falling open slightly. That was it though. Just... oh. And I couldn't make out if it was a good "oh" or a bad "oh" and she was just standing there staring at it.

I shuffled my feet. "Fee," I said, needing an answer, needing her to end the torment.

"This is what you think of when you see me?" she asked, her voice low, her eyes still on the mirror.

"Yeah," I said. Because it was true.

Her head turned suddenly, her eyes finding mine. "You see right through me," she said, shrugging a shoulder. "I love it."

I couldn't keep the smile off my face. It was a big, goofy, high school cheerleader smile. "I'm glad you like it."

Her smile matched mine for a second, before it slipped slowly away. Something else rose up on her face, making her emerald eyes look glassy and bright. "Hey Hunter..."

"Yeah?" I asked, sure that she was just going to thank me. But then...

"Take me to bed."

FIFTEEN

Fiona

As soon as the words were out of my mouth, I wished I could suck them back in. I wanted to hit rewind, slap myself really hard across the face, and say something... anything other than that. It wasn't that I didn't want him to take me to bed. Of course I did. It was all I had been thinking about while he was working on me.

And then seeing what he had done... well... that just pushed me over the edge. It wasn't just because it was good. Every woman was turned on by talent and he was very talented. Every line was clean; the saturation was perfect. But it wasn't the skill. It was what he had chosen to do.

I swore those light eyes of his saw right down into my soul and the tattoo was proof that he did. He saw past the bitch persona. He saw past the seemingly extroverted phone sex operator. He saw what it all really was: fear, someone who was afraid to let herself feel anything so she kept it all under lock.

The only problem was, I lost the key.

I looked back at Hunter who looked as stunned as I felt. How hard would it have been to take it back? I could have told him I was joking. I could have told him I misspoke. I could have said that I was just riding a high from all the endorphins that stabbing me repeatedly with a needle had caused to flood my system. The only problem was... I didn't want to take it back. I didn't want to lie. I didn't want to have to keep denying myself the first thing I had really wanted in a long, long time.

"Hunter..." I started.

"It's alright," he said, shrugging a shoulder.

"What's alright?" I asked, confused.

"If you want to take that back." He shook his head at me. "Fee, you looked freaked the fuck out when you said that. So if you need to take it back..."

"I don't," I said, looking down at my feet. "I don't want to take it back. I want you. Like..." I said, looking up at him, "really want you."

"I really want you too, baby," he said, making my belly feel all fluttery again. How was he able to do that so easily? "But I want you to be ready." He paused for a second, looking pained. "If something has happened to you that has made sex... difficult..." he trailed off.

"What do you think happened to me?" I asked, not sure where his mind was going. There was a tightness in my chest at the idea that he might have had a clue.

He ran a hand over his eyes. "Did someone... rape you, Fee?"

I felt the word fall heavy against me. Rape. It was one of those words that made every woman tense, even women who hadn't lived through it, even women who had never been anywhere close to it. You felt it. It settled somewhere deep in your stomach, right behind your bellybutton, like a hole had opened up and was sucking energy in. Strong and strange, but somehow familiar.

I felt sick at thinking it, but I almost felt like that would be easier. That would be so much easier to explain. But that wasn't it and I couldn't let him think that.

"No," I said, shaking my head, taking a deep breath. "No."

"Okay," he said, reaching out toward me, taking my hand and holding it. "Well, whatever it is, Fee, you can tell me."

"I know," I said. I could. I knew I could. He wouldn't judge. He wouldn't think less of me. It was just hard to find those words. What words could ever explain it?

They couldn't.

I squeezed his hand once before letting it drop, reaching for the bottom of my shirt and pulling it up.

"What are you doing?" he asked, moving back a step, eying me like I had lost my mind.

"I need to show you... something," I said, praying he didn't ask. Because I was already a mass of panic. I just needed to get it over with.

"Okay," he said, leaning back against the door jamb.

I reached behind my back and unclasped my bra, pulling the material off in one quick motion and tossing it to the floor. I saw him look for a second, not seeing. Then his eyes squinted, looking closer and his face went to mine. And there was a question there.

"I didn't do it," I told him, "to myself. I didn't do this."

"Okay," he said, nodding.

I swallowed hard past the tightness in my throat and reached for my pants. I slipped my thumbs underneath the band of my tights and panties and pulled downward.

"Fee..."

"Please just... please," I said, shaking my head.

"Alright," he said, sounding tense.

But he was not one one-millionth as tense as I felt. That was the first time I had ever actually taken all my clothes off in front of someone. In the past... the two times I had tried to be intimate with someone, I had kept my skirt on. It had been easier that way. And they hadn't even stopped to wonder why we weren't getting naked. But they still found out.

Christ, how they reacted.

I remembered the first one. I was on his futon in his room. His mother was asleep two rooms away. I was eighteen and brand new to the city. I was curious. And such, such an innocent. I barely understood the concept of sex, let alone the feelings involved. He had quickly ripped my panties down, and shoved his bright blue condom-wrapped penis inside me without any pretense. I remember the pain like it was yesterday, sharp and burning at the same time. Then his hand had pushed up my skirt so he could watch and he sprang back like I had stabbed him.

"What the fuck?" he had exploded, looking at my sore and scarred vagina like it was the ugliest thing he had ever seen. I had been so humiliated that I got up and ran out without explaining, without grabbing my panties.

The next one had been a year later. I liked him. I really liked him even though he was city-roughened and a nasty drunk. By then, a year and a half of living on the streets had given me quite an extensive knowledge about sex. Regardless of my traumatizing first time, my hormones were begging for me to try again.

"I have some... scars," I had told him, feeling shy.

"Whatever," he said, and shoved himself inside. It was quick, mostly painless, but wholly unsatisfying at the same time. Afterward, he reached down and lifted my skirt to look. He looked for so long that I felt a swell of hope that he wasn't repulsed. But then he had dropped my skirt, looked at me, and shook his head. "That's the ugliest pussy I've ever seen."

I couldn't bring myself to ever face him again.

I shook my head, trying to clear it. That was the past. This was the here, the now. This was with Hunter. And I was going to face the issue head-on no matter how much I felt like throwing up all over my own feet.

I pushed the material down, stepping out of the legs and straightening.

His eyes stayed on mine for a long time and I could feel myself trying to project the need for him to look. *Please, please look. I need to get this over with. I'm dying little by little.*

His eyes finally started to trail downward, stopping slightly at my breasts then going down my belly. Then his gaze stopped. I heard his breath exhale out sharply. I tensed against the sound, sure I knew what was going to follow: revulsion.

Then he was moving, walking closer. He stopped right in front of me and went down on his knees. His hand moved up the front of one of my thighs, reaching the spot where my leg met my hip, just an inch away from where his eyes were planted.

Where the word "wicked" was scrawled in huge, ugly, uppercase print across the triangle above my sex.

"Why do I get the feeling that this wasn't you trying to say you have a wicked cool snatch?" he asked, attempting levity.

The tension in that moment was as thick as honey when I didn't laugh. "I didn't do it," I said again.

Maybe I should have just... owned up to it, said that I did. I self-harmed all the time. It would be completely believable. But I had my hands full with my own depravity, I suddenly didn't want to claim his as my own anymore. At least not with Hunter.

"What happened to you, Fee?" he asked, his hand moving to cover the scars as he tilted his head back to look at me.

I took a deep breath, closing my eyes against the tears. I wasn't going to cry. But it wasn't because I was embarrassed to; or because I was afraid to let Hunter see that side of me. I wasn't going to cry because my father didn't deserve that.

I swallowed and looked down at him. "I grew up in a very religious household," I started, my words sounding robotic. "My father raised us in a shack with no running water, no electronics. No... nothing. Even though he was from a rich family. We needed to know humility. I... wasn't even allowed to learn to read. But my mother taught me in secret. It was a rough life but we didn't really know any better." I paused, taking a breath. Hunter's blue eyes were still on mine, patient. Expectant. "I have an older brother. Isaiah. He's about two years older. We shared a room and when he was twelve... he started to... watch me change," I said, watching Hunter wince slightly. Because it was gross. I couldn't blame him for thinking how disgusting that was. It totally was disgusting. I knew that, even though I had long since come to understand that Isaiah hadn't known any better. He was a kid, just like I was. "One night, my father came in and saw him watching me..."

"You don't have to tell me," he said when I paused, when the words failed me, "if it's too much. You don't have to."

"I want to," I said, surprising myself. "He saw Isaiah watching me and he grabbed me. He dragged me through the house and threw me out into the snow. Naked. I was naked. And he was rambling on about the wickedness of Eve. Of women in general. He beat me. And then he... he got on top of me and he pulled out a knife and he did this," I said, touching the scars under my breasts. "Then he did this," I said, reaching down and touching his hand that was still covering the word. "He told me that I was dirty and wicked. He told me that I was leading my brother into the temptations of the flesh. He said I was evil. He told me that he would make me so ugly that no man would ever want me. So I couldn't lead another man to sin against God like I had with my brother."

My heart was pounding in my ears and every inch of my skin felt hot, feverish.

Hunter ducked his head. "You were ten years old," he said quietly.

"Yeah," I agreed, trying to focus on breathing. In. Out. In.

Out.

His hands moved, slipped around my hips and touched my ass, settling there softly. He leaned forward, planting a kiss on the center of the awful word. "You're not wicked," he said, shaking his head and I felt his hair brush my thighs. "Your father was a sick fuck and your brother was warped," he said, sounding angry.

"I know," I said. I knew that. I did. I had known that for a long time. But it didn't take the sting away. It didn't take away the years of believing he was right about me. It didn't erase thinking about how I was going to burn in hell for my sins; or how I was a punishment to my family. How I was a penance that needed to be paid so they could go to Heaven. While I rotted.

"He was also wrong," Hunter said. "You could never be ugly," he said, looking back up at me. "And I want you." He slowly got onto his feet, one of his hands reached out toward my face, stroking my cheek. "Thank you for telling me."

"Thank you for not telling me I have an ugly pussy or running away like I was a demon," I said, thinking of the other boys. They were boys. Because a man acted the way Hunter was acting.

"Whoever did that was a dickhead and had no idea what they were missing out on," he said.

"What were they missing out on?"

"You."

Then he leaned forward and kissed me, soft. He gave me a bunch of little kisses across my lips before pressing down. I sank into it, into him. My arms went up and around his neck, pulling him closer. His tongue slipped between my lips, teasing mine and sending a flood of desire to my core. He kissed me for a long time, until I felt like I was floating, until I felt it all the way down to my toes. Then he pulled back, his eyes hazy. "We don't have to have sex," he said and the pulsing need between my thighs was in complete disagreement with him.

I smiled slowly at him, shrugging a shoulder. "All talk, huh?" I asked. "Can't get it up without the phone in your hand?"

He snorted, leaning down and planting a kiss on my forehead. He reached down, grabbing my hand and turning it so the palm was out, then placed it down on his crotch. His cock was straining against the thick material of his jeans. "Can't get it up, huh?"

"I'm afraid I'm going to have to see it to believe it," I said, pursing my lips at him.

He chuckled, taking a step back, reaching for the hem of his shirt and pulling it off in one swift motion.

He was too good looking. Like, seriously. It wasn't right for one man to be that perfect. The face alone was enough. The face should have been paired with some flabby man boobs or a beer belly just so the other guys stood a chance. But, no. Hunter was perfect everywhere. His shoulders were wide and strong. His chest was defined. And then, of course, because no God would be complete without them... he had abs, the kind that you could sink fingers in between. And that glorious, beautiful V that half-hid beneath the waistband of his jeans. There was a thin black trail of hair that disappeared underneath his top button.

As if sensing my need to see more, to see everything, like he got to see me, he reached down, slowly unfastening the button and pulling down the zipper. He pushed the material down and it fell with a slight whooshing noise to the floor. His dark boxers were all that was left. Beneath them, his legs were solid. His cock was hard, pushing against the thin material and I could make out the perfect shape of the head.

He grabbed the waistband and pulled it open, letting the boxers fall to the floor.

Yup, perfect. Head to toe. Every little space between.

"Okay, I believe it," I said, glancing at his long, thick cock with a surge of anticipation. What would it be like? Without the fear? Without the shame?

All I knew was I wanted to find out.

"Come here," he said, tilting his head to the side, looking down once then back up to my face.

I did. My feet moved across the cool floor with a weighted feeling. "Hi," I said, my feet next to his, our bodies a whisper from each other.

"Hi," he said back, smiling. Then he leaned forward and kissed the tip of my nose. "So, wanna go to the bed?" he asked, reaching down and taking my hand.

I laced my fingers between his and nodded.

He pulled me into the hall then to his room, still bare-walled and dominated by the huge bed with rich black blankets and sheets. He closed the door, turning to me and wrapping his arms around my hips, pulling me against him. I felt myself shiver as our bare skin touched. He leaned down and breathed in the smell of my hair, then started moving forward, making me slide backward blindly across the floor.

The backs of my knees hit the bed and I untangled myself from him and slid up on it, moving toward the center, my knees to my chest. He stood there looking at me for a minute before moving closer, crawling across the bed toward me. I lay backward against the pillows.

He sat back on his heels, running his fingertips up the tops of my feet, my calves, the sides of my thighs, not even hesitating over the cuts and scars. Like they were normal- a part of me, a part of my skin. I felt my thighs part around his hips, my knees touching the sides of his stomach. He pressed forward sightly, letting his hands settle on either side of my shoulders.

"Guess what?" he asked.

"What?"

"I've thought about you naked a thousand times," he admitted, lowering down to trail kisses across my shoulder, my collarbone, "and my fantasies didn't even come close to the reality of how perfect you are," he told me, sinking his lips into my neck and sucking the skin into his mouth.

I knew I wasn't perfect. Far from. But, for the first time in my life, that was okay. Because Hunter thought I was and that was more than enough.

My hands moved up his back, enjoying the hard muscle beneath. His erection was pressed up against my lower belly, as needy as I felt. But Hunter was taking his time. His lips moved to mine, pressing into them and I kissed him back with every bit of passion I was feeling. Then he was trailing downward, touching my throat, moving between my breasts. His hair fell forward, tickling my nipples as he slowly planted soft kisses across the scars under each breast. I arched away from the strange sensation, noticing the surge of panic at the contact.

He moved upward, taking one of my nipples into his mouth, running his tongue over the peak until it was straining, until there was an impossible tightness there, then moving to the other one to do the same. Then he was trailing his tongue down the center of my belly and I felt my legs fly out on the mattress around his legs.

Every muscle in my body felt tense as desire pinged off of each nerve ending, making me feel frazzled, overwhelmed with each new sensation. He moved his lips across my hips, his hands reaching down to press on my thighs, holding them open against the mattress. Then his tongue was touching the edge of the W, tracing it down then up, then down, up, before moving on to the next letter.

And all of a sudden, they felt different. They didn't feel like a brand, like a curse. They felt cherished. They felt like something that was a source of desire, not shame. I almost cried. But then he looked up at me, a devilish smile was toying at his lips for a second before his head dipped and I felt his tongue sneak between my delicate folds, sliding upward. His lips closed around my clit, sucking. My thighs strained against his hold as I let out a surprised yelp. My hips arched into his mouth, begging for more, begging for things I was barely familiar with. The pressure built until it was painful, before his lips pulled away, his tongue stroking over the sensitive bud quickly side to side. My hands went to his hair, grabbing it and twisting, but pushing him closer. Holding him there.

"Hunter," I whimpered, my toes curling, my whole body straightening as I felt my orgasm build higher and higher.

He opened his mouth, breathing warm air over my clit for a second before his tongue started working in small circles. Then I felt his finger press against my slick entrance, pausing for the briefest of seconds before pushing in, turning, and stroking against the top wall. He did it over and over until I couldn't fight it anymore and my body exploded into orgasm, making me cry out and push his head harder against me.

I fell back against the mattress after, feeling sweaty and weak, like my limbs were too heavy to move. He went back on his ankles, looking down at me with heavy-lidded eyes. "You're so sexy when you come," he said, running his fingers up and down my inner thighs, giving me time to recover and making my body come alive at the same time.

When I was panting again, whimpering against his exploration, he leaned over, reached into the nightstand and pulled out a condom foil. I watched as he slid it on, watching me with a fierceness that was almost scary.

He moved forward, going down on his forearms, and taking my lower lip between his teeth. I felt his weight settle on top of me, his chest hair teasing my hardened nipples. His hips pushed against mine and I felt his hardness against my inner thigh.

"You ready?" he asked, then smiled. "I mean, I know you're ready," he said, licking his lips, tasting me there still. "But are you sure?"

I smiled up at him, my arms going to his shoulders. "Never been more sure of anything in my life," I said, leaning up and planting a quick kiss to his lips.

He reached down between us, settling his cock at my threshold, pausing there, pressing but not penetrating. I rocked my hips against it, shameless with my need. He made a chuckling sound somewhere deep in his chest then, with his eyes on mine, he thrust once forward, pushing all the way inside.

A surprised cry escaped my lips as I felt his thickness spread me, just shy of painful, a tight pulling sensation that felt foreign but right. Like I had been missing it all along. "Fuck," he said, dropping his forehead to mine, taking a deep breath. "You're so fucking tight," he ground out from between clenched teeth.

I felt my insides pulling at him, begging for the motion I needed. The motion he wasn't giving me.

"Hunter, please," I whimpered, my hands grabbing at his shoulders.

He lifted his head, looking down at me, a smirk on his face. "Please what, baby?" he asked, innocently.

I half-laughed, half-groaned. "Please fuck me," I said, digging my nails across his back.

"Well, if you insist," he said, pulling out and slamming forward again.

He smiled down at me then withdrew again, rocking his hips into me quickly. We were both too desperate to take it slowly. We were both too close already. My hips rose up to meet his thrusts, pulling him deeper. I felt myself tightening around him with each thrust forward.

To my ears, everything sounded muted: his harsh breath, his quiet groans, my own moans. But I knew I was loud enough to wake the neighbors, completely lost in him, in the sensations I had never felt before.

"That's it," he said, sounding winded. "Come for me baby. I

want to feel your pussy grab me."

My hips rose to meet his one more time and I felt myself teeter on the edge then plunge over, my body shooting into my orgasm so hard that I saw white. My fingers raked across his back as I cried out his name, burying my face in his neck.

"Fuck, Fee," he growled out as he slammed forward, twitching deep inside me as he came.

We stayed exactly that way for a long time, our hearts slamming in our chests, our breathing ragged on each others skin. Hunter turned his face slightly, kissing my jaw, before pushing up and looking down at me. "Not that the phone sex wasn't great," he started, smiling in a tired way, "but Jesus Christ, Fee," he said, leaning down and kissing me once more before moving off of me, out of me, and turning away for a moment.

I felt oddly empty when he was gone, completely aware of my nakedness, but unconcerned with it. I watched his back until he turned back to me, sliding into the empty space next to me. He slipped a hand under my shoulders, turning me onto my side and pulling me across his chest.

We stayed like that for a long time, my leg moving up over his hips. His hands moved lazily up and down my back, stopping just below my tattoo that was burning sightly from all the squirming around. "You alright?" he asked, sounding half asleep.

And I was. Maybe for the first time ever, I was fine. Good even.

Beneath me, he drifted off to sleep, his hand still and heavy at my hips. I traced shapes on his skin as I breathed in his sawdust soap smell that still clung to him despite not actually being around any sawdust that morning.

So that was what sex was supposed to be like. That was what I had been missing, what my body had begged for until it gave up. Until it forgot to want it anymore. Now the floodgates were open, and I wanted. Oh, how I wanted. I almost felt bad at how much I was going to take advantage of Hunter. Up and down the hall and through the floor.

I woke up a while later on my back. The arm thrown up over my head was asleep and throbbing painfully. Hunter was on his side next to me, his hair wild and his eyes hazy. He was staring at my chest. When he noticed I was up, he reached out, touching one of my scars.

"How do you feel about these?" he asked.

I pulled my arm down, feeling it drop heavily to the mattress. "Feel about them?" I asked, still struggling against my sleep-cloudy brain. "I hate them."

He nodded, still stroking the soft skin. "I could cover them," he said, looking up at me.

"What do you mean cover them?"

"Well you know what underbust tattoos are, right?" he asked. "They're really popular now."

I thought of all the pictures I had poured over online. So many of them with girls holding their hands up to cover their nipples as the tattoo draped under one breast, moved up between them, then draped under the other. They were always intricate, lace-like. Beautiful.

"Yeah," I said carefully, not letting myself hope too much. "But...these are... big scars. Can you even tattoo on a scar?" I asked, knowing how I had never grown hair on the marks between my legs when I hit puberty.

"Yeah," he said, stroking again. "A lot of women tattoo to cover mastectomy scars now. Some even tattoo ink bras over their breasts to hide them. It covers."

There was a heaviness in my chest as the realization settled in. I wouldn't have to live with them. I wouldn't have to pretend they weren't there. I wouldn't have to avert my eyes when I looked in the mirror. I wouldn't spend every day of my life with my awful past etched into my skin. All thanks to Hunter.

"Will you do it for me?" I asked, my voice sounding more emotional than I wanted it to.

He looked up at me for a second, then bent down at kissed the center of each scar. "Of course I will." He said it easily, like that had been the plan all along. "I could maybe do something about these," he said, touching the word without a trace of hesitation. "I saw a woman tattoo a phoenix across here. It went up her belly and the tail went down over the side of her thigh," he said, stroking his hand down over my self-inflicted cuts. "These could be a memory too."

And I would think twice about slicing into something beautiful that he had painstakingly made a part of my skin. True, maybe I would just find a new place to cut open. But there was a chance, albeit small, that the sayings were right: time does heal. Maybe that was what this was. Maybe this was healing.

"Hey," I said quietly and his eyes met mine. I found no strangeness there. No disgust. But, better yet, no pity. I leaned down, grabbing his face and pulling it to mine, letting myself kiss him with every failed hope, lost dream, every frustrated moment of low self-esteem, every hidden, dark, secret, shameful thing. I kissed him like therapy. Like I could pour it all into him and finally be free.

And he sensed it. His hands went to my face, cradling it softly as I purged all the old away, leaving room for the new, for him, to sink in.

He pulled away slowly, giving me a small smile. Then lying down on the mattress next to me, rolling us both on the sides to face each other.

"So," he started.

"So..." I said, smiling.

"Tell me your story, Fee."

"My story?" I asked, sounding confused. Because I was. I had already told him the awful, ugliest parts of me. I told him things I had never told anyone and he wanted more. "You want more?" I asked, feeling uncertain.

"Oh, Fee," he said, reaching out to touch my cheek. "I want everything."

SIXTEEN

Fiona

How were you supposed to start? How do you tell someone the entire story of your life? How do you find those kinds of words?

As if sensing my dilemma, he let his hand drop, grabbing mine. "How about your mother. Tell me about her."

My mother. I had such guilt about my mother. I remembered when I left, how I had learned to hate her after. Almost as much as my father. More at times. She was supposed to protect me. She was supposed to save me from his torment. And I hated her for letting me suffer while she stood by and did nothing.

It took me a long time, maybe a year after I found what had happened, to forgive her. To understand. "My mom was damaged. She was raised with an abusive father. I think it was easy for her to just... continue the cycle, bow down before another abusive man. And she was never good enough for my father. He was always picking at her about how she cooked, how she cleaned house, raised us. But, most of all, how she wasn't a religious enough woman."

"She must have had a rebellious streak to teach you to read," Hunter said, nuzzling his face into my neck.

"Yeah. And she named me Fiona. I was supposed to be Mary, but because my father didn't go in the delivery room... my mom named me Fiona. After her mother. And," I said, thinking of her running out barefoot in the snow, her eyes wild, "when my father was doing this," I said, waving toward my crotch, "she... set the living room on fire."

"What?" he said, popping his head up.

"Yeah. I guess she knew she could never make him stop. And he seemed like he would be happy to carve into me until there was nothing left, that's how angry he was. So she took a stick and set the side of the chair next to the fireplace on fire. She waited until it was going good and ran out and screamed for my father."

"Wow," Hunter said, reaching out and rubbing my hip.

"Yeah. I felt so bad for not realizing what she had done for me while I was growing up. The small ways she had looked out for me. Protected me."

"You see it now," he said, shrugging.

"Too late though," I said. "I was so angry when I ran away from home. So, so angry. I had been beaten that morning for not getting my chores done early enough. I had to go have breakfast with my grandmother and my father was in rare form. I couldn't even sit down when I got to Gram's house with my backpack that I said was filled with my sewing, but was actually spare clothes and the money I had stolen out of my father's bible. When my grandmother went into the kitchen to get the tea, I ran. I ran and ran and ran, every step of the way cursing my father and mother."

"It's never too late to tell her you saw what she did, Fee."

"But it is," I said. "The day I ran away, just hours after she knew I was gone, she knew I would never be in his grasps again, she took my father's hunting knife, the same one that cut me up, went out into the woods and killed herself."

"Jesus," Hunter hissed. "Fee... I'm so sorry."

I shook my head. "No. Don't be. I realized after I heard about it... two years later... that that was all she had wanted to do for twenty years. Twenty years she spent being belittled and beaten and forced into humiliating sex with my father. She had thought about death every day. But she endured it. For me. Because she needed to protect me. She needed to prepare me for the day when I would escape. Like she never could. And once I did, she got to have her own sort of escape too."

Hunter scooted closer, wrapping his arms around me and pulling me close. "So what happened after you ran?"

"I ran here. Even living like I lived, shut off from the world, I had heard about the city. My father ranted and raved about the sinners here. About it being the new Sodom and Gomorrah. People fornicated on the streets. Men sodomized each other. Women lifted their skirts to good, religious men who crossed their paths, pulling them into their debauchery..."

"Sounds like a fun place to be," Hunter said against my shoulder.

"Exactly," I said, smiling. "I figured if there was one place he wouldn't go to find me, it would be a place damned to be consumed with fire and brimstone. So I made my way here, taking a bus for the first time, a train for the first time. Then I stepped out of the station onto the streets and I knew I was home."

"Where did you go?"

"Well, that's the thing," I said, shaking my head. "I wasn't exactly prepared. It had been such a rash decision and I knew so little about money and how to take care of myself..."

"You were on the streets," Hunter supplied, moving away to look at me.

"Yeah."

"For how long?"

"About two years. It wasn't as bad as it sounds. I mean it was bad. I was so hungry and cold and scared... all the time. But I was on my own. No one was going to beat me for not being godly enough. No one was going to carve me up like a turkey. And no one told me I couldn't do things. Like read. Learn. I went to the library and I read... everything. I ate what people felt bad enough to feed me. I put up my walls and I tried to figure out a way out of it." I thought about the makeshift showers in the fast food bathrooms, cleaning myself up so I could go for interviews. They always ended up being jobs I could never keep for very long. But they offered me some money. I saved enough to get a phone and to buy rental time on a computer cafe. Eventually, a way to start my business.

"I did my first phone sex calls while living in a box between a office supply store and a pharmacy. I had been so green..."

"Were you still a virgin?" he asked.

"No," I said. But, oh, I wished I was. "But I might as well have been. I was able to get this place just a couple weeks after."

Hunter gave me a small smile. "You've made a really good life for yourself here, Fee."

I thought of all the designer clothes in my closet, the money I spent like water, the freedom I had to go out all night and sleep all day. He was right. It might not have been a wild, grand life and it might have been fraught with all my demons... but it was good. It was mine.

He was silent for a moment. "I think your mom would have been happy with this," he said, smirking a little. "Aside from you just getting away from your father. I think what you've done would have made her laugh. What a slap in the face to everything your father tried to beat into you to become a phone sex operator who drinks a lot and tattoos her body and has sex with the trouble that lives next door."

"You're not trouble," I said, an image of him beating that guy flashing into my head before I pushed it away.

"You don't know me that well, Fee," he said, sounding almost sad. "Trust me... I'm trouble."

"Well," I said, reaching out and wrapping my arms around his neck, "maybe I like trouble."

"Oh yeah?" he asked, his eyebrow raised.

"Yeah."

"How much?" he asked, smirking.

I smiled, sitting up, pushing him onto his back and putting my legs on either side of him. His hands moved to my hips, sinking into the hollows and wrenching a moan from me. I leaned down, turning my head to the side and trailing my lips across his neck like he had done for me, wanting to see if it felt the same to him as if did to me. He exhaled roughly, bolstering my self-confidence and I slowly moved downward. Between his ribs, over his stomach. Lower.

I had been faking oral sex long enough to know what I was supposed to do. I knew my instructions. I was supposed to tease the head then take the shaft into my mouth. Deep. Deeper than was comfortable. They liked to hear you gag slightly on it. That turned them on. Then start moving your mouth from the base upward in a twisting motion. You could intermittently go up and down, but the twisting was what got them really going.

I knew what to do. But I had never done it.

Uncertainty was like a churning inside, like a hand grabbed my insides and twisted. I paused for the barest of seconds before my hand reached out to grab the base and hold it as my tongue snaked out to swirl circles across the sensitive head. I heard his breath hiss out and his hands slam down on the bed next to his body. Encouraged, I slid my mouth around him, slowly moving downward, tilting my head slightly upward to look at his face.

"Oh fuck," he said, reaching down to put a hand on the back of my head. Not pulling or pushing, just resting there as I took more and more of him into my mouth. "Yeah, baby," he said, sounding pained, "take it all." I hit the base with an involuntary clenching feeling in my throat, tight and uncomfortable, but not sick. Not like I had expected. I closed my lips down harder, turning slightly to the left, then right as I slowly moved back upward. I got to the head, licking my tongue once over the tip, tasting him there, before moving quickly back down again.

In that moment, I didn't understand the complaints I had heard from endless callers about how their wives didn't give head; or only gave it on special occasions because they didn't like it. How could you not like it? How could you not feel powerful? How could you not get off knowing how good you were making them feel? How at your mercy their pleasure was?

It was the hottest thing I had ever experienced, watching Hunter's face contort, feeling his body tense under me, hearing his breathing become ragged. I couldn't wait for him to come. I wanted to hear him, to feel him lose control. I wanted to taste him, to take him in.

But then his hand moved into my hair, grabbing it and pulling me upward. His cock slipped out of my mouth and I made a whimpering sound. Hunter chuckled. "Don't worry baby," he said, moving to sit up, still holding my hair, watching as I licked him off my lips, "one day I am going to love coming in that pretty mouth. Down that throat. But right now," he said, letting me go and moving toward the end of the bed, "I want to fuck you until you can't walk right for a week."

It sounded like a threat. Like a promise. I felt my desire like a stabbing inside, like a white-hot need.

He moved to the nightstand, slipping another condom on before turning back to me. He reached out, grabbing my hips and pulling. My arms flew out to brace my fall as I landed face-first against the mattress. He pulled backward until I felt myself hanging off the edge of the bed. His hand reached out, slapping my ass hard once. "I've been thinking about this ass since that first day on the balcony. You had on those pink panties that only covered half of it. I wanted to jump over to your balcony, rip them off, and fuck you from behind right there where anyone could look up and see us."

He slapped me again, making me jump, groan a little. "You like that, baby?" he asked, slapping me again without waiting for an answer. "Does that get your pussy wet?" he asked, his hand pushing between my thighs and, finding wetness there, he plunged his finger inside me. "Yeah it does," he growled, thrusting his finger quickly inside me before pulling out. His hands grabbed my hips, pulling them off the mattress, making me stand on my shaky legs.

His hands moved between my thighs, pulling them slightly apart. Then his cock was pressing against me, holding there still, making the tension build unbearably. Then, with one quick thrust, he was buried inside me. Impossibly deep, deeper than he had been before. I felt him everywhere. I clenched around him, needing the fullness, needing him deep, and rocked back against him.

"You like it deep, baby?" he asked, pulling my hips back and upward slightly, making me yelp. Because it hurt, a sharp, pinching feeling. It hurt, but it felt so good at the same time.

"Yeah," I groaned, wiggling against it.

"Make yourself come," he instructed, holding still inside me.

I didn't need any further encouragement. I was too far gone to feel shame or self-consciousness. I pulled forward and shoved back, I moved my hips side to side, I swirled them in circles. I could feel the tension build, the tightening that was threatening to explode. I was so close and he still hadn't moved at all. "Am I going to make you come too?" I asked, hearing his ragged breathing.

His hands bit painfully into my hips. "Not until you make yourself come," he said, barely words at all, more like a growl.

Empowered, I moved faster, slamming back into him, pushing in fast, frantic circles. I felt my orgasm slam into me, making my legs give out and Hunter grabbed my hips and held them up as I clenched around his hardness over and over, an endless wave of sensation.

As soon as I stopped moaning, I felt him pull out of me and slam forward. Hard, so fucking hard my entire body jerked forward. My feet went back on the floor, bracing, trying to not go flying with each powerful thrust. I held still, my body rigid as his cock thrust into me in a slow, but forceful rhythm. Fast, hard in. Pause. Quickly out. Pause. Harder, faster in. I was a puddle of need under him, a screaming, panting mess. His hand let go of one of my hips, spanking my ass before each thrust and I arched up into it, enjoying the sting more than I could have ever known. I needed it. It pushed me forward toward the orgasm that threatened to make me dumb.

Then the spanking stopped and he picked me up off my feet, his thrusts becoming faster, more demanding. I couldn't move. I couldn't rock against him. I couldn't help us each reach the impending oblivion. I was completely at his mercy as he slammed into me over and over, making my insides tighten around him, become a vise-like grip that he groaned at, staying deep and plunging further in.

"Oh my God," I cried, almost fearful as I teetered in the nothingness for a second before he pushed forward, hitting the front wall and making me completely lose what little control I had. I screamed his name loud enough for heaven and hell to hear me as I came around him, pulling him, clenching him.

He groaned, slamming forward once more, burying deep. "Fuck," he growled out. "Oh, fuck... Fee," he yelled out as he came deep inside me.

My feet fell hard onto the floor as he dropped them, pushing forward, his chest landing on my back. Spent. He was spent. I struggled for breath through my own exertion and the weight on me. My heart was beating so fast in my chest it almost scared me.

Above me, his breath was fast in my ear. His cock slid out of me and, after a minute, he slowly lifted himself off of me.

I felt his hand slap my ass once, not hard. Then he leaned down and I felt him kiss one of the cheeks. "Jesus fucking Christ, Fee," he said, sounding disbelieving as he moved away from me.

I couldn't move. Literally couldn't. I was a mess of flesh and aftershock, lying there, half on the bed, my ass at the edge of the mattress, my knees collapsed against the side of it. I felt half dead, but more alive than I ever had been before.

Hunter came back, stroking the sides of my hips. "You okay there, Sixteen?" he asked, sounding amused, sounding pleased with himself. He fucked me into oblivion and he knew it.

I made a weird sound, a garbled mumbling nothing that he chuckled at. I felt the mattress give way to his weight as he moved in beside me. He reached out, grabbing my sides and pulling me up on the mattress fully. He reached down and pulled the tangled blankets up and over my suddenly very cold body, resting a hand at my lower back.

A long time later, I turned my head to face him, a few inches to my side. "Well you made good on that threat," I said, wincing as I curled up on my side facing him.

His brows drew together. "What threat?"

"I'm not going to walk right for a week," I said. He threw his head back and laughed at my pain that wasn't quite pain, it was soreness, a deep, deep ache that started to smart anytime I tried to move, so I decided to stay completely still.

"Well that's fine," he said, recovering, reaching for my hand and kissing it, "because you're not leaving this bed for a week." At my look of strain he smiled. "There are so many ways I still need to fuck you. On all fours. Riding me. And," he said, his voice sounding deep as his hand slid down my back to cup my ass, the cheeks red and sensitive. "I would like to bury deep inside this ass at some point too."

"Oh, really?" I asked, not opposed to the idea. I wanted him everywhere. I wanted him to claim every inch of me. Besides, I heard of the kind of orgasms you could get from anal sex, especially if you pushed your fingers inside to stroked your G-spot while he worked your clit. A triple zone orgasm. I heard they could make you spring out of your body with their intensity. And I was really eager to give that a try.

"Yes," he said, pausing, "really," he said the word harshly, like he had never wanted something so much.

"We'll have to see what we can do about that then," I said, inching closer and snuggling up to his chest. "But first," I said, yawning, wrapping my arm around his back, "sleep."

SEVENTEEN

Fiona

I didn't go home for three days. I took my calls in Hunter's bed, gloriously naked while he watched on. Sometimes he would lay next to me, a sketchpad on his lap as he worked on the designs for my upcoming tattoos.

No matter how much I thought about it, I couldn't get over it. I couldn't believe how I went from my usual self: cold, brittle, don't-fuck-with-me-while-I-self-destruct Fiona to this one, the one who was okay with letting someone else see her completely bare. Completely vulnerable.

I felt Hunter in every fiber of my being. And it wasn't scary. It wasn't awkward. It was right. It felt right.

"I love it when you sniff my panties, baby," I said and Hunter's head shot up, a brow lifting, a smile playing at his lips. I rolled my eyes at him and he went back to drawing. He didn't question me about work. He didn't think it was weird or perverted or a terrible way to make my ends meet. I would occasionally hear him snort or chuckle when I needed to say something especially unusual, but he kept his opinions to himself.

"Yes, my pussy is so wet," I said and I saw Hunter out of the corner of my eye setting his pad down on the nightstand and moving toward me.

He stood at the edge of the bed, staring down at me for a long time and I sent him a confused look. Then he grabbed my ankles, pulling me closer to him and spreading me open. A smile played at his lips as he kept his eyes on mine. His finger slipped between my folds and I had to bite down on my lip to keep from crying out.

"Yeah," I said into my phone, my voice sounding breathy. "I'm touching my clit," I said and Hunter's hand shifted, running over the sensitive bud. "Yes. It feels so good," I said, squirming against Hunter, reaching down to push him away. But he just slapped at my hands and continued his torture. "I think I'm ready for you," I mused and Hunter's finger slipped deep inside me, making me arch up. He nodded, pulling his finger back out and I almost died of laughter, bringing a hand to my mouth and pressing down.

On the other end of the phone, my caller was sounding breathy. "You want a dick deep inside right now, don't you?" he asked.

I took a long, slow breath. "Mmhmm. I want it so bad," I murmured and watched as Hunter slipped a condom on. No way. No fucking way was he going to screw me while I was on the phone with a client. That was so, so unprofessional.

I shook my head at him and he smiled and nodded. "How are you guys doing it?" he whispered and I blushed crimson.

"How do you want me, baby?" I asked, not even having to fake the desire in my voice.

"Yes, I love being on top," I said, watching as Hunter shrugged and lay down on the bed, patting his lap. He was so adorably sexy sometimes. I climbed over to him, straddling his waist. His hand went to the base of his cock, holding it in place so I could lower down on it. "Oh," I cried out, sliding slowly down on him. "Oh, that feels so good," I groaned, feeling my hips drop down on his.

Hunter's hands moved up my belly and grabbed my breasts, squeezing them in his big hands as I started moving back and forth. "It's so... deep," I moaned, to Hunter. The phone was all but forgotten in my hand. Hunter's fingers swiped over my nipples and his hips drove up into mine, making me gasp and fall forward, one hand bracing against the bed the other still holding my cell phone.

I lifted slightly off of him, holding still as he thrust upward into me over and over until I was crying out, needy and frantic. I heard my caller curse, make a garbled sound, thank me and then there was only silence.

I dropped the phone to the mattress, my hands moving to Hunter's belly to brace myself as his thrusts became more wild and needy. Once I got the rhythm, I moved too. As he thrust upward, my hips slammed down, making me take him as deep as my body would allow. "Hunter..." I groaned. His hand reached between our bodies, stroking my clit, trying to drive me up higher. Below me, he was tense. His jaw was rigid, a muscle ticking there as he fought for control.

"Oh, God," I ground out as I felt my muscles grab him once before spasming with my orgasm, falling forward on his chest.

His hands went to my hips, holding me still as he slammed into me a few more times, his fingertips bruising into my skin as he came.

I took a deep breath that broke off on a fit of giggles. "Well that gives a new meaning to mixing business with pleasure," I said against his neck.

His hands patted my ass, then squeezed. "Your job leaves a lot of room for office nookie," he murmured.

"Nookie?" I asked, pushing up to look down at his face, my hair falling forward to curtain us. "Did you just say... nookie?"

"Hey not everyone has a filthy mouth like yours."

"You like my filthy mouth," I said, leaning down and biting his lower lip.

"Fuck yeah I do," he agreed. "As soon as I have some strength back, I am going to bury my cock in there again."

"Mmm," I said, slowly licking my lips.

Hunter cursed and half-laughed. "You're killing me, woman."

"Hey, you initiated it this time," I said, sitting up and looking down at him. I was never going to get used to the sight of him. Flawless. He was truly a flawless male specimen.

"What?" he asked, his hands moving up and down the sides of my thighs.

"Nothin'," I said coyly, leaning back on his thighs as he brought them up behind me.

"Tell me," he said, squinting his eyes at me.

I shrugged a shoulder. "You're pretty," I said, smiling.

"Pretty?" he asked, rolling his eyes.

"Yes, very. Like... it's unfair."

He shrugged. "You're prettier. Stunning actually."

"Oh, stop," I said. But I didn't mean it. I would never get enough of hearing it. From him.

He rose up toward me, planting a kiss between my breasts and wrapping his arms around my back. "Never," he said, with feeling.

I slid upward, off of him, putting my weak legs on the floor.

"Get back here," he said reaching for me.

I dodged away from his arms. "Nuh-uh," I said, finding the t-shirt and pants I had discarded three days ago. "I need to go and shower and change..."

"I can help you soap up," he suggested, putting his feet on

the floor as he watched me.

"You told me that you have work later today," I reminded him.

"I'll cancel," he said immediately.

"No, don't," I said, laughing. He meant it. He would have canceled his client for me without thought. "You go to work. I will catch up on some... work..."

"You mean filling pantie sniffer orders," he smiled. "That business is going to suffer."

"Why?" I asked, my brows drawing together.

"Because I plan to keep you naked pretty much all the time," he said nonchalantly.

I pulled my shirt down, stooping to grab my bra and panties, then walked over, kissing the top of his head. He smelled like him. Sawdust. Soap. Even though he hadn't been near either in days. His arms went around the back of my legs, pulling me against him. His face planted in my chest as I stroked his hair.

It was silly, but it almost felt like goodbye. I was irrationally scared that if I walked out of that room, out of his apartment, that we would lose what we had found, that it could never be the same again. So I leaned forward into him, letting my arms encircle his body, trying to hold on just a moment longer.

I took a deep breath, stepping away. "You get some work done," I said, "and I'll get some work done. And then..."

"And then," he agreed.

"My apartment?" I asked.

"Chinese," he added.

"Sounds good," I agreed, leaning down for a quick kiss before turning and walking away. I had to go before I could think better of it and run back into his arms.

I felt different. It was a total teenager thing to think. But that was how I felt. Different. Like myself, but improved. Happier. Lighter. I closed his front door behind me, leaning against it for a moment.

Hours, I reminded myself, it would only be a few hours before I saw him again.

I was being ridiculous. I was a strong, independent woman. It was unacceptable to bemoan a few hours on my own. I took a deep breath and moved the couple feet toward my own door, slipping my keys into the locks.

I closed the door behind me, kicking out of my shoes and walking into my living room.

"You really do bring shame to our family," a voice said, making me move back a step, a hand flying to my chest. But it wasn't him. It wasn't my father. My eyes shot up, finding eyes as green as mine.

"Isaiah," I hissed out his name like a curse. "How the hell did you get in here?"

He looked older than I remembered him. He was two years older than me only, but hardened. His blond hair was short but choppy from cutting it with the edge of a knife. His skin was darker than mine, a bit ruddy in the cheeks. There were lines next to his eyes, etching deep from hours spent squinting in the sun, squinting at bible verses.

"I picked the locks," he shrugged.

"What a regular criminal you have turned out to be," I said, holding my phone tight in my hand. I could call the police if it got messy. But they would take too long. It would be better to scream. Hunter would charge over in a heartbeat. I took comfort at that.

"At least I'm not a harlot," he seethed, his eyes dropping down to my hand.

"What's the matter," I started, holding up my hand, "never seen a bra or panties before? Still not married? Can't find someone to put up with your particular kind of insanity? Or," I said, feeling downright empowered around him for the first time in my entire life, "are you and your father sharing a more than familial bond out there all alone in the woods?"

"Don't be disgusting," he said, looking like he was going to spring off of the couch and throttle me.

I dropped my bra and panties on the floor, leaning back against the wall. "Never could get out from under his thumb, could you Isaiah?"

There was a flash of something in his face, something that was gone too soon for me to analyze. "Not everyone is as ungrateful as you, Fiona Mary."

I felt myself smile, shaking my head. "It's hard to be grateful for beatings and mutilation."

"Discipline," he countered.

"Child abuse," I shot back.

"Where did you get ideas like this?" he asked.

"From the real world, Isaiah," I said, almost feeling sorry for him, waving a hand out, "not some isolated shack in the woods so cut-off from everything else that we didn't even know how we were being abused. It is sick what we accepted as normal."

"Godly," he objected.

"God, or more accurately, the counsel of men who decided what to put in the Bible," I said, rolling my eyes, "said a lot of things father skimmed over. Did you ever notice that? We didn't keep slaves. He didn't insist Mom be silent at all times or else he would put her to death. He didn't go out on the town and kill the homosexuals."

"Because it's illegal," he said.

"It's illegal for a reason. Because it's wrong to have slaves. It's wrong to kill your wife. It's wrong to kill gay people. And it is just as fucking wrong to carve up your daughter. It's just as wrong to deny me an education."

"You seemed to manage well enough," he said, ignoring everything else I said.

"Yeah," I said, raising my chin. "I have my mother to thank

for that."

"Mother?" he asked, sitting forward, looking suddenly interested. "Mother taught you to read?" He said it with almost wonder, like maybe he had never even considered that our meek, submissive mother would be able to defy our father.

"Every day when you went out into the woods we would sit on the floor and work on letters and, later, basic math. Because she knew I was going to get out of there one day... like she always wanted to, and that I would need to be prepared."

"Mother was happy with Father," Isaiah insisted, but it didn't have the edge to it that it usually did. He was grown. He knew the things he had deluded himself into believing as a child were wrong.

"Mom cried every single night after our father went to sleep. And then she killed herself, Isaiah."

"That was because you..."

"No," I said, shaking my head sadly. Because it was useless to be angry with someone when they were so brainwashed. "Mom didn't kill herself because she was ashamed of me. Mom killed herself because she no longer needed to protect me. I was free. So then she got free."

"She's in hell for it," Isaiah said firmly. Some sins couldn't be forgiven.

"Yeah, well, maybe she prefers it there," I said and his face shot to mine like I had struck him. I took a breath. "Why are you here, Isaiah? You obviously didn't want to come here to have an argument with me about religion and our shitty upbringing."

"No," he agreed, scrubbing his hands over his face. "Father is sick."

Good. That was the first thought that came to my mind and I felt like an awful human being for it. It was petty an vengeful to wish someone unwell. But I couldn't ever bring myself, allow myself, to feel bad for him. "And?"

"No, Fiona Mary... he's in the hospital, looking more and more frail by the minute. It's cancer."

I hated that word. Everyone hated that word. It was ugly and cruel and unforgiving. Three words that also described my father. "How long does he have?"

"Days, weeks maybe," he said. "They say it is advanced bone cancer. It must have went undetected for years."

"Yeah because he refused to see a doctor," I said. Because you didn't mess with God's will. "Is he refusing treatment now?"

"Yes. He's half delirious with pain all the time."

"Okay," I said, setting my phone and keys down. "Thanks for telling me. You don't have to come again when he dies... just send me a letter."

Isaiah looked up like I had slapped him. "You can't be that cold."

"I can," I said. "I am. Maybe it's from not knowing my mother, the only person I ever loved... the only person that ever loved me, died. Split to pieces in the woods while I fought over food to stay alive. That might have something to do with me not needing to fall into nineteen-fifites dramatics over this."

"He wants to see you," Isaiah tried again.

"To see how many more insults he can hurl at me before he finally croaks?"

"For goodness sakes, Fiona Mary, it is his dying wish," he said, getting to his feet. "Would it kill you to take a day out of your busy little life in this godforsaken place to just... come for five minutes and say goodbye?"

More like: I hope you rot in hell you evil fucking bastard.

"He's at Saint Mary's hospital. Room three-fifteen."

"Ironic isn't that?" I asked as he reached for my door.

"What?" he asked, looking over his shoulder at me.

"For someone who hates women so much to be put in three-fifteen?" At his confused look, I smiled. " 'She is more precious than rubies, and all the things thou canst desire are not to be compared to her.' "

"Proverbs?" he asked, like maybe he had thought all of those words had just been cleared from my mind like an etch-a-sketch.

"I'm sure that didn't escape his notice."

"No," Isaiah said, shaking his head. "I think it might be why he wanted to see you," he said, opening the door and jumping back a step.

Because there standing in the hallway was my big, scary, hulking, sexy, dangerous neighbor. He was staring at Isaiah for a long minute, his eyes landing on Isaiah's with a look of realization on his face. He glanced over my brother's shoulder at me. "You alright, Sixteen?" he asked.

"Hunter," I said, trying to keep my calm. "This is my brother, Isaiah. Isaiah, this is Hunter." Hunter inclined his head at my brother, a typical macho man type greeting, then looked back over at me. After a second, Isaiah's eyes followed. Both of them looked at me like I had all the answers. "Isaiah was just leaving," I said and saw a look of relief on my brother's face. Hunter paused for a minute then moved out of the way and I heard Isaiah shuffle quickly down the hall.

"What the fuck, Fee?" Hunter asked, stepping inside my apartment and closing the door. "I didn't think you were in contact."

I walked into the kitchen, suddenly in dire need of some coffee; or maybe just something to do to settle my nerves. "We're not," I said, moving around the room. "When I got this place, my grandmother somehow got mail sent to her about it. So I got a letter from her that pretty much just blackmailed me into calling her every Sunday."

"Or what?" Hunter asked, sounding angrier than I probably ever was about it.

"Or she would give my father and brother my address."

"Well I guess you aren't making any more Sunday phone calls," he said, watching me like I was about to burst into a million pieces.

That was true. I hadn't even thought of that. No more slinking down dark alleys. No more paying people to interrupt my call early. No more nights trying to drown myself into oblivion. That part of my life was over. My father would be dead soon. My brother wasn't the threat I had feared he would be. So she had nothing on me.

"My father is dying," I said, watching the first drops of coffee drip into the pot.

"Good riddance to bad rubbish," he said, his tone cold. I actually felt cold hearing it. I turned to him, my brows drawn low, my arms crossed under my chest. "I'm sorry. Was that not true?" he asked, shaking his head. "He's a miserable piece of shit who should have spent the last thirteen years rotting in a cell for what he did to you. I'm glad he's dying. And I hope it hurts like hell."

"Hunter..." I said, at war with myself. Part of me felt almost offended even though I knew he was right. He was absolutely right. But the other part felt nothing but warmth. Warmth at the fact that he cared enough to be mad for me, be spiteful for me. "You don't need to be angry for me," I said, walking over to him and wrapping my arms around his middle, resting my face against his shirt.

There was a long exhale of breath on the top of my head before his arms went around me, pulling me close, and crushing me to his chest. "Okay," he said, kissing the top of my head. "So how was the reunion? I think I heard some yelling."

"Oh, we discussed religion and our mother's suicide and the difference between discipline and child abuse."

"I'm assuming that didn't go over well."

"You know... it was weird. He didn't fight me like I expected him to. Like my father would have done. And he was always my father's little protege."

"Maybe he's just worked up about your father being... sick? I assume he's sick."

"Cancer," I agreed. "They said he maybe has days."

Hunter took a deep breath and I felt him tense, like he was going to say something and he needed strength to do it. "Fee... maybe you should go."

"What?" I said, pulling against his arms, but they only held me tighter. "You think it would be what? Kind? To fulfill his final wishes?" I struggled harder to no avail. His arms were like weights around me. "Fucking let me go, Hunter."

"No, listen," he said, his tone infuriatingly reasonable. "This isn't about him. Fuck him. This is about you."

"What about me?" I asked, not quite believing that this was the same guy who had just told me he hoped my father dies in agony a few minutes ago. I had never met someone so all over the place in my whole life.

"It's just... you're doing better, Fee," he said, letting me go enough so that I could look up at him. One of his hands reached up briefly to touch my cheek. "You're doing so much better. You're not cutting. You haven't been drunk in days. You're sleeping. At night. Like the rest of the world. You're doing so much better and I think it's because you are dealing with your past, facing it, sharing it... instead of bottling it up and taking it out on yourself in private."

I didn't want to tell him that the only reason I was doing better was because of him. Because he was there to accept all my damage. Because he was there to keep me safe from myself. Because he was there, when all other things had failed, to fuck me into an exhausted sleep. I couldn't tell him that. It was too much. It was too dependent. It was too needy. I wasn't going to let myself be that girl. At least not outwardly.

"So your answer is to throw me right back into the situations that caused me to cut and drink and be afraid of the dark..."

"No," he said, letting me go finally. "Because this is different. You're not ten years old anymore, Fee. You're not a helpless, brainwashed kid. And he's not your father. He's just a man. A deeply disturbed, worthless pile of flesh. You're everything. You're the fucking sun and stars and moon. So you should go there. And you should face him. And you should tell him that no matter how hard he tried, he couldn't break you. Because I think you need that. I think you need him to know that you're not his whipping boy anymore. That he didn't win."

He was right. As much as I wouldn't let myself think that before, he was right. I did need that. I needed that closure. I needed to give him a none-too-subtle "fuck you" before I wouldn't have the chance to again. He didn't deserve peace. He didn't deserve to leave this life thinking he did good, that he was a man of God, that he lived a righteous life. He needed to know he was wrong, that he had sinned against the God he had devoted his life to by abusing me and our mother and, in a lot of ways, Isaiah as well. And then, if he felt the need, he could repent. It wouldn't do him any good. Not in my eyes. There are some things that you do in life that could never be forgiven. There were some cuts that went too deep to heal. And I wasn't going to tell him I forgave him. I wasn't going to brush it under the rug.

God could forgive him. Not me.

"What's up, Fee?" he asked, watching me as I leaned against the counter.

"I know I need to go," I said, shaking my head, "but I really, really don't want to."

"I could go..."

"No," I said immediately. Hell to the no. I was not dragging perfect, amazing Hunter into my fucked up past. I wasn't going to let him be there in case I lost my shit and started beating on someone trapped in a hospital bed. Or, worse yet, falling into a puddle of nothingness on the floor. I couldn't... wouldn't let him see me like that. The me I might be around my family might be nothing like the me he knew and cared about. I couldn't risk losing the way he looked at me. It mattered too much. "No," I said again, less urgently. "Thank you, but I think this is something I should do alone."

"I get that," he said, pulling me to him. "So when are you leaving?"

That was a good question. From what Isaiah said, I didn't exactly have a lot of time. If I dawdled, I might miss my chance. I would need to get on a bus as soon as possible. "The first bus out I guess."

I felt him sigh against my hair. "I think I might miss you," he said, his voice barely above a whisper.

"Oh yeah?" I asked, breathing him in.

"Yeah, but you know..." he said, his voice trailing off, sounding way too amused given the circumstances.

"I know what?"

"Well you seem to have this particular line of work that makes a situation like this much more tolerable."

"Oh," I said, trying to hide the smile in my voice. "You need a pair of panties to hold you over, huh?"

He chuckled, reaching town and swatting my ass. "No, I'm good on that front. But keep that phone of yours charged. And be prepared for a big bill."

"You know phones don't really work that way anymore," I teased.

"Shut up, you're ruining the moment," he said, his hands squeezing my ass before sliding up toward the waistband of my pants and slowly pulling them down.

"What moment is that?" I asked, stepping obediently out of the legs.

"The one where I give you something to remember me by," he said, reaching for my shirt and pulling it up. He dropped my shirt to the floor, standing back and looking at me for a long time. It was long enough to make me shift uncomfortably, to want to cover myself. Then he reached to pull his own shirt off, followed by his pants. "Alright," he said, nodding, clapping his hands once.

"Alright?" I asked, my brows drawing down. "Alright what?" I asked, expecting him to reach for me.

He stepped back, waving toward his body. "You'll remember this," he said, looking pleased with himself.

"Oh, gee," I smiled. "I don't know. I may have seen better," I said, shrugging and started to walk away.

His arm reached out and grabbed me, pushing me forward against the counter. I felt his cock slide between my legs, stroking my slick heat. "Have you... felt better too?" he asked, sounding hoarse.

My hands slapped down on the counter top, the cold shocking against my overheated skin. A million times no. Nothing. No one could ever feel as good as he did.

"I don't know," I said, biting my lip to keep from groaning.

I expected him to pull back and slam deep inside me. I was bracing for that, for that powerful surge of lust. That was what I had come to expect from Hunter: wild abandon. But he pulled slowly away and stroked forward again, the tip of his cock brushing over my clit. Soft, gentle. Over and over. "You don't know?" he asked.

All I wanted was for the teasing to end, to feel him inside. To feel us both lose control. But I balled my hands into fists and shook my head. "It's hard to tell," I said.

"Hmm," he said, pulling away from me and I had to fight not to beg him to come back. "Well," he said a long couple of seconds later, grabbing my shoulder and turning me around. His hands brushed down over my breasts then slid around my back, grabbing my ass and pulling me up off my feet.

I wrapped my arms around his neck, my legs going to the

sides of his hips as he walked, finally pressing me back against the wall. "Has anything felt better than this?" He asked, reaching between us and bringing his cock to my entrance, pushing against it for a second before pressing in, but only slightly.

My head fell backward and I let out the groan I had been holding in for what felt like ages. "I'm not sure yet," I whimpered, trying to push further down on him, but his hands were on my hips, holding me hard against the wall.

"Well I guess it's always wise to gather all the evidence before making a decision," he said, leaning down and kissing me until I forgot all about him inside me, until all I could focus on was his lips and tongue and the strange lightness in my chest.

And then he pushed forward, quickly but achingly gently and I cried out against his lips. Once fully inside, he stilled and continued his exploration of my lips. Like he was trying to press the memory into my skin. As if I could ever forget. Every inch of me was clinging to him as if I wanted him to sink into my skin, as if I wanted to sink inside his. Like I would never be satisfied until I did.

It was fucking terrifying.

"Hunter..." I whimpered out, not sure what I was saying or what I was asking. Did he feel it too? Was I alone in the scary new sensation?

He pulled back slightly, looking at me with his gorgeous blue eyes for a second before finally slowly withdrawing out of me and pushing back in. Then there was no more thinking. Just feeling. Just him and his delicious, frustratingly slow pace and my body pulling him, trying to drive us both upward but in an unhurried way. Like I had all the time in the world to get there, like it was something that would add to the experience, but wasn't the only reason we were doing it.

I leaned forward, burying my face in his neck as I felt my body pushing toward the peak, a sensation of being pulled downward until I burst up, whimpering his name into his skin.

"I'll remember you," I said as he came, holding him tighter. It was a promise. A vow.

EIGHTEEN

Fiona

It felt wrong. That was all I could think after Hunter slipped out of my apartment. The sound of the door closing had felt like a pain in my chest. He said he would call, kissed me almost chastely, then was gone. I stood there dumbly for a few minutes, staring at the door, before turning to go check bus schedules.

Because I wasn't the girl who pined over guys. I wasn't that pathetic. Nope. Not me. But even as I typed into my computer, his face kept popping into my mind.

I got up and went to my closet, trying to decide what to pack. What did you wear to go face the man who made your life a living hell after four years away from him? What could you wear that would be a slap in the face to his opinions on how a woman should dress as a silent 'fuck you'? But, also at the same time, be somewhat respectful of the fact that you were visiting someone dying in a hospital?

Eventually, I packed a few outfits and set aside the one I

would be wearing: a skintight, knee-length black pencil skirt and a form-fitting pale pink scoop-neck, three-quarter length sleeve shirt. Low black heels. I showered, fixed my hair, applied a little makeup, grabbed my purse and suitcase and headed down to the bus stop.

I could smell Hunter's cigarettes as I walked out of the building. I knew he was out on the balcony smoking but I refused to let myself look back. If I looked back, I might run back. And that couldn't happen. I pulled my shoulders back and kept walking, a lump the size of a fist in my throat.

The bus ride was long and nerve-racking. I tried to keep myself focused, calm. It was a couple hours. That was all I needed to get through and then I could jump on the next bus back to the city. I was the one in control for once. But that didn't stop the rolling in my stomach, the tension headache, the sensitivity to loud noises around me. It didn't stop the ghosts of the past from creeping in.

The bus led to a hotel which led to a cab which dropped me off outside of the massive, sprawling white and sparkling window building. I looked up at it, feeling small. Feeling, irrationally, that if I went in there, that I would never get out.

I took a deep breath and moved into the revolving door toward reception. I was almost done. Getting there was the worst part. Getting there was full of all the anxiety and the fear. The part that would follow would only be a couple minutes. I just needed to say my piece. Then I could leave. I could leave at any time. No one could stop me.

The elevator dropped me off on the floor. I walked onto the worn, but pristine linoleum floor, my heels making a clicking noise that sounded deafening to my own ears. One of the nurses in deep purple scrubs, looked up and offered me a small smile.

"Fiona Mary?" My grandmother's voice called, shrill and disbelieving. She rose up out of her chair outside of my father's room, dressed in a simple but expensive gray pantsuit with a single round diamond at her throat. Her perfectly dyed ash-blonde hair was pulled back from her face in a chignon. Everything about Joanna Meyers screamed simple, sophisticated elegance. She had the house and car to match her wardrobe.

"Grandmother," I said, my voice was cold and betrayed as I felt.

It had been a long time since I saw her. Two years. I had still been sporting the dark brown I had dyed my hair that year, and wearing nothing but thrift store baggy men's clothes, desperately trying to disconnect from my old self. My face had been burned and I was gaunt thin from living on the streets.

I had been a mess.

It had taken me eight months after getting a roof and food to slip back into my more natural state. I stripped my hair; I put on some weight; I bought clothes that fit. I put myself together. She had only seen me when I was still in pieces.

"You're here," she said, sounding like she was in complete shock.

"I'm here," I agreed, inclining my head slightly. "Wasn't that the intention when you sent Isaiah to break into my apartment?"

"He broke into your apartment?" she asked, sounding genuinely concerned.

"Oh yeah we had a... nice little reunion," I said, feeling the nurse's eyes on us. The tension made the air thick and sharp. It was like at any moment, someone might lose a limb.

"That explains his dour mood since he returned," she said.

"How dare you?" I started, walking closer so I could lower my voice. "We had a deal."

"I might be a lot of things, Fiona Mary," she said, lifting her chin much the same way I did and I wondered fleetingly if that was where I had picked up that habit, "but I am not stupid. When your father passes on to Heaven, you will have no reason to keep calling me. So I really didn't have anything to lose by giving Isaiah your address." There was a certain sadness in her voice when she said I would stop calling her, like she would genuinely miss it.

I exhaled my held breath through my nose and shook my head. "You know, Grams," I started, "if you had just once cared about me... not as your son's daughter, not as a soul that needs to be saved, just me as a person... I would have happily kept in touch. I don't have anyone else. But all you want is submission and obedience. And I'm not your fucking puppy," I growled, watching her face jerk back like I had struck her.

A shadow moved from the room behind her, coming out into the hall. "What is all the racket out here... Fiona Mary," Isaiah said, looking surprised. He was ragged, his eyes heavy and red. He looked past me, over my shoulder with a look of trepidation.

"Don't worry," I said, shaking my head. "I didn't bring him."

"Bring who?" Grams asked, perking up. "You told me you didn't have any respectable gentlemen in your life."

"Well," I said, smiling wickedly, "he's not respectable. And he's certainly not a gentleman," I added.

A strange look came over my grandmother's face then, a light in her green eyes that almost seemed amused. "Have you... sinned with him?" she asked, only sounding half-concerned as she usually did about the idea.

"In every room and every position," I agreed and one of the nurses coughed to cover her laugh.

"Well," Grams said, waving a hand, "God will forgive you of that. He wouldn't have been so forgiving of you not saying your last respects to your dying father."

"Respect wasn't what I came here to give him," I said, taking a deep breath, "but I promise I wont pinch his IV lines," I said, winking at the nurses. There was a pained silence that I finally broke. "Is he awake?" I asked, looking at Isaiah.

"Yeah," he said, watching me like he was trying to study me, like there was something about me that confused him.

"Good," I said, moving toward the door. "I can get this over with then," I saw my grandmother moving to step in behind me and I blocked the doorway. "I can handle this alone," I said firmly then went inside and slammed the door.

There was a curtain pulled, blocking his bed from view but I could hear his machine beeping and his breathing, raspy and slow. I leaned back against the door, taking a deep breath. The encounter with my grandmother had bolstered my confidence a bit. I could do it. I could walk over there and dish it out as much as I used to have to take it.

I took a long, slow breath, pushed off the door and walked around the curtain. To say it was a shock would be the biggest understatement of my life. My memories of him were like that of a child: he seemed huge, imposing, powerful. But there he was, completely swallowed up by the bed, his body swimming in its hospital gown. He looked old and frail.

At the sound of my heels, he turned expecting, I imagined, to see my grandmother. His eyes squinted for a second, uncomprehending before they went wide. "Fiona Mary," he said, reaching for the button that slowly bent his mattress upward. "What are you doing here?"

"Well your mother thought it was important enough for me to be here that she broke our deal and sent your son up to see me."

"Isaiah? Isaiah was up in that godforsaken place?"

"Yup. Plenty of things to see to pervert his mind on his way to my apartment," I agreed.

"I'm dying," he said, sounding very matter-of-fact about it.

"Yes, you are," I nodded, putting my purse down on the windowsill.

"So you're here to make amends?" he asked, nodding, "for all the heartbreak you have caused this family?"

"Not even close," I said, watching as his jaw tightened. That was always how it started. If you watched him close, the anger would start in his jaw. Then he would flush. His eyes would turn to slits. His fist would clench. I spent a lot of time watching him when I was growing up.

"Then why are you here?" he asked, his voice deceptively calm.

"Closure," I said, shrugging a shoulder. "To show you that you didn't break me. I know that was always the plan."

"Willful," he spat the word like it was a curse, "you were always so willful. Like your mother."

"Yeah," I agreed, glad for the comparison. "I haven't purposely set the living room on fire yet. But I'm still young."

"Purposely," he repeated, looking perplexed.

"Oh, you didn't think it was an accident, did you?" I laughed, the sound taunting. "It seemed Mom had a bit of a problem with you mutilating her only daughter."

"It was discip..."

"It was child abuse," I cut him off, my voice raising enough to make him shut his mouth. "It was child abuse. You were a predator who hid behind his bible. You were a weak and pathetic man..."

"You ungrateful shrew," he started, his face turning bright red, "coming in here dressed like a common street whore and throwing your city ideas around like you know more than your father..."

"Listen," I said, glancing out of the window, watching the night take hold across the sky. "I know there is no making you see how evil you were," I said, holding up a hand when he went to speak. "What you did was evil. And you can resolve that with your God. But I don't forgive you. For what you did to me and to my mother. Even for the way you have warped Isaiah. I just needed to tell you that before you died and I didn't get the chance to," I said, grabbing my purse off the windowsill and walking toward the door.

"You'll burn in hell for this," he yelled as I opened the door, making everyone in the hall look at me.

"That's fine. So long as you're not there," I called back, slamming the door. Outside, Isaiah looked like he was in genuine pain and my grandmother's mouth had fallen open. "I'm assuming that wasn't what you had in mind when you told me to come here," I said, looking at her, "but, damn, it felt good."

I walked out of the building feeling ten pounds lighter than I had when I went in. That was what closure felt like: lightness. Like weight that had been holding you down had finally been lifted.

I walked down a few blocks to wait for a cab out front of a coffee shop. It was done. I had done it. I had faced the person who made me wake up screaming when I tried to sleep at night, the person who made me carve into my skin, the one who made me look for answers at the bottom of empty bottles.

Maybe I would never be completely free of him. Maybe I could never be as whole and well adjusted as the average person. But maybe I wouldn't have to spend my life just inches from self-destruction. Maybe I could build a life that didn't revolve around trying to avoid my past. Maybe I could sleep at night and have healthy relationships.

Hunter. I could be with Hunter.

I grabbed a coffee, checking my phone with the silly hope that maybe he had called or texted. I had only left him a few hours before. It would have been too soon for a call or text. For all he knew, I hadn't even arrived yet, let alone arrived and had my last words.

The cab took half an hour to take me back to my hotel where I paced around my room in endless circles, feeling too anxious to sleep.

I could have just taken another bus back to the city, been done with the town I had tried desperately to escape from. But as I sat down on my bed, slipping my feet out of my shoes, I had to admit that things didn't feel finished. I didn't know why even as I slipped out of my shoes and under my covers, but I knew I couldn't leave yet.

—

      I woke up the next morning and before my eyes even opened, I knew what I had to do. I had to go back. I had to go to the woods. I had to see the shack I grew up in. I had to face the nightmares that were caused by living in those walls. I needed to look at it from the eyes of a survivor, not a victim.

      I dressed in a pair of high waisted jeans and a tight blue crop top, slipping into a pair of low boots, and tying my hair back. My phone had remained stubbornly silent throughout the night and I couldn't bring myself to be the one who called first.

      Before I set off, I sat down on the bed and took a few work calls. It wouldn't do me any good to lose clients because I was on some tour of my past. Besides, it distracted me from the fact that Hunter still hadn't called. Even though I knew he was always up before six and it was well after eleven.

      I grabbed a cab, giving them the address to my grandmother's house. It looked like I remembered: big, white, full of secrets. My grandfather had died young and left my grandmother sitting on a boatload of money and a massive family estate that had been in his family for generations. It sat on a fifty acre plot and I walked up the driveway on the right side and slipped into the woods. It had been so long and the trees and bushes had matured beyond recognition, but I still knew my way back. I could probably walk it in my sleep.

It was a good twenty minute walk before the trees started to clear and I saw the outline of the house that built me. Plain, still as simple as I remembered. It seemed smaller. If I thought my apartment in the city was a shoe box, this was a matchbox.

"Isaiah," I called, but knew there would be no answer. He wasn't going to leave our father's side when he was so close to the end. My grandmother had never stepped foot into the house. She had always been more than a little embarrassed that it was on her property, but she had always indulged every whim of my father's. Which was probably why he was so screwed up in the first place.

There were flowers dying in the front beds. Flowers my father had always told my mother were frivolous and unnecessary. I remembered her insisting that God wouldn't have given us plants that were useless if he didn't mean for us to enjoy them. I walked over, kneeling down and picking a few. Then I got up and turned away from the house, walking further into the woods.

My grandmother hadn't given me a lot of details about it, but I remember her saying something about a lilac bush. And there was only one on the entire property. I came upon it a few minutes later, a simple white cross right in front of the old unruly lilac bush. I felt a tightness in my throat and struggled against it as I walked closer. I knelt down in front of it, feeling more than a little angry at the lack of care that was put into her grave.

Deena Mary Meyers. There was no date of birth or death. There was no mention of her being a beloved mother or devoted wife. There was just a name. In death, that was all my mother was worth to my father. I put the flowers down at the base of the cross, touching her name with a sort of reverence I didn't know I was capable of.

"I don't know if I believe in an after life. Or that you can hear me," I said, feeling awkward, but bold. "I'm sorry I wasn't here. That I didn't mourn you the way I should have when I found out. And I'm sorry that you suffered for so long just because of me. I was never grateful enough for everything you did for me. If you hadn't been brave enough to defy my father, I never could have had the basic skills I needed to start my own life. And I'm just..." I trailed off, blinking away the tears. No tears. She was free. She was where she wanted to be. There was no use crying over her decision. "Thank you, Mom," I said, touching the cross once more and getting to my feet.

I felt better as I made my way back to the house. I felt like I had finally been given the chance to pay my mother her respects. I felt the years of guilt slowly start to slip away.

Opening the front door, I stepped into the darkness I had grown up in. The literal darkness. The light only came from the few windows my mother used to scrub mercilessly but now were covered in a layer of film and filth. Everything was the same: the dirt floor, the worn sofa, the wooden furniture, the plain walls. I ran my hand over the dining table, coming away with dust, as I made my way into my old bedroom. Now Isaiah's room.

It was his now. The curtain was gone. My old bed was missing. But there was a small chest in the far corner and I walked over to it, remembering it as a Christmas present one year. We got one gift and it was always handmade by one of our parents. One year it was new heavy knitted blankets for our beds. Blankets that I had never seen her working on so she must have done late at night or early into the morning. Another year it was a hunting knife for Isaiah and a rag doll for me.

The chest was probably the only thing my father had ever actually taken the time to make me. It was from the year I was born. When there was still hope for me, I guess. It was small, two feet long and a foot wide. It had always been more than enough room to store my meager possessions. It was made of light wood and the top had a big cross burned into it. The front had Proverbs 29:15 burned in: "'Whoever spares the rod, hates his son, but he who loves him is diligent to discipline him.'"

Why he even bothered to put that there when he had no intentions to teach me to read was completely beyond my comprehension. I ran my hand over the lid, wiping the dust away before opening it. Inside smelled like the dried lilacs and mint my mother had always kept inside to keep the moths from eating our clothes or blankets.

Nestled neatly on top were my knitting needles, and a circle of embroidery I had been working on when I left. There was a collection of fabric headbands I had made from scraps of clothing material, an indulgence I was allowed only because my father didn't like anything to go to waste.

I pulled out the bible resting there, meaning to throw it on Isaiah's bed when I noticed it felt weird. The spine was loose and the pages felt like they might fall out. Curious, I flipped open the first page, to find all the bible pages had been pulled out and replaced with small scraps of paper, ones with my grandmother's watermark on them. Ones that my mother must have stolen when she went over there for holidays.

Fiona,

I wish I could find the nerve to be less of a coward and tell you these things... like all mothers do while raising their children. But I couldn't take a chance that you might slip up and say something in front of your father. The punishment would be beyond your comprehension as a girl. But if you are a woman reading this, you know what I mean. And you never get used to it. And I can't bring myself to risk it.

I hadn't wanted to marry him, you know. I was just shy of eighteen and I was planning of running as far as fast as my legs could carry me. Away from my father who was fond of the rod himself. Fond of making me feel like I was inconsequential. Then, as if sensing my growing departure, he handed me over to John like a prized sow. I was bought and sold, Fiona. My father got two deers a year for the first five years, and your father got me.

He wasn't such a monster then. Your father. He was still young, uncertain. Insecure. I think having me to boss around and discipline gave him confidence, gave him purpose. And, oh, how he enjoyed that. Your brother was born ten months after we married. A huge, squirming baby boy that your father had cried over. For the first year after him, I was the beloved wife. I was the woman who gave him a son. Then I got pregnant again. I knew you were a girl, I was carrying different than I had with Isaiah, but I dared not tell your father.

I named you Fiona after my own mother. Someone I hoped you turned out like. Someone I hoped I had turned out a little bit like. Someone with her silent rebellions. Someone who got away with things the abusive men in her life never found out about. That's why I knew enough to start teaching you things: reading and writing... some math, some history. I knew because she defied my father. You know because I defied yours.

My greatest hope in life is that you never have to know what that is like. My greatest hope is that you can break free from this pattern of subjugation- that you bow to no man.

- Mom

I had to rest my hand against the wall to keep from falling over. My mother had destroyed a bible to finally get the chance to tell me her story. My mother must have been writing and hiding letters for years. She must have piled them in with all my possessions the day I left, right before she went out to the woods and finally got away from the men she had needed to bow down to for her entire life.

I slipped the first note back on top of the pile and flipped the book to reach for the last one.

Fiona,

God, I hope you're gone. Good and gone. Miles and miles away. I know your stubborn spirit. I know your pain. And I know you would rather die out on the street than live another moment in this house. I hope that drive keeps you warm and keeps you hungry for your independence. You're resilient and you're smart. A few weeks or months of hardship will be nothing if it leads you to a better life than you had here. I pray you'll be happy in whatever life you build for yourself.

And I hope that you can forgive me. For what I am going to do. I hope you'll understand. You needed to get out. And I do too. Isaiah is a grown man now. He doesn't need his mother. And he never really did. It was you I had always worried about. And now my worry can transform into hope and I can finally let go. Please don't think of me as a coward. I have endured so much. Much more than I would ever tell you. This has been something I have been planning since you were born- the day when we could both be free in our separate ways.

I love you. I love you more deeply than I thought my rotten bones ever could. You are everything good and right in this world. I hope you found that out for yourself before reading this. And I hope some day we can meet again. Goodbye, Fiona.

- Mom

PS: The lilacs are beautiful this time of year.

I closed my eyes. Not because it was, essentially, her suicide note. But because of how calm it sounded; how free of sadness or anger or regret. Her handwriting was perfect: neat, not rushed. There were no tears smearing the ink and warping the paper. She had very deliberately sat down just hours after I ran away and wrote the last thing she would ever write, knowing she was about to go into the woods and take her own life.

I looked down at the last sentence. *The lilacs are beautiful this time of year.* Maybe she was worried that my father would move her, would put her body somewhere other than where she had chosen to die. She wanted me to know, just in case.

Slipping the page back into the book, I closed the cover and put it down on the floor. I pulled everything else out: my old rag doll, handmade mittens and a matching hat made by my mother for my seventeenth birthday, and finally, that knitted blanket that had kept me warm every night for most of my life. I laid it out on the floor, putting all the other items inside, and wrapping it back up. I wouldn't leave them behind. They were the proof that my mother existed, that she had always loved and taken care of me and they belonged in my life. The chest, however, could be torn apart and used for firewood for all I cared.

I paused in the dining room, reaching into my purse and pulling out the glossy magazine. I smiled as I placed it on the dining room table and flipped it open to a particularly scandalous image.

Opening the door, I screeched, flying back a step and almost falling over. Isaiah was in the doorway, his arm perched high on the door jamb. I had a sudden and frantic surge of panic seeing him that I quickly pushed away. He was slumped forward, his head hung.

"Isaiah?" I asked, trying to draw his attention.

"Fiona Mary," he said, not bothering to look up, like he knew I was there. "He's gone," he said, looking up at me. But there wasn't just grief there. That was there, though, in the redness to his eyes. But there was more; there was a lack of tension in his shoulders, in the slackness to his jaw.

"Good," I said, but not with as much anger as I felt.

Isaiah's eyes shot up to mine. "That is extremely..."

"I know that you loved him, Isaiah. But I know that you feel a sense of relief too. And that's okay. It's not wrong."

"Yes it is," he said, shaking his head at himself.

I felt myself reaching out, touching his arm for the briefest of seconds. "Grieve. Bury your father," I said, "but then move on. Okay? You need to have your own life outside of all of this," I said, waving a hand toward the house as he moved inside and past me, looking around. He reached a hand up to run through his hair and my mouth fell open. "Isaiah," I said, my breath a whisper, "what is that on your hand?"

His arm fell quickly, automatically. Shamefully. But then he looked at his palm for a second before holding it up and out at me. There, etched in the center of his palm, was a huge, raised scar in the shape of a cross. And I realized with blinding clarity that I hadn't been the only one to get punished that night when I was ten. When I was carved into. I didn't even remember Isaiah crying out or coming in bloody. But I had been slipping in and out of consciousness that night and then in and out of hallucinations from an infection fever for the week following.

And after that incident, we had been kept apart as much as possible. Isaiah went out with my father before I even woke up in the morning. They came in only for dinner and prayers and, I realized when I thought about it, he had always kept his hand curled into a fist. Always. I was pretty sure that for the eight years that followed, I had never seen that hand uncurled. Whether it was from shame or self-consciousness, I had no idea. Scars. We both had our own kind of scars.

"He wanted to make sure I saw God anytime I even thought about..."

He couldn't even say the word. That was how much of an influence our father still had on him. "Masturbated," I supplied and he jerked back, wincing slightly. "That's the word," I said, "masturbating. And it isn't bad and wrong and sinful," I said, then waved a hand out toward the dining room table. "In fact... I left you a present there," I said and watched as he slowly walked over and saw the naked woman, her large breasts soft and fleshy, her leg propped up on a chair to the side Captain Morgan style so you could see right to her naughty bits. Isaiah's breath hissed out of his mouth and he slowly sat down, his arms resting on the table and unable to look away. "When you decide to leave all this shit behind," I said, "and you want to know more about real life, you can contact me. Okay? I can ease you into it so you don't get overwhelmed or, more likely, freak out the normal people."

He looked up at me then, his green eyes intense. "Okay," he said.

"You have my address," I said and he nodded. "You can write. Or even just show up. I'm almost always there."

"Alright. Thanks," he said, nodding at me. "The funeral is going to be the day after tomorrow. Grandmother is burying him in the plot on the other side of Grandfather," he told me, which went completely against my father's wishes, but he was dead... he couldn't object. "Nine in the morning."

"Alright, thanks. I'll see you around Isaiah," I said, walking out the door, the slam it made sounding off somewhere deep in my soul.

I was done. Finished. With all of the pain and the guilt. It was all settled. I had said my piece to my father. I had found a piece of my mother. And I had figured out that my brother, who had always seemed spoiled and condescending toward me, had been almost as tortured as I had. Which took away some of my anger at him. He would be alright. He would need a few months to put himself together and figure out what he wanted out of life. And then he would come to me. Some day. I was sure of it.

NINETEEN

Fiona

In the end, I had stayed for the funeral. It only felt right. I had stood back from the ceremony that was already pitifully small, just the priest and the distant relatives that were conned by family obligation stood next to my grandmother and brother.

I grabbed the next bus back to the city with a different kind of knot in my stomach. Because he hadn't called. Well, that wasn't entirely true. I had one missed call when I got back from the woods. There was fucking no reception out in the boonies. But there was no message and no texts. I had called back three times but got nowhere and I couldn't bring myself to leave a message.

If he wanted to, he would call.

But he didn't and I couldn't shake the awful feeling in my belly. I needed to get back to the city as soon as possible. I needed to see him, to feel him again.

The bus ride felt five times longer on the way home as it did on the way there. I sat silently, trying to concentrate on my mother's letters. But Hunter's face kept invading my thoughts. I couldn't shake them so I eventually gave up on the letters, tucking them safely back into my suitcase and staring out the window the rest of the trip.

I had to hold myself back from running into the building. It looked the same as I left it: worn, old, shitty. But home. It was home. I let myself into my apartment, dropping my things in the entryway and going to make a pot of coffee. He would be there any minute. As soon as he heard me there, he would come over and welcome me home. Preferably with hard, punishing sex. The sexual tension I had built up over the past few days had made me hot and antsy all the time.

When I was done with my second cup of coffee and I still hadn't heard from him, I went about putting my things away, taking a long hot shower, primping myself up to look my best for him. I slipped into a bright blue thong... and nothing else.

And waited. And waited. And waited.

Before I knew it, night was coming down fast and I still hadn't seen him. I tried not to freak out. He was probably out. Maybe he had booked extra work when he thought I would be away so he could take me to bed for a week straight when I got back. Maybe that was the plan. In which case, I couldn't be mad. I hadn't even told him I was on my way back.

I threw a shirt on and curled up in front of the television. But sleep wouldn't come. Whatever hiatus I had from the bad thoughts and nightmares I had had while back in my hometown, and around Hunter was gone.

My thigh was driving me crazy. The itchiness meant I was healing. Physically, scabbing over. The thing I never realized about cutting was the addiction connected to it. Especially for someone who already struggled with addictive issues. Your body got used to that rush of endorphins. It craved them. It needed them to deal with the bad sensations.

But I didn't want to cut into myself anymore. I wanted to heal. I wanted to feel better, to treat myself better. I didn't want Hunter to have to find me on the floor in a puddle of my own blood again. I didn't want to have to wake up and realize I could have killed myself without even meaning to. I didn't want that life anymore.

I got up off the couch, slipping into workout clothes and going into the basement to run. It would help. It would give me a surge of endorphins that my body needed. It would exhaust me. And then I could sleep.

Then the next day, I would see Hunter. I half expected to be woken up by the sound of his hammer slamming against my wall. Because that would be a fitting welcome home by him. It was exactly what I thought he would do.

I showered, slid on a different thong, a red one, and pulled out my mom's letters. It was still dark out. And I was having trouble even thinking about going to sleep.

Fiona,

Not all men are bad. I want you to know that. I realize the only male presence you have had in your life is your father and that he has been your only example of manhood. And I wish I could have changed that for you. I wish there were someone else, anyone else, you could have met to show you. To prove to you that there are good men out there. There are men who are kind and sweet, full of love words instead of hate, men who would never think about raising their hands to you in anger.

Maybe you are wondering how I know that. Knowing at this point how my father treated me. Knowing how my husband treated me.

But there was a time... when I was seventeen, when I was still living at home and enduring the punishments I was convinced I deserved... I met a good man. My mother had convinced my father that I should volunteer at the church for a year. For humility. To teach me to be selfless for my future husband and children. I knew what the real plan was: to show me the world outside. To show me the town so I would be familiar with it when I eventually ran away.

The church at that time was a revolving door of volunteers. Kids from the catholic high school. Recently released convicts. Just plain good people wanting to do good.

I was there for four months. I was in the food pantry, organizing donations when I heard shuffling behind me. And in walked a man, his arms full of boxes from the truck. My teenage heart pounded at the sight of him. He was older. In his late twenties with big, kind eyes. He was a convict, Fiona. But he was a reformed man. He was sweet and gentle with me. He made me see how good a man could be.

I hope one day, darling, that you will know the touch of a man who loves you. I pray you will know how wonderful that is. How rare and beautiful. How godly. Even if it isn't within the union of marriage. It isn't wrong. Nothing is more right.

So, my precious girl, when I tell you that not all men are bad, I hope you believe me. I hope you don't close them all out. I hope you give yourself a chance to be loved.

- Mom

My mother had been in love. With a convict nonetheless. She was so in love with him that she was willing to ignore her father's orders and sleep with him. I wanted to know more about him. What had he done to land in prison? What happened to him? Were they separated because of her marriage? The reality was... that was probably the case. One day she was there, loving him. The next, she was dragged away to live with my father. Without having the opportunity to explain to the man she loved. With no final words.

And then she was thrown into an awful loveless marriage, forced to endure the touch of a man who despised her but used her nonetheless.

That was the life my mother had lived. My heart hurt in my chest at the idea. Twenty years in a life you hated. Twenty years clinging to the memory of an old love to get you through the drudgery. Twenty years knowing that you would never, ever see him again. Twenty years of constant heartbreak.

I fell asleep a long time later, tossing and turning in fitful dreams. I woke up past ten in the morning, feeling restless and moody.

My phone rang suddenly, making my heart fly into my chest as I stumbled through the house to grab it.

"Hello?" I said into the receiver, sounding way too eager.

"Get on your knees," a voice said. Familiar, but not who I had wanted to hear.

There was a sinking feeling in my belly as I reached for the closest phallic-shaped object I could stick in my mouth for him; which ended up being a wine bottle I had never gotten around to recycling.

"Yes, sir," I said, falling easily into the role. I could do it. I could throw myself into work.

"Open your mouth and stick your tongue out you dirty little slut," he growled. This wasn't one of the doms who got me a little warmed up. This one made me think of cruelty and debasement. But he was a paying customer and a regular.

I took three calls, showered, changed into yet another thong. Pink. I dressed in a simple gray t-shirt dress, grabbed my keys, and went next door. Because at that point, I was getting worried. Maybe something had happened. Maybe he was hurt or laying unconscious or God-knew what next door just waiting for someone to come by. I chose not to think of the fact that if he was hurt, he would yell.

I knocked.

And knocked.

And knocked.

I called his name. I told him to open up. I went from lighthearted and flirtatious to downright frantic in a matter of minutes. When I finally reached for the knob, I felt it turn, unlocked, in my hands.

I paused. I don't know why. Fear or nervousness. But I paused for a long time, feeling my heartbeat pound frantically in my chest, throat, wrists. Then I stepped in and my legs gave out. Literally gave out. I dropped numbly to my knees right there in the doorway, the backs of my feet still in the hall.

Because his entire apartment was cleaned out. The dining room set he had made, the coffee table, the couch, the television. Everything. It was all gone.

Hunter was gone.

The reality of that broke through the shock like a bolt of lightning, too bright, too powerful to ignore. Hunter was gone. Not just for a couple days. Or weeks. He was gone with the intention of never coming back. He was gone forever.

I placed my hands on the floor and pushed myself up, willing myself to look. I walked toward the kitchen, looking in the cabinets and the fridge. There was nothing, not even a leftover box of baking soda in the back of the fridge. I moved down the hallway to the bedroom. His giant bed with all its comfortable sheets and blankets was gone. His clothes and even the hangers were gone out of the closet.

I stood there for a long time in the empty space the bed used to occupy. I missed it. I missed the softness and the memories. I missed the sex I had learned I could enjoy there. I missed the nights

I was able to sleep there.

I took a long, slow deep breath and walked back into the living room. And that's when I saw it. It was sitting right in front of the sliding balcony doors so it could get light and heat. The cactus I had bought him. I walked over to it, getting on the floor beside it, touching the skull planter it was in.

Then I was crying. It was the kind of crying you only did when you know you are going to be unobserved: loud, ugly sobbing. I pulled my knees to my chest and rested my forehead against them, my body shaking more with each passing moment. It was a violent kind of breakdown that was almost scary. Because I couldn't stop it. I couldn't fight it. I just had to sit there and let it wash over me.

A long time later, I uncurled from myself, scrubbing furiously at my face with my hands. The urge to cry was still there, but the tears weren't coming. I felt dry, like all of the moisture had seeped out and I was brittle inside.

It hurt. Oh, God how it hurt. And, what's worse was, I didn't expect it to. I hadn't realized just how much he had started to mean to me in such a short amount of time. He shouldn't have. I mean... with how closed off and distant I was... he shouldn't have been able to mean so much. But he did.

The absence of him was like a black hole inside, constantly turning and pulling everything good into its hollow depths.

Would I be able to sleep through the nights anymore? Would the lure of sharp objects come back with the same intensity that it used to? Would I ever again feel the way I felt around him... fully naked and completely comfortable?

Or was security something I buried in him?

Taking a deep breath, I looked out onto his balcony. He even took his goddamn ashtray. But he left my cactus. Which, the more I thought about it, felt like a fucking slap in the face. Was it a pointed move? What else could it have been?

So... what? He wanted me to know he wanted literally everything else in the world except something that was from me?

Well... *fuck him*. Fuck him seven ways to Sunday. And then once more for good measure.

I stooped down, grabbed the cactus and stormed out of his apartment, slamming the door and making it rattle in the jamb. I turned and went down the elevator, outside and down the street. I walked right back to the same store I bought the damn thing to begin with. The woman at the counter watched me storm up to the closest, most girly freaking planter I could find which was hot pink with purple hearts all over, turned the skull upside down and swiftly stuck the cactus into the new pot. I handed her a twenty, headed right outside and into the closest empty alley, taking the skull and hurling it with everything I had at the wall.

Watching it splinter all around was the best feeling I had felt in days.

He didn't want me? No big deal. I didn't want someone who didn't want me back. I was better than that. I deserved better than that. He could rot in hell for all I cared.

I would be fine. Eventually. Once the betrayal dulled. Once the anger died down. Once I had a few nights under my belt... I would be fine.

I went back into my apartment, putting the cactus on my coffee table and sitting down on the couch. I kept trying to breathe deep, to suck air into the hole inside. I had a sneaking suspicion that despite all my convictions, all my intentions to be a good scorned woman, that there would always be that feeling. And, with it, the fear to ever let myself open up enough to be put in the position to feel it again.

I thought of the tattoo he had done on me; my pretty heart with its chains. In that moment, I swore I could feel the chains tightening, wrapping around, keeping it even further out of reach.

Not all men are bad.

My mother may not have led a life of greatness. She might not have broken out of the shackles of her prison and built a life on the other side. She might not have been an idol.

But she was all I had. And I owed it to her to take whatever lessons she had for me and trust in them; put my faith to rest in them.

So, no... not all men are bad. But Hunter was a particular kind of asshole.

How do you treat a person, so obviously, painfully damaged, like that? How do you kiss their scars and tell them you want to know everything? Every sordid detail of their damage?

Maybe I was just a sucker for a sweet talker after all.

And maybe that whole scene in my kitchen before I left, about remembering him and whatnot, maybe that was because he knew something I didn't. Maybe that was because he was planning all along to leave.

I ran a hand underneath my breasts, thinking of my scars, thinking about his plans for them. He had spent hours working on those sketches, getting them just how I wanted them. The bastard couldn't at least have left the final product so I could go get it done by someone else?

Well, fuck him. Again. He wasn't the only tattoo artist in the city. Hell, he probably wasn't even one of the best. I got up from the couch and grabbed a stack of printer paper and a pen. I could try to recreate it. I could get it as close as possible and bring it to a professional. It would give me something to focus on.

Because I knew that if I let myself slip for a second, if I let myself think of anything other than the bitterness, if I allowed even a drop of the good that had been between us get in... I would fall face forward into the grief. I would wrap it around myself like an old favorite sweater. I would sink into it and settle. I would never get better.

Because the truth of it all was, I loved the jackass.

So what other option did I have but to *deny, deny, deny*?

I absolutely, positively, did not in any way shape or form love Hunter from apartment fourteen.

TWENTY

Hunter

I was such a fucking asshole. There was really no other way to put it. That was what I was. I grabbed my last box off the floor and put it on the kitchen counter. The cactus was sitting on top in its absurd skull planter.

I should have left her alone. The first week in this place, I knew she was trouble. I knew I was *in* trouble. She wasn't part of my plan. Which had been simple: get the fuck away, new city, new apartment, new life. I was supposed to spend my time getting my career on its feet, tinkering with my home improvement projects, and keeping to my goddamn self. I had no business getting acquainted with my neighbors. If they knew what I was running from, they would want nothing to do with me anyway.

But, damn, that woman.

All it took was one look at her drinking her coffee on her balcony, leaning on the railing with her ass sticking out in those panties. Then she opened her mouth and spit fire. I was hooked.

Men like me didn't like good girls, and Sixteen was far from a good girl. Having loud (what I thought at the time) sex several times a day, going out drinking to complete oblivion every night dressed in those crazy sexy outfits. No, she wasn't a good girl. But good girls were overrated.

Maybe if I hadn't been so blindingly attracted to her from the first, I would have seen the damage sooner. Not that it mattered. Actually, she was all the more attractive to me when I could see she had demons of her own. There's nothing in the world like a heart that's been cut up the same.

I wasn't lying when I said that nothing, not even her scars, could make her anything other than beautiful. She was perfect and flawless.

I reached into the box and took out the cactus, looking at it. She was right, I did think about her every time I saw it. But not because she was prickly, but because she had been thoughtful enough to get it for me for being a bitch. That was what Fiona was like... she would cut you and then patch you up and kiss the bandage.

I walked over to the glass door and put the pot down. I wanted to keep it, bring it with me. I really did. I wanted a piece of her with me. I wanted a physical representation that she was a part of my life. But I couldn't bring any part of bright, perfect Fee into my fucked up past.

The door made a hollow sound as I closed it and made my way down the hall. Which was fitting. It was how I felt inside too- like I was leaving an important part of me behind.

I hadn't meant to be such a fuck. I really meant it when I said I would call her while she was away and that I would take her to bed when she got back. I meant that. I couldn't think of spending a day in my apartment without her there. Preferably naked.

But that was before I got the knock on my door the morning after she left.

I opened the door, half expecting the super or maybe even her, having decided she didn't want to go after all; or that she wanted me to come with her. There might have been a leap of hope as I pulled it open. But it quickly got dashed away as I felt my stomach drop. Because there in my doorway was one of my own ghosts- all six foot three inches of unnecessary muscle and ink.

"You thought you could just leave?" he asked as a greeting, his blue eyes so much like my own.

"Shane," I nodded, knowing it was the end. I wasn't going to get away from him. From them. I was going to have to go back.

"Pack your shit," he said, looking past me into the apartment, "or I'll have some of the guys come up and toss it all. You have eight hours to get this all handled and meet me out front. I'll drive."

And then he was gone. I closed the door, resting my forehead against the inside of it. How was that for a family reunion? But given the reputation of my family, it actually was quite fitting. Shane, my brother, was a year younger and a hell of a lot more ambitious in the eyes of our father. It was a constant bone of contrition that I was still somehow the favorite despite all Shane did for him.

I made a few calls and walked to the closest U-Haul station to pick up a truck. I did all this without a fight; without question. Because it was useless. I hedged my bets when I ran. There was always a chance of being found, of being pulled back.

I guessed a part of me had been holding out hope that my father would let me go. He had other sons; four others to be exact. He didn't need me. He had his oldest and his youngest; he could just let the useless middle ones go. But, no. That couldn't happen because it wouldn't look good. It wouldn't send out a good message that he couldn't keep a handle on one of his own children.

The door opened just as I adjusted the cactus into place. "It'll die," Shane said, completely overtaking the doorway.

"No," I said, shaking my head, "someone is going to stop by eventually and see it."

"Shit," Shane laughed and as I turned back to him, I found him shaking his head at me. "You went and got yourself a girl? Amateur move, bro." And for a second, we were brothers again, familiar, teasing. But then his face settled into hard lines and he walked back into the hall. "Let's go."

The ride back was long and tense. Shane had taken my phone and tossed it then spent the rest of the time Shane staring out the window, his metal blasting from the radio so he wouldn't even have to make an effort at conversation. I sat there in silent resignation, watching as my new life became a dot in the rear view. I would never get back to it.

To her.

And if I thought living in the past was bad, being forced back into it was going to be a million times worse. Because I had gotten a taste of freedom, of a life by my own terms. I knew what it was like- infinitely better than I had imagined. I got to be the person I had always wanted to be, the man I knew I was underneath it all. I got to find a woman who didn't know who I used to be. And she liked me for who I really was.

My fucking family was taking that all away from me. I had been able to forgive them for what they had done to me in the past, but I could never forgive this.

"Unclench those fists, bro," Shane said, parking the truck, "we're here."

From the outside, the bar looked harmless enough. It was just your average everyday watering hole for bikers, as evidenced by the dozen or so black and chrome beauties parked out front. It was a long and low red brick building with a plain wooden sign saying only "Chaz's". The windows were small, the front door black. Nothing interesting.

I climbed out of the truck, taking a long, deep breath. That was it. I should have been terrified. I should have been shit my pants worried. But I felt nothing, just numbness and a vague imprint of misery I tried to snuff out. Keeping any kind of attachment to the City, to Fee, wasn't going to do me any good there.

I swear as I walked, if you listened close enough, you could hear the wind whispering "dead man walking". The front door made a familiar groan as Shane opened it, walking through first so he could show off the big fat mouse he brought home to his master.

The inside of the bar was sleek and upscale, not the typical dirty, disease-ridden joints most bikers frequent. The bar itself was located to the right of the door with a large blue felt pool table next to it. The walls were painted a gray that reminded me a lot of Fee's walls, but here they felt cold and unfriendly. The wood floor was stained to almost black and the walls were free of any clutter. There were just tables; they were small and black with matching chairs. I had spent months making them all after finally convincing my father the old ones needed to go.

"Dad," Shane called and the voices in the room quieted immediately. Everyone knew. They knew all the Mallick boys.

I saw my other brothers, various ages and looks but all tall, dark haired, and light eyed. No one would mistake our family resemblance. They moved away from the table where I knew my father was sitting, where he always sat, facing the door with a gun on the table in front of him. My oldest brother's face gave nothing away. Silently intimidating, that was Ryan. The second oldest, Eli, softer, gentler, but with a fierce temper, sent me a sympathetic look for a moment before dropping his eyes. Then there was Mark, who glanced at me then back at our father.

Shane slammed into my shoulder as he went to stand near the others, watching me with a sneer on his face.

My father looked up slowly, as if he had all the time in the world, as if my disappearance hadn't been the single most important thought on his mind for the past six months. Charlie Mallick. He was an older version of all of us- tall, lean, light eyes, dark hair with a bit of gray at the temples. He had wrinkles between his brows, but otherwise had aged well. In plain ole jeans and a black t-shirt, he was the most intimidating sight I had ever seen.

"Hunter," he said, raising a brow at me. "It's so nice of you to come pay us a visit."

"Wasn't as if I had much of a choice, Dad," I said, sending Shane a sideways look.

"Where was he?" my father asked Shane whose spine immediately straightened at getting to be the golden boy.

"New York. In this shithole of an apartment, all gaga over some woman."

God, he was such a dick. As if my running away wasn't bad enough. Now I got to be the pussy who had fallen for the first skirt who came my way in my new life. Great. Just great.

"Is that so?" my dad asked, his tone almost amused, motioning me toward the chair across from him. "Why don't you have a seat?"

"Why don't you cut the bullshit and stop acting like I have a choice in any of this?" I asked, sitting down, lounging back in my chair and making the front legs pick up off the floor.

"Shane," he said, "why don't you invite our guests to come back at another time?" he asked and Shane rushed to kick everyone out of the bar. I heard the shuffling of feet, the grumbling, the slamming of the door, the sliding of the lock, then finally... the silence. Shane walked back over to stand closer to my father. "Did you really think you would get away with it?"

"Get away with living my own life? As a grown ass man? Yeah, I thought I might," I shot back, beyond caring that all I was doing was provoking his anger.

"You know the deal here, Hunter," he said, his voice calm.

"You work here. In exchange you get a nice place, cars, a certain amount of protection from your actions..."

"A life sentence doing something I don't enjoy..."

He smiled then, a slow, strange smile. "Hunt... don't even try to tell me you don't enjoy it. I've seen you. I've seen how much you like the job."

He wasn't wrong. That was the scary part; the part I was running away from. That was the part that made me promise myself I would stay away from people in the city until I could get it under control- the anger. The anger that he had instilled in me. The anger that made me enjoy all the awful things he made me do.

"Not anymore," I said back, choosing not to think about the time outside my apartment. Trying to not think about the guy with his hands on Fee, the guy who would need a lot of plastic surgery to have his face look like it had before I got my hands on him.

"Well that's an easy enough fix," he said, shrugging. "You'll be back in shape in no time." He took a deep breath then, looking almost sad. "I'm afraid you know what happens next," he said.

And I did. Oh, I did. And I hated him in that moment, for making it be this way, for pitting brothers against each other.

Beat-ins were common when we were younger, to find friends who were strong enough to take a beating from all of us, and therefore could be a part of our twisted little family.

Beat-outs weren't as common and were as close to lethal as possible to discourage disloyalty.

What I was about to get was somewhere in between. It was something we didn't really even have a name for. What was about to happen was what you got when you fucked up: when you lost money, when you got an outsider involved in our shit, and, apparently, when you tried to escape. If it had been as easy as a beat-out for me, I would have endured it a long time ago. But that couldn't happen. Not to one of his sons.

I slowly got up out of my seat, watching my father. Shane

got closer, his voice taunting. "Want to take a minute to tape up those artist hands of yours? We'll wait," he said, close to my ear.

"Fuck you, Shane," I said, holding my arms out wide at my sides, palms out. It was clear to him, to them: I wasn't going to fight back. They could beat me. But it wasn't going to get them anywhere because I already accepted my circumstances.

There was a tension in the air as they all looked at me, at each other, then my father. This wasn't done. I didn't have a choice. I had to fight back.

My father sighed, closing his eyes for a second, then waving a hand.

I tensed for the first punch which I knew Shane had been waiting years to give me. The others hesitated, Ryan breaking free of his shock first to join in. Mark was next, and lastly, Eli. I couldn't blame them, not even as I felt myself fly back onto the floor, had a boot land in my side and felt my ribs breaking. That was what we were raised to do. A call to fight was like the bell to Pavlov's dogs. We salivated for it. We could feel the anger rise up in our blood, some like mine and Eli's, stronger than the others. Maybe it was because we weren't, by nature, fighters. Because he was softer, because I was resistant. Maybe the need to fight to gain validation from our father had warped us into becoming monsters.

So I knew it was his fists that took to my face. Just like I knew it was Ryan, with his cool, detached temper, who eventually pulled him off.

Because we knew one another. Even though we were forced into hurting one another, even though our lives felt like a competition for our father's attentions and affections, even though we were all cold and hard- we knew one another. Ryan knew that Eli would bash my face unrecognizable. He also knew that Eli would never forgive himself for it.

I rolled onto my side when my father finally called them off, spitting blood out onto the floor. It was bad. It was worse than I had been expecting. My face was on fire. My ribs were throbbing. I could feel soreness and stiffness in every inch.

My brothers stepped away, walking out the front door and leaving me alone with our father. "I understand why you left, Hunt," he said, coming up next to me, kneeling next to my blood stain. "And I know you understand why I couldn't let you leave. Not like that," he said, touching my knee then standing up and following my brothers outside.

Through the pain, I felt hope. He couldn't let me leave... *like that*. Which meant that maybe I could leave. Somehow; under his terms. When he was done punishing me. When he was done proving to everyone that he still controlled me. Then and only then, he would let me go. But it was something. It was something to cling to.

I tried to curl up on my side but my sore ribs sent white bursts of pain through my body. I ended up lying flat on my back, staring up at the ceiling, still tasting my own blood for a long time.

A while later, hours, it had to be hours; I heard footsteps. It was a set that didn't belong to my brothers or father, but still familiar. The click-clicking of heels, heavy and deliberate could only belong to one person. "Mom," I grumbled.

"Hunt," she said, walking up to stand next to me, her heeled foot brushing my leg as she stared down at me. Now, my father was terrifying. He was a scary man to know. It went to follow that the woman who spent her life dealing with him would be submissive and kowtow to his whims. This was not true of my mother.

Helen Mallick was five-foot-nine inches of steel. She was also always one of the prettiest women in the room: long legged, thin, with sharp features, hazel eyes, and long black hair. She also had the distinction of being the fiercest human being I had ever met. Which, given all the unsavory characters I met in my line of work, was saying something.

And my father loved her. He loved her with a passion that I had always found uncomfortable; with a passion that was evidenced by the five sons she gave him in under a decade. We were boys she raised to be rough and tough and loyal. We were boys she let beat the ever loving shit out of each other over toys, or girls, or cars. We were boys she let run wild and get into all kinds of trouble. But we were also boys she would knock across a room if we ever dared to smart-mouth or disrespect her rules. Even as teenagers. I distinctly remember "falling" (or at least that's what we told the doctors at the hospital) out of a window when I was seventeen and thought it would be a good idea to skip out on Sunday dinners. That was unacceptable in our household.

"Having a good homecoming?" she asked, kneeling down on the floor by my stomach and pulling up my shirt. Her fingers pressed into the bruised skin over my ribs and I let out a string of curses that had a smile toying at her lips. "Glad to see they didn't break your spirit even if they did break a rib or two."

"So what's next?" I asked, shaking my head. "Gonna throw me down in the basement? Chain me up like one of the scumbags who don't pay back their loans?"

"Don't be silly," she said, reaching down to grab my arm and help me up. "You'll be back at your old place. Your brothers should have your new crap all unpacked by the time you get there. I suggest slapping on some elastic bandages and some triple antibiotic because your dad is probably going to have you out on a job tomorrow."

"Tomorrow?" I growled, the sound coming out jumbled with my swollen lips.

"He thinks it will be good for you to get right back in the thick of it. Won't leave you time to get all resentful."

"More so than I am now?" I asked, reaching up to touch the side of my face, which felt particularly damaged, and feeling the swollen flesh underneath my hand. "I don't think that is possible at this point, Mom. But thanks for the warning."

"Hunt," she called as I slowly wobbled toward the door.

"Yeah?" I asked, half turning to her.

"Talk to your father. I know you think he's just a monster, but he's a man. And though it's hard to see sometimes, he's not a bad man either. He wants you boys to be happy."

"Yeah, maybe I'll give that a try," I said, lying through my teeth and she knew it. No fucking way was I showing that kind of vulnerability in front of him.

"Hey Hunt," she called again and I stopped but didn't look at her. "Please tell me she's not some meek shrinking violet," she said walking and opening the door for me.

"How did... did Shane..."

"No, baby," she said, shaking her head and giving me one of her rare motherly smiles. "I can see it in your eyes. I am your mother, you know."

I nodded, stepping outside. "No, Mom. She's a fucking blonde-haired, green-eyed spitfire. The second time I met her, she was breaking in and stealing my tools so I couldn't wake her up anymore."

"Good," she said, nodding and closing the door.

Why it was good that I had a woman my mother approved of when she damn well knew I would never see her again was completely beyond my comprehension. But it mattered to her. It always had. Any time one of us would show interest in a girl or woman who seemed timid or altogether too average, she would make a big deal about it. Because boys like us needed women who could handle us. So she became best friends with every juvenile delinquent, every drinking/smoking/ fighting trouble maker, every purple haired, pierced and tatted girl we brought home. And she shunned the ones who cheered in high school, or worked at a tanning salon, or wore demure knee-length skirts.

She really would have liked Fiona. She would have

approved of all the skimpy dresses, the tattoos, the phone sex job, the selling her dirty panties, hell... she would have even liked the scars. And Fiona wouldn't put up with her shit... or my brothers' for that matter. She would fit right in. But now they would never get to meet her.

The walk back to my old place was long, painful and exhausting. I could barely get five feet without having to stop, bend forward and curse the entire fucking universe. It was a walk that should have taken me fifteen minutes, but took me the better part of an hour and a half.

My old place was an apartment above a liquor store that my parents and I owned. It was one of our their many legitimate businesses to fund our their less than legal one. I wondered who they got to keep an eye on it while I was gone since each of my brothers had their own gigs: a gym, a lawn service... whatever niche my father wanted to get in on next.

The stairs up the side of the building were steep and dangerous on a good day so I let myself in through the store, grabbing a huge bottle of whiskey off a shelf, and slowly made my way up the staircase in the backroom.

My apartment in my hometown was a lot like my apartment was in the city. I had spent endless hours trying to get it right. The walls were painted a cappuccino brown. The furniture was all stained a perfect antique walnut shade as were the kitchen cabinets. It was a studio and I used bookshelves to divide my bedroom from the main area. My brothers had piled everything from my other apartment into a corner next to my dining set, making the space feel cramped and claustrophobic and full of old memories.

I dragged myself to the bathroom, grabbing the plastic container of medical supplies out of the closet and dropping them onto the counter. I twisted the top off the whiskey and took a long swig before starting the cleaning up process. It was nothing new. It was impossible to tell how many times I had stood in that bathroom and fixed mine or one of my brothers' busted faces. That was the business, the life.

I took as deep a breath as my ribs would allow and looked into the mirror. It wasn't pretty. My lip was busted and swollen; one whole side of my face raised and bruised; my nose was bent slightly out of shape and I grabbed it and pushed it back where it was supposed to be. It wasn't my first broken nose and it probably wouldn't be my last. I grabbed the alcohol and dabbed at the cuts, cleaning the blood away. I glued the worst of them, swabbed antibiotics on the others. I chugged a fifth of the whiskey, wrapped my ribs, and fell into my bed.

--

The pounding in my head was what eventually woke me up. The sun was shining brightly in through the windows that had the blinds drawn when I had gone to sleep. I blinked past the pain behind my eyes, turning my head to the side and seeing my father sitting there on one of the dining room chairs from the City beside my bed.

"So what's her name?" he asked leaning forward.

"Fiona," I said, trying to rise up off the mattress and falling back with a curse. "Mom told you?"

"Shane might have mentioned something about a cactus," he said, shrugging a shoulder. "What's the deal there?"

"She gave it to me... because she's prickly."

"Prickly," he repeated, smiling a little. "Sounds like someone I would like to meet."

"Fat luck with that, Dad," I said, finally sitting up and nearly throwing up all over my feet from the pain. "She'll never forgive me for leaving without a word." Shane had tossed my phone which was a burner to begin with so there was no way for me to get the records and find her number. Sure, she ran a phone sex line in NYC, but there had to have been at least a hundred of them. What was left? A letter? By the time it got there, would she even read it?

"I think you'd be surprised, son, what a woman can forgive a man who loves her."

"Speaking from experience?" I asked, taking the whiskey off my bedside table and tipping it up for a drink.

"You're not falling into a bottle over this," he said, snatching the bottle from my hands.

"Good luck stopping me," I said, shaking my head. "There's an entire liquor store downstairs."

"Look, Hunt," he said, his voice softer than it usually was, "I know you think I'm a real dick, but I really do want what is best for you."

"Which is a good solid beating?" I asked.

"Once in a while, yes," he said, smirking and I almost laughed. "You can't just run away, Hunt," he shrugged. "It's bad for business and you know it. But if you had come to me and talked about this like men, we could have figured something out. I don't need you. I ran this business all by myself while you and your brothers were still pissing yourselves. I don't need all five of you here. And I know Ryan and Shane can hold things down. And, what's more, they want to. If this wasn't the life you wanted..."

"It's not."

"Then you can consider this," he said, gesturing toward my face, "your beat-out. For lack of a better term. You're out. But you're still my son and I want you around."

"What's the catch here, Dad?" I asked, knowing that when things sounded too good to be true, they usually were.

"I don't know if you can call it a catch," he said, shrugging. "Call it family obligation. I want you to be in touch. I don't want you sneaking off to some city and not even calling your mother to tell her you're alright. She was worried sick."

"Mom has never worried a day in her life," I countered.

"She worries about you boys. Mostly you and Eli. She knew you guys weren't meant for this life. You had your art thing, Eli has his books. We were just waiting for you to come to us."

"Maybe you should have made it seem like that was an option."

"Maybe you should stop acting like a boy and start being a man. Take responsibility. Running away was a chicken shit move. That's why you knew I would send for you. That's why you knew you needed a beating for it. I wouldn't have lost respect in this town if I allowed one of my boys to go off and live a different life. Having one just take off, however..."

"I get it, Dad," I said, feeling guilty. He was good at that. He was good at guilt. Which, more so than the threat of violence, was probably what made him such an efficient parent. "So what now?" I asked, knowing it wasn't going to be as simple as he was making it out to be. "You're not just going to let me take off back to the City after all the trouble you went through to get me here."

"No," he agreed, offering me his arm as I tried to stand, "you're right. You're not going back yet. I need you to show your face around here for a while. At least until it heals up. Lex and V are flexing their muscles; we can't have them thinking we have any kind of weakness right now. So you're going to stay and show everyone that you're back, punished, and starting your own life, but with my blessing, not because of your defiance. Then you can leave." he followed me to the kitchen, reaching into the cabinet to bring the coffee grounds down for me. "Though your mother and I would really like it if you stayed, of course. Go get your girl and bring her back. You'll be welcome here always."

I turned back and looked at him, my father. He was a man who I had, for the most part, only seen be ruthless and methodical. The only softness about him seemed to exist when he looked at my mother. But maybe I had always been so wrapped up in my own misery and my own anger that I couldn't see how much he actually cared about his kids.

"You know," he said, a strange smile playing with his lips, "we have been waiting a long, long time for one of you to get your shit together and give us some grandbabies."

I found myself smiling back at him. "Don't push it."

In the end, I had to stay three months. I worked at the store. I went to the bar and drank with my family. I went to Sunday dinners. I rebuilt the bond I had snapped when I left. Everyone seemed to let bygones be bygones. My face healed as did my relationships with my brothers, even Shane.

I couldn't call Fee. I missed her with a fierce sort of passion I didn't know I had within me. I wanted to hear her voice. I sat down to start and toss at least two dozen letters. But by the time I was moving around enough to even get to the post office, I knew she would have already been home. She would have already seen my empty apartment. And if I knew anything about her, and I fucking did, she would have been furious with me. She would have ripped it up without opening it. She wouldn't have given me a chance to explain. And I couldn't blame her for that.

So, I didn't send a letter.

I waited. I got better. I got my shit together.

Then I planned to go back to the City and talk to her- face to face.

My mom met me at the car one morning, her maternal sixth

sense somehow knowing that that day was the day. She had a take away coffee in one hand and a small blue jewelry box in the other. "Go get her," she said, "then bring her here to meet me, you hear?"

I leaned forward and kissed her cheek. "Yes ma'am," I said, climbing in my car and heading back to the City.

To Fee.

She was going to be so pissed.

TWENTY-ONE

Fiona

There was a new tenant in the apartment next door; in the apartment it had taken me ten weeks to not call "Hunter's apartment" anymore. I saw the moving truck the day before and a guy about my age dragging endless boxes inside. I probably should have helped. That's what neighbors did, right?

I was really trying. Since I got back. Since I got over my little stint of half-insanity over Hunter's disappearance. I had blasted raging chick music. I went out drinking. I flirted with other men. I cried myself to sleep. I became a stereotype that I hated for a good two months before I snapped out of it.

There were other men. Good men. There were men who didn't just fucking take up and leave out of nowhere. So I was trying. I went out at night, but I didn't get trashed. I had a drink or two, but nothing more. I had, for the most part, stopped trying so hard to self-destruct. I was healing.

I grabbed the potted plant I had went out to grab that

morning and went into the hall. As much as I tried to deny it, there was a twisting in my chest as I raised my hand to knock. But that was stupid and the past. I needed to get over it.

"Hi," the man who opened the door greeted me. He had light brown hair, a handsome face, and big honey-colored eyes. He looked friendly. He seemed nice.

"Hey," I said, giving what I hoped was a friendly smile, not a creepy serial killer one. I held out the plant. "I'm Fiona... from sixteen," the word was painful to say still. *Damn him.* "I just wanted to welcome you to the building." God, I felt stupid. Every word felt awkward and forced. "I... ah... stay out most of the night and run a phone sex line during the day." There. That felt more natural.

He stood there dumbly for a second then threw his head back and laughed. "Alright, Fiona. I'm Jake. I... work at a hotel and my boyfriend and I like to have loud sex all night."

"Well, that works out nicely," I laughed.

"Want to come in for a minute?" he asked. No. Oh, God no. I couldn't. Even though it was empty for months, I hadn't been able to step foot inside again after the day I took my cactus back.

"Sure," I said, squaring my shoulders and walking through the doorway.

"I was expecting to have to do a ton of work in a neighborhood like this. But the last tenant must have done a lot of work..."

"Yeah," I agreed, running my hand over the kitchen cabinet, "he did."

"Oh, crap," Jake said, looking at me warily. "He didn't... die in here did he?"

"No," I laughed, shaking my head. "This one just up and left one day." Left *me* one day. "But the guy before him did die in here. Heroin is a bitch."

"Oh, okay. Well... I'll just burn some sage or something," he smiled.

"Well, it looks like you still have a lot of unpacking to do," I said, moving my way to the door. "I won't keep you. If you want to maybe come over for dinner tomorrow, I'd be happy to cook. I know you'll probably be living on take-out till you get all this sorted out so maybe..." I needed to shut up. I was rambling.

"Sure," he said, eagerly, saving me from any further embarrassment. "That sounds great."

—

Jake ended up going with me the next afternoon to pick up groceries, helping me with the bags back to my apartment. I reached for my keys but the door was slightly open. I rolled my eyes at Jake and pushed the door open. "Isaiah, you need to stop fucking leaving the door open. Isaiah," I called, dropping the groceries on the counter and walking around my apartment looking for him.

He had a habit of dropping in without calling, using the keys I had given him the week he crashed on my couch while he was trying to deal with losing our father... and then our grandmother within a few weeks. He was still withdrawn, awkward with conversation, and apparently, completely unable to shut a goddamn door, let alone lock it.

"Well," I huffed, walking back to the living room where Jake was looking around. "He's graduated from leaving the door open while he was here, to forgetting to close it when he leaves."

"Your boyfriend?" Jake asked, running a hand over my

couch.

"My brother," I clarified. "He's not from around here. He doesn't understand that in the big bad city... we need to lock the..." I trailed off, looking to the center of my coffee table with a dropping feeling in my stomach.

"What's wrong?" Jake asked, eying me. "You look like you've seen a ghost."

"Nothing," I said, shaking my head, looking around the room. "I just... there is usually a cactus on that table. He must have... moved it." But even as I said it, it felt wrong. Why would he move my cactus?

It was, however, the only logical explanation seeing as nothing else in my apartment was missing. No one would break in and steal my eight dollar cactus but leave my five-hundred dollar television.

"Alright," I said, shaking off the weird feeling. "How does vegetable alfredo over pasta sound?"

"Fabulous," he said, putting a hand over his heart.

It was late when we finally decided to call it quits after a bottle of wine and more pasta than two people should ever have eaten by themselves. I walked him to the door, agreeing to let him accompany me to the gym the next morning.

As I walked back into the kitchen, there was a knock at the door. "Did you forget something?" I asked, sliding the chain and pulling the door open.

I almost passed out. Literally. Like... I had to grab the door jamb to keep myself from falling flat on my face.

Because there in the hall was fucking Hunter.

"Oh hell fucking no," I said, moving back and slamming the door in his face. My hands fumbled as I tried to get all my locks into place.

No no no no no.

"Open up, Sixteen," he called, sounding lazily flirtatious.

How dare he? How dare he act like I was being unreasonable by closing the door on him? You didn't just disappear one day and then show up three months later like nothing had happened.

"Go to hell," I shot back, moving into my living room, holding a hand to my chest. My heart felt like it was going to explode in my chest; the frantic pounding making me feel nauseated.

That literally could not be happening. I had just finally gotten over it. Well, not over it. But I was doing better. I was moving on. A lot of shit had happened since the last time I saw him. I had plenty of things to focus on beside what he did to me, about what an idiot I had been about him.

I was pacing the living room floor when I realized something. I looked back at the door. I knew he was still there. Don't ask me how I knew, but I knew. "Give me my goddamn cactus back, asshole," I yelled.

There was the sound of a chuckle and it made my insides feel uncomfortably wobbly. And I got all the more angry with him. He wasn't allowed to have that power. Not anymore. "It's my cactus," he called back.

"You abandoned it," I said, "so schoolyard rules come into play."

"You can't call 'finders keepers' on another person's property."

"It was in an abandoned apartment. So technically it didn't belong to anyone anymore. Besides, I bought it in the first place."

"Where's my skull planter?" he asked, ignoring what I had said. And it was every bit annoying as it used to be.

"Smashed to splinters in an alley," I shot back. "Hope you

like pink and purple heart planters."

"In fact, I love them." There was a pause, the lump in my throat was too hard to talk through, so I didn't try. "Open the door, Fee," he said, his voice soft and reassuring. It was a voice that touched something deep inside that I had been trying to forget existed.

"Go scratch at someone else's door, Hunter. You're not welcome here anymore. And don't fucking break in again."

I wrapped my arms around my middle that felt like it was falling apart, like all my insides were going to fall out if I didn't hold them in.

"Is this about your new boyfriend?" he asked, his voice with only the slightest edge to it when he said that word.

I felt myself snort, shaking my head. He didn't have a right to be angry or jealous or... anything. He up and left. And, not for nothing, but he knew how fucked up I was. He knew how damaged I had been. He knew I was going into a situation that could have easily screwed me up worse. Then to get back and see him leave his "f-you" cactus in his empty apartment...

I could have done something really, really stupid for all he knew.

So if, instead, all I had done was go out and find myself a normal relationship... then good for me. And fuck him if he thought I had done something wrong.

I wasn't about to tell him that Jake was just the new number fourteen and was gayer than Christmas. He was attractive enough to be a threat to Hunter. So, good. I was glad he was threatened.

"Never mind him," I said, willing my voice to be calm. "This is about you being a coward."

"If you would just let me explain, Fee," he said instead, sounding sad. As sad as I felt, in fact.

"No," I said, sliding open my balcony door. I didn't care that it was twenty degrees out and that I was barefoot. I just needed to get away. I was just barely holding it together. "It's too late, Hunter," I said, sliding the door and blocking out the sound of whatever he said.

I lowered myself down onto the cold cement, wrapping my arms around my legs and rocking myself back and forth, trying to take some comfort in the motion. *Goddamn it all.* I thought things were okay. I thought it was all settled. I thought I had found some kind of equilibrium.

But right then, it just felt like it had felt right when I first knew he was gone. It felt like there was a swirling hollowness in my chest, like someone was ripping out the insides of my belly. Like I was falling fucking apart.

A strange injured animal sound came out of my lips, halfway between a scream and a cry that had fourteen's balcony door opening and Jake stepping out, looking around. "Fiona?" he asked, sounding worried.

"I'm fine," I lied, closing my eyes tight against the tears, but they streamed out anyway.

"Fine? With a fine piece of man like that outside your door begging like a dog for a bone? I think not." I saw him move toward the side of the balcony closest to mine, leaning against the railing and looking down at me. "Spill, neighbor."

I took a deep breath. "He's the former fourteen," I told him.

"And former... boyfriend?"

"He wasn't my boyfriend," I said automatically. That was a phrase I had said to myself all day every day like it was on repeat endlessly: *he's not your boyfriend, he's not your boyfriend, he's not your boyfriend.*

"He seems pretty torn up for a non-boyfriend."

"He can rot in hell."

"Aw, Fee," a voice said that had me jumping, "you don't mean that."

"Jesus! What the fuck?" Jake exploded and I knew where

Hunter's voice was coming from: Jake's balcony.

"Sorry, babe," a third voice, unfamiliar, broke in. "I thought you knew him. He was knocking on your door when I came up."

Jake's boyfriend. It must have been positively cozy over on that tiny balcony. I buried my face into my knees harder. I wasn't going to let him see me cry. No way.

"Dude, get the fuck out of my apartment," Jake said, sounding meaner than I thought he could.

"Yeah, one sec, guys," Hunter said. His voice held a mocking tone when he spoke to me again. "So it seems that your new boyfriend is gay." I bit hard into my lower lip to keep from talking. It would only lead to another argument. Also, he would know I was upset. "You're gonna get pneumonia sitting out here like this," he reasoned.

Like he'd care. "Just go, Fourteen."

"Fee..."

"I think it's time to leave, bud," Jake's boyfriend said and I sneaked a glance at him, big and burly. Jake had a thing for bears. He was just big enough to give Hunter a run for his money.

"Fine," Hunter said. "Fee..."

"Now," the boyfriend said again, holding an arm out toward the open sliding door.

Hunter sighed but went in through his old apartment. I heard the door to the hall close and let out my breath. "You sure you don't want to give him a second chance?" Jake asked, wiggling his eyebrows at me.

Nope. Not at all. "Yeah," I said, getting to my feet. "Never been more sure of anything in my life." I opened the door to my apartment, shivering in the cold. "Tell your boyfriend thanks for me."

And with that, I went straight for my razor blade for the first time in weeks.

TWENTY-TWO

Fiona

I winced as I slid opaque black stockings up over the fresh cuts, cursing myself fiercely. It was stupid. It was so incredibly stupid to backslide over something as pathetic and predictable as a broken heart for Christ's sake. I used to do it because of my horror story worthy past. Because it was the only way to cope. And there I was slipping into old destructive habits over a guy? Seriously? How weak could I get?

I hadn't left my apartment the whole day after he showed up. I worked out with Jake. We did the punishing, ass breaking two hour workout I had started after Hunter left. They were workouts designed to replace the endorphins I wasn't getting from cutting. They made me drop perhaps a bit too much weight, but were a way for me to stay focused. They helped me look forward instead of behind. They allowed me to fall into bed too drained to even consider not sleeping.

Then I had cooked. I had taken a bunch of extra calls I didn't need to. Actually, I didn't need to take any calls anymore considering what went down after my father, and then grandmother's deaths. But I needed to do something to occupy my time and my mind.

It was two nights later, and I needed to get out of my apartment or I was going to go crazy. Besides, I hadn't heard from Hunter since Jake's balcony so I figured I had gotten my point across.

I pulled a red wine colored dress on and black boots. I fixed my makeup. I dried my hair. Then, with one slow, deep breath, I headed out for the night. The goal was dinner, a open mic at a coffee house, a drink at a bar, then home. I was not, absolutely was not, going to get drunk. Not even though oblivion sounded really, really good right then. That was until, of course, I opened my door to find a note pinned to it. I knew who it was from. And I had every intention of ripping it right up and dispensing of it in the dumpster outside the building. Yeah, that was the plan. But I had barely made it out the front door before I was opening it, the pit in my stomach growing by the minute.

Fee,
You have every right to hate me. I never would have left like that if I had a choice. Please believe me when I tell you I truly didn't. If you would just speak to me, I could explain everything.
Hunt

Explain what? How he couldn't find two minutes to call and tell me he was sorry; or send a text saying he had to go and he'd explain everything when he got back? I could have accepted that. I would have taken any tiny scrap he fed to me. I would have made a fucking feast of it. But, no, he had chosen to starve me instead.

I crumpled the note and threw it in the trash. There was no excuse for what he did. What? Was he chained in a fucking dungeon somewhere? Locked up? What could possibly explain not taking the time to call me? Nothing. Literally nothing. So he could take his explanations and shove them up his ass. Because I wasn't going to listen to them.

Okay. So maybe I got a little drunk. And by "a little drunk" I meant fucking plastered. I was gone before it was anywhere near last call. I was so trashed, I was asking random strangers how drunk I was and laughed until I couldn't breathe at their words.

Sloshed. Pissed. Wrecked. Bombed. Loaded.

And my personal favorite: *schnockered.*

"Drunk Girl," Guy, my favorite bouncer, nodded at me as he sat down in front of his drink. "Been a while."

"I was trying to be not-so-drunk-girl," I slurred, toasting him with my glass.

"Well, it was worth a shot," he said, nodding.

"Shot! That's a good idea. Shot me please!" I called out and the bartender raised a brow, but reached for the vodka.

"No," a voice called out behind me. "Don't you think she's had enough? She won't be able to walk as it is."

"Fuck off, Fourteen," I said, rolling my eyes dramatically at the bartender. "Don't listen to him. I can walk just fine. See?" I said, getting up off the bar stool and demonstrating my major walking skills. And to my credit, and thanks to one too many nights drunk walking home, I only stumbled slightly. "And in heels nonetheless!" I declared happily, walking back to the bar and slapping my hand on it.

"No, Fee," Hunter said, grabbing my hand.

"Hey," Guy cut in, looking like he was ready to get out of his chair. "Drunk Girl, do you know this guy?"

"He's..."

"Her ex," Hunter said and I stumbled back a step.

Ex? He was *not* an ex. 'Ex' implied boyfriend status at some point. He was never my boyfriend. "He's my ex neighbor," I corrected.

"Aw, sugar," Hunter said, holding a hand over his heart like my words wounded him.

"Want me to walk you home, Drunk Girl?" Guy asked and I was seconds from agreeing because the bar was starting to spin. And I knew only two things came after the spinning: throwing up or passing out.

"I'll take her," Hunter insisted, moving closer to me.

"Nuh-uh," I said, pointing a finger at him. "He can't take me. He stole my cactus!"

Guy's eyebrows went up as he looked at Hunter. "She's not wrong," he shrugged, "but it was mine first."

"Alright," Guy said, holding a hand up, "you two seem to have some... thing going on. I'll let you handle it. These shoes are new," he said, looking down, "I would prefer to keep them puke-free for a week. Take care, Drunk Girl," he said and walked toward the back room.

I spun back toward Hunter, slamming my hand down on the bar to keep myself standing at the sudden motion. "Don't even think about it," I warned him, holding up a hand. "I am taking myself home. You are not walking me."

"Fine," he shrugged, tucking his hands into his pockets.

"Fine," I said, storming toward the door.

"I'll just walk behind you then," he said, sounding positively tickled at the idea.

There was really no use fighting about it. I couldn't stop him from following me. So I pushed outside, shaking once violently against the rush of cold on my hot skin. I shook my head at sober-me who thought a coat would be too much of a hassle. *Fuck her. Stupid, stupid sober me.* I pulled my sleeves down over my hands and hunched forward against the wind.

The puking idea was becoming more and more of a possibility with each passing moment. My body was shivering and making my already shaky insides even more wobbly. I stopped, grabbing the metal pole of a stop sign over the wave of unsteadiness.

"Fee," Hunter said, coming up close. "Here, put this on," he said, shrugging out of his leather jacket and trying to wrap it around my shoulders. I twisted away and he sighed. "Come on, baby. Your lips are turning blue."

"I'm not your baby," I objected, my teeth chattering too much to have the effect I intended. At his ever patient gaze, I looked away from him, but slipped my arms into the sleeves. It was so warm from his skin that I felt my frozen skin tingle against it. And it smelled like him: sawdust and soap. He reached for the zipper and pulled it up until the collar popped and engulfed my neck in its warmth.

"Come on," he said, turning his head back toward the sidewalk, "we're almost there."

He stayed about two feet out to the side of me the rest of the walk as my eyes got heavier and heavier and my steps more and more unsteady. "I don't know where you think you're going," I said as my heel caught a grate and I stumbled. His arm reached out to steady me. "Because you don't live here anymore," I went on, gesturing toward my building.

"I'm just getting you home safe, Fee," he said, shaking his head at me, his light eyes sad.

"You have no right to be sad," I said, climbing up the front stairs and looking down at him. "You're the one who left. You're the one who left me all alone. When you knew I needed you. I fucking *needed* you, Hunter," I said, my lips trembling, dangerously close to crying.

"I know. Fee, fuck. I know. I just..."

"No," I said, shaking my head. "It doesn't matter. It's over. It's done. I'm fine. I'm good. Better anyway. So just leave me alone, Fourteen," I said, turning back to the building. "And I am keeping this coat as retribution."

—

I woke up the next morning on the floor next to my bed, curled up beside the heat grate in a jacket that wasn't mine, still wearing my shoes from the night before.

Fuck. So much for not drinking. I pushed myself up, looking down at the jacket and not comprehending its existence for a moment. That was, until I took a deep breath and I smelled him. And then the memories flooded back.

There had been drinking. Oh, dear lord, had there been drinking. I might have actually broken a personal record that night. I didn't even want to think about how much vodka was in my system. An image of Guy flashed into my mind, offering to walk me home. And then... yup... there was Hunter. Arrogant, helpful fucking Hunter.

I put a hand over my eyes. I had admitted that he hurt me. I let out a long, low groan at that. So much for having the upper hand. *Stupid, stupid drunk me.* As I stood up, slipping out of my shoes and unzipping the coat, I remembered telling him I was keeping his jacket as punishment. One of my finer nights, for sure. I grabbed clean panties and a tank top and headed to my shower. It took the better part of half an hour to feel like I had washed the night away.

Walking into the hall, I got the distinct smell of brewing coffee.

Oh, that bastard.

"Good morning, sunshine," he said, moving into the doorway of the kitchen with two cups of coffee. His hair was wet.

I glanced outside and, seeing no rain, felt my anger reignite. "Did you take a shower here?"

He shrugged a shoulder, holding out a cup of coffee to me. "I didn't want to leave you."

"Leave me?" I asked, grabbing the coffee. "I left you," I reminded him, remembering turning and leaving him outside the building.

"Yup," he agreed. "And then I came in a few minutes later to check on you because your light didn't go on in your apartment, and you were asleep against your door."

Of-fucking-course I was. Because the night hadn't been humiliating enough without that little tidbit. It also explained why I had passed out fully dressed. "Why was I in front of the heating vent?"

He raised a brow, smiling slightly. "That was all your own doing. I had you on the bed."

"Great." I took a sip of my coffee. "Well, I'm awake now. You can go," I said, walking past him into my kitchen.

"Those look fresh," he said instead, following me and gesturing toward my thigh.

"Yeah," I agreed, going in my fridge for the mixed berry

parfait I had learned were infinitely better than leftover take-out in the morning. "I had a slip up."

"You were doing better."

"Yup."

"Until?" he asked and I shrugged a shoulder and put a spoonful of food into my mouth. "Until I showed back up," he guessed. He looked down at his coffee for a long minute and was about to speak when there was two sharp knocks on the door before it unlocked and opened.

"Fiona," Isaiah called, strolling in. There was no more 'Fiona Mary' nonsense. He and I had spent a lot of time talking in the past few months. He told me things about what our father had done to him that I didn't know about. He expressed the long-held desire to know about a life outside of our sheltered upbringing. As such, I'd introduced him to the library and the news. I got him as up to date as possible on current events and the holes in his education. He was almost, but not quite, normal.

"What the fuck?" Hunter asked, looking between the two of us.

"Oh," Isaiah said, looking at Hunter for a second before looking at me. "Were you two... in the middle of something?"

"Ew gross," I scrunched up my nose. "You're not ever allowed to imply that, dude."

"Sorry. Still new at the whole sex talk stuff," he shrugged and I knew he had actually come a long way since I left him the porn mag back at the house. He had shown up a week later full of questions and I had steeled my stomach to answer them. Eventually, I had pointed him to a "friend" of mine for some hands-on experience. And by "friend" I meant a hooker I paid to teach him the ropes. It was a fact which I still hadn't told him. Maybe I would in a couple years, when he would find it funny. "So..." he said, looking at Hunter, "you're back."

Hunter nodded. "I'm back."

"This is where I am supposed to be a good big brother and tell you to not break her heart again or I..."

"Break his face," I supplied.

"Right... I break your face. I think we both know that that's not gonna happen, but you know... don't be such a..."

"Dick," I added.

"This time," Isaiah finished, handing me a bound pile of paperwork. "No rush on these," he said, glancing again at Hunter. "You want me to hang out or are you alright?"

I considered it. I could have told him to stay. Maybe Hunter would eventually give up on the whole talking to me thing with my brother around, especially given that he had no idea what had happened between us. But, a bigger part of me knew that there was no deterring Hunter. He was a stubborn jerk when he wanted to be.

"No, I'll be fine. I'll call you about these once I've read them over."

"Alright," he said, nodding stiffly at Hunter. "I'll see you later, Fiona."

"Bye," I called, but he was already out the door. He was still a little lacking in the manners department.

"Fee... what the hell?" Hunter asked, turning back to me with a disbelieving look. At my raised brow, he sighed. "Please, Fee. Can you just... stop hating me for five minutes and talk to me?"

Maybe it was the 'please'; or maybe it was just the tone. But a part of the wall slipped. "Fine," I said, going into my living room. "I went and said my piece to my father. He died a few hours later. Don't," I said, holding up a hand out of habit whenever I told people about my father, "tell me you're sorry. I know it's fucked up, but I'm glad he's dead. But anyway. I went back to my old house and found my old bible filled with letters to me from my mom..."

"That's great, baby," he said, looking down at me as he leaned against the wall. "Did she say anything interesting?"

"A lot actually. But the highlights were: she had been in love before my father; my brother was just as abused as I was though I didn't see it, and that not all men are bad. That last one though," I said, looking at him pointedly, "is still proving to be false."

I won't lie; I took a little pleasure in his wince. "What about you and your brother?"

"He came by while I was in the house. He was wrecked. I left him a dirty magazine and told him to contact me when he wanted to learn about the real world."

"He obviously took you up on that."

"Only after my grandmother died," I said, holding up the pile of paperwork. "She left us her estate. Isaiah needed help figuring it all out. And then once he was around here for a few days, he started to see that he did want this normal kind of life."

"You're really amazing, Fee," he said, shaking his head at me. "To help him like that. That's really big of you." He paused, looking down at the paperwork. "That's a lot of paperwork for some little old lady's estate."

"Yeah, well," I said, smiling down at the paperwork that would tell me that I would never have to worry about money again for my whole life. For two lifetimes. Five maybe. "Grams was loaded. And we were the closest relatives."

"That's really great news," he said, but sounded sad. At my raised brow, he looked down at his feet. "I just... I wish I could have been here for you, to see things finally falling into place for you, to watch you start to heal..."

"You could have been," I reminded him, not caring about the bitterness in my voice.

Hunter rubbed his chin, taking a deep breath, then walked over and sat at the edge of the coffee table in front of me. "Are you going to let me tell you what really happened?" he asked.

"I'm all ears," I said, not quite believing that anything he could say would make up for what he did.

"I never really told you anything about my past because...

well, because it's kind of fucked up..."

"Umm..." I broke in, holding up a hand, "hello?"

He smiled. "Yeah I know, baby. But your past is fucked because of something that happened to you. Mine is fucked because of the things I have done."

"What have you done?" I asked, not sure anything he said could make me think he was as messed up as I was.

"My father, ha," he said, rolling his eyes. "There's really no good way to say this. He owns a lot of businesses. But the only way he funded those businesses was by starting a money loaning business."

"Your father is a loanshark?" I asked, unable to stop myself from laughing at the word.

"I know," he laughed too. "It sounds ridiculous. But it's true."

"So he like... what? Broke peoples' kneecaps when they couldn't pay up?"

"He used to," Hunter nodded and I felt a rock in my belly, starting to understand where this was going. "Until me and my brothers got old enough to pitch in. And by 'pitch in' I mean we fucking loved it, Fee. I loved it. In a sick and twisted way, we were taught to love doing the job."

Which made his anger at that guy on the street that night make a hell of a lot more sense. "Okay. So both of our fathers screwed us up," I said, shrugging, knowing he needed me to not be horrified. And I actually wasn't. Loansharks were necessary in the sleazy underground. Beatings were needed to keep people from welshing on their deals. It all made a sick kind of sense.

"You can't possibly be so calm about this," he said, squinting his eyes at me.

"Hunter," I said, leaning forward. "I grew up with a man who beat and carved into me. I really don't think a little violence is going to shock me." I went to reach out, to reassure him, then remembered I wasn't supposed to do that and let my hand fall down at my side. "So that's it? You had to take off because you didn't want to tell me about your past? That's kinda cheap, Fourteen."

"No, see... you don't just get to leave that lifestyle. And I just ran off one day. I tried to start my own life here. But the day after you left... one of my brothers showed up and dragged me back. My father wasn't... pleased. I got a nice solid beating from my brothers. And then I got a visit from my father the next day. He told me that if I had wanted out, I should have went to him first. But I wasn't allowed to come back until I stayed there for a while. I needed to parade around my busted face, take care of my business, show everyone that my father was letting me go... that I wasn't defying him."

I sat there quietly for a long time after he stopped speaking, not sure if I was going to accept that. True, it seemed completely fabricated and unlikely. But, then again, so did my own past. "So in... three months," I said, making his face snap to mine, "you didn't have access to one phone?" I asked, my eyes on his, begging for some kind of explanation that I could believe in.

He reached out, placing a hand on my knee and I didn't push him away. "My phone got destroyed. I didn't have your number. I was going to write, but I figured that by the time you got it, you would have ripped it up."

"You have a point," I smiled, thinking of how much pleasure I would have taken ripping up his bullshit apologies.

His hand was starting to whisper back and forth over the skin of my thigh, reminding my body of how much it missed it. Him. Being touched. Everything. "So..." he said and I knew how vulnerable he was feeling, like I had felt when I had told him my story.

"So," I said, looking down at his hand, feeling my chest get tighter with my desire. "I am afraid I am going to need proof."

"Proof of what?" he asked, looking up at me.

"Proof about your story," I clarified.

"How the hell am I supposed to do that?" he asked, his hand moving higher on my thigh and I could see his eyes getting heavier.

"You're going to take me to meet this family of yours," I decided and his eyes went wide.

"What? Fee... no."

"I'm afraid it's a deal breaker," I said, standing. "But first," I said, reaching for the bottom of my tank top and pulling it up and over my head. I watched his eyes automatically go up toward my breasts, but stop short.

"You got the tattoo," he said, reaching out to touch the intricate black ink underneath my breasts. He had been right; the scars had completely disappeared. "I wish I could have done it," he said, skimming his hands over the design that was exactly the one he had drawn up himself, "but it came out really great, baby."

His hands slid down my ribs and landed on my hips for a moment before pulling my panties down, letting them drop to the floor, before pulling me forward and planting a kiss right above the scars there. "God, I missed you," he said with a quiet kind of fierceness that made me almost sway on my feet.

My hand went to his hair, stroking it down toward the back of his neck and allowing myself to say something I promised myself I would never say to him. "I missed you too."

I felt his warm breath on my heat and, before I could process what he was doing, his hands were pushing my thighs apart and I felt his tongue find my sensitive clit. My hands slammed down on his shoulders, trying to keep myself standing. "You taste so good," he said before going right back to his torturous exploration.

"Hunter," I groaned, reaching down his back to start pulling his shirt upward.

He pulled backward, planting a line of kisses up my belly, between my breasts, taking my nipple into his mouth and making me cry out when he sank his teeth into it. He stood up slowly, pulling off his shirt and my hands went for his zipper, pulling his pants down desperately. It had been so long and my body had barely gotten a taste of what it had wanted before he left. I needed him. Right then. There.

My hand reached out for his cock, stroking it until he made a growling sound in his throat, reaching for me. "Get on your hands and knees," he told me and I quickly lowered myself down to the floor. I saw him stoop down into his jeans for his wallet, heard the crinkle of the condom wrapper, then felt him move up behind me. His hands went to my hips for a moment and I felt his cock press against my ass. He reached forward, pulling my hair away from my neck so he could see the tattoo he put on me. He twisted my hair in his fist and pulled slightly so I arched up.

"Tell me how much you thought about me," he said, one of his hands slipping between us and bringing his cock to slide between my slick folds.

"Every day. Every other moment," I admitted. "No matter how hard I tried not to, I couldn't help it."

"I thought about you too," he said and I felt his cock slide backward and press against the opening. "And, fuck how I wanted you again. Like this."

Jesus Christ. I needed him inside of me five minutes ago. He was killing me. "I wanted you too." I wanted him more than anything I had ever wanted before.

"Like this?" he asked, plunging forward and burying deep inside me.

"Fuck," I cried out, my hand slamming down on the floor. "Yes."

His hand pulled my hair harder as he started thrusting into me wildly. There was no particular rhythm and my body didn't care. I just needed him. I needed the fullness inside. I needed the friction. My orgasm built quickly, tightening around his cock with each thrust.

"You're so fucking tight," he ground out, slapping my ass hard once.

"Don't stop," I pleaded, pressing my thighs closer together, trying to push my body closer to the climax, trying to feel him as fully as I could.

He pushed harder, each thrust sending my body slightly forward across the floor. "Come for me, Fee," he said, sounding close himself. "I want to feel that pussy grab my cock."

Holy hell. I tried to suck in a breath but my orgasm slammed into me hard, making my breath come out in a strangled yelp.

"Fuck, baby, yeah," he hissed, letting go of my hair and grabbing both my hips, slamming me back against him as he thrust forward. I heard his breath catch and felt his cock slam in fully, twitching slightly as he came deep inside me.

My legs were weak and wobbly from the unexpectedly intense orgasm, and I started to slide slowly down toward the floor. Hunter wrapped his arms around my middle, pulling me up and against his chest.

I looked down at his arms and felt my heart drop slightly. I had spent hours studying his tattoos. There was a family coat of arms on his shoulder; a Dante quote on the inside of his right arm. There were dozens of them I was as familiar with as my own skin. But there was a new tattoo on the inside of his left wrist, running right up over the vein that goes up the arm. It was just about four inches long and already healing.

It was an antique locket key with very familiar filigree and a heart in the top of the key where a rope of chain would fit through.

"Hunter..." I said, not sure what to say; or what to ask.

He looked down over my shoulder, kissing my neck as he did. "Yeah?"

"What is this?" I asked, my fingers reaching to run over the key.

"It looks like a key tattoo," he said.

"It looks like a key tattoo that matches a locket tattoo of mine," I said.

"Mmhmm," he said, resting his face against mine. "I think we both know I am the only one who will ever have the key."

"That is a bit... presumptuous," I said, not quite ready to say it; not sure I would ever be ready to.

Luckily, he saved me from having to do so first. "I love you, Fee," he said simply. "I think I loved you the morning you stormed in and stole all my hammers. I think I have only loved you more each day since then."

There was a strange sensation inside, starting in my stomach and moving up toward my chest. It was something that felt like tightness and lightness at the same time. It felt foreign and yet familiar. It felt like it was something I had been waiting for all my life.

I hope one day, darling, that you will know the touch of a man who loves you. I pray you will know how wonderful it is. How rare and beautiful. How godly. Even if it isn't within the union of marriage. It isn't wrong. Nothing could be more right.

I put my arms over his on my stomach, squeezing as much as the awkward position would allow. "I love you too, Hunter," I admitted, closing my eyes against the rush of feeling. "Even if you did steal my cactus."

TWENTY-THREE

Fiona

"You sure you want to do this?" he asked me for the fourth time since we hit the road. We were already several hours outside of the City and I was staring out the window watching all the new leaves start to break out of their buds on the trees.

"Yup," I said simply. I had been planning on meeting his family since the day he told me about them. At first, because I wanted to validate his story. But as time went by, it was pure curiosity. I wanted to know them: these people who made Hunter who he was. Wonderful. Perfect. And, also... who didn't want to meet a real life friggen loanshark? That sounded like a blast.

We had waited for the winter to pass. We spent those cold days and nights curled up in bed, keeping each other warm, enjoying the blissful cozy feeling that was new love. But spring was well underway and there were no more excuses he could throw at me that I would accept.

I had spent hours agonizing over my wardrobe all the while

Hunter had insisted that the more "me" I looked, the more his family, and especially his mother, would like me. So I had thrown a bunch of mini skirts, tanks, crop tops, and heels in a bag and called it a day. I had slipped into a peach mini skirt with a white and robin's egg blue vertical striped crop top with nude heels for the meeting.

Hunter had nodded at me, took the bags out of my hand, lifted my skirt, shoved me against the wall, and fucked me from behind until my legs were shaking. Then we casually went down the stairs and got in his car.

"Alright," Hunter said, pulling into a bar parking lot and cutting the engine. I eyed the bikes parked out front, chrome and black, suggesting a particular kind of clientele. I sat there for a second fighting the image of Hunter in head to toe leather and studs. "What's so funny?" he asked, looking over at me.

"So..." I said, biting my lip to keep from laughing, "do you own some leather pants I don't know about?"

"Oh, shut up," he said, getting out of the car and walking around to meet me. "You're sure about this? We could just turn around and head back right now," he said, reaching for my hand and pulling it up to kiss it.

"Take me to your mother," I said instead. Hunter sighed and pulled me in through the doors. The inside wasn't what I had been expecting; it was sleek and sophisticated. Several stereotypical bikers sat at the bar and stood around the pool table to the right. Toward the back of the room was a group of tall, dark haired guys that were, unmistakably, Hunter's four other brothers.

"Hunt!" one of them called and the rest turned, four sets of blue eyes on me and I almost took a step back. Almost.

Hunter's hand went to my lower back, firm and steady. I turned my head to him and he smiled down at me. "Out of the frying pan," he said, nodding past his brothers.

"Into the fire," I whispered back, watching his parents break through the group and walk up toward us.

"Mom, Dad," he said, leaning forward to kiss his mother's cheek. "This is Fiona. Fee, these are my parents: Charlie and Helen."

They stared at me for a long minute, his father a glimpse at what Hunter would look like in twenty years and his mother a gorgeous, albeit intimidating woman, in her six inch stilettos and tight black jeans.

The silence stretched on and I glanced from the parents to the brothers. "So," I said, breaking the impossible silence, "if I walk out on my tab tonight..." I saw the knowing smile on Hunter's face while I spoke, "which one of them is gonna break my kneecaps?"

Hunter's father was the first to laugh, reaching out and grabbing me into a hug. "I like this one," he called over his shoulder at Hunter as he pulled me over toward the other Mallick boys. "Alright, this is Ryan, Shane, Eli, and Mark. Boys," he said, tightening his arm around my shoulders, "this is Hunt's new girl. He's gonna be the first one of you worthless lot to get me a grand baby."

"Dad," Hunter warned.

"I got it, Hunter," I called back, beaming up at his father.

Maybe I had never given motherhood any thought before. It always seemed like an impossible goal, seeing as getting pregnant generally meant I needed to get naked around someone and before Hunter, that was not even an option. But I wasn't going to lie, I had been giving it a little thought since Hunter and I had mended bridges. Perhaps you could blame my mother's letters: to finally feel that connection with her without the threat of my father finding out. I would like the chance to pay that forward; to break the cycle. I wanted to raise kids in security and comfort and warmth. And love. Oh, the love. Especially with someone as giving and good as Hunter.

"Give it a few years," I said close to his father's ear and he chuckled, nodding down at me.

"Need the honeymoon phase. I get it. When I met that woman," he said, looking over at his wife with a look of wonder and pride... even after all their time together, "I didn't let her out of arm's reach for five years before I got her with Ryan."

The brothers groaned, rolling their eyes, and I laughed. "So," I said, turning to all the Hunter look-a-likes, "which one of you is Shane?" I asked and watched as they all tilted their heads to the biggest of them.

"'Sup Fiona?" he asked, inclining his head at me.

I looked back at Hunter's father then stepped out of his arms, closed the few feet between us, and slapped Shane as hard as my much smaller frame would allow across the face. The other brothers' eyes went wide, then they laughed as did their father. "Don't even act like you didn't have that coming," I said.

He reached up, rubbing the skin on his cheek that had turned a satisfying shade of red. "Yeah, I guess I did."

"Damn straight you did," I agreed, not stepping back though I had to crane my head up to speak to him. "And if you ever feel like some stupid fucking sibling rivalry gives you the right to play God in his, in our, lives... then you'll be answering to me."

"You better listen to her," Helen said, coming up on the other side of me. "I hear she is pretty ruthless with a knife."

My eyes went to Hunter who looked as every bit as guilty as he was. "Sorry Sixteen," he said, rubbing the back of his neck.

"So, Fiona," Ryan broke in, "what do you do?"

I felt myself smiling and Hunter held his hands up as if letting me know he hadn't told anyone. Good. He saved the juicy bits for me to share. "I'm a small business owner," I hedged.

"What business?" his father asked, looking curious, being a businessman himself.

"Phone sex," I said matter-of-factually and one of the brothers, Eli, who had been drinking a beer, choked on it. "And let's say... supplies for certain fetishists."

"What kind of fetishists?" Shane asked, smirking.

"Panty sniffers."

Helen was the first to laugh. "Oh, Fiona," she said, putting an arm through mine. "I think you and I are going to get along perfectly. Why don't we take a little walk? Get away from all these men for a while..."

"Sounds good," I said, letting her lead me out the side door and into the back lot where there were a few old picnic tables. "So, Fiona," she said, letting my arm go.

"Is this the part where you ask me my intentions toward your son?" I asked, climbing up on the top of the picnic table. "It would be only fitting. My brother attempted to do the same kind of thing."

"Actually, no," she said, sitting down next to me. "I am more curious about why you are here."

"To... meet all of you?" I said, turning my head to look at her.

"Right," she agreed, looking off toward the bar. "But why? I'm sure Hunt told you what he was running from... what happened when Shane brought him back."

"Yeah," I agreed. "Did Hunter tell you about my family?"

"Yeah, honey," she said and I fought the urge to tell her not to feel sorry for me.

"Well... you guys might not be perfect, but I think you all really care about each other. I just... I don't know. I wanted him to keep in touch with you. And I wanted to meet you myself."

"For any particular reason?" she asked and I had the feeling she knew what I was getting at. Even though that was impossible.

"Yeah," I said, smiling at her. "I just needed to make sure first."

"So we passed the test?"

"So far, so good," I agreed.

"What is the plan from here?" she asked.

—

"This is your place?" I asked as we climbed the steep stairs up the side of my building. Anyone below could see right up my skirt. I tried not to focus too hard on that fact as my heels kept getting stuck in the grates.

"Yeah," he said, opening the door and flicking the light on.

"It's very... you," I said, looking around. If things worked out like I planned, we would be spending quite a bit of time there.

"You're... off," Hunter said, dropping my luggage off next to the bookshelves. "Everything alright? We can leave if you need to."

"No, actually," I said, turning back to him. "I want to talk to you about something."

"Alright," he said, looking terrified. "What's up, Fee?"

I walked over toward his table and sat down, resting my arms on the top. "I have an idea."

"Spit it out, baby. You're killing me here," he said, resting his hands on the back of the chair across from me.

"Well, first. Let me ask you something. Why are you in the City?"

"That's a stupid question," he said, rolling his eyes. "For you."

"No other reason?"

"No."

"Okay. So if... I didn't want to live in the City anymore..."

"We can go anywhere you want to go, baby."

"Good," I said, looking around his apartment. Soon to be *our* apartment. "I want to move here."

"What?" he asked, looking down at me like I had just said the most ridiculous thing he had ever heard.

"I want to move here. I want to leave the City and come here. Be by your family. You can open a tattoo shop. I can open... something to keep me busy."

"Are you crazy?" he asked, laughing humorlessly and sitting down.

"Maybe," I smiled, shrugging. "Look, Hunter... I don't have much family left. You have this huge gaggle of people here who love you and want you to do well..."

"Fee, have you forgotten that they beat people up for a living?"

"I sell my dirty underwear for money I don't need," I laughed. "None of us are saints, Hunter."

A part of me had expected him to jump at the opportunity. Now that he didn't have to work with them, I figured he would want to be around them in his more independent capacity. And yet he was acting as if I had suggested we go live in my old childhood home.

"Have you really given this thought?" he asked after a few minutes.

"Yeah," I said, getting up and wrapping my arms around him. "I talked to your mom about it too."

"What?" he asked, his brows drawing together.

"Well I needed to work some things out logistically. You'll keep a thirty-percent share of the liquor store. And your tattoo shop will be completely your own thing. They won't have any part in that. We can live here for a while," I said, gesturing out into the apartment. "Until we decide on something more... house-like."

"A house, huh?" he asked, wrapping his arms around my

ass. "You feeling an urge to nest, Sixteen?"

"I did sort of promise your father a grand baby."

"Oh, did you now?" Hunter smiled, leaning down to plant a kiss on my lips.

"Mmhmm," I said, resting my face against his chest. "I told him to give us a couple years."

"Good plan," he said, squeezing my ass. "But you know..."

"Hmm?"

"We really should probably practice making one. Just so when we are ready, we do it right."

I smiled, tilting my head up to him. "That's probably for the best."

"I love you, Fee," he said and my insides did a little flip-flop. I hoped I never got used to hearing that.

"I love you too, Hunter."

EPILOGUE

Fiona

I walked into Chaz's bar with an arm full of take-out food and a bursting baby bag. All of the Mallick men were congregating in a circle on the floor around a little black-haired, green-eyed two year old. Her hair was braided down the back even though I had left it wild when I had dropped her off. I wondered which one of the huge, hulking men had fumbled with her delicate baby hair to get it so perfect.

Becca sat in the center of their little circle in her bright pink sundress with her little plastic tea set all around her. She had all the Mallick men eating out of the palm of her pudgy hand and she knew it.

"Mama!" she yelled, pushing herself up off the floor and rushing over toward me, toppling forward and all five of the men yelped and lunged to try to break her fall.

"She's fine," I said, shaking my head at them. "You can't protect her from every scrape and bruise."

"Hell we can't!" Shane insisted, scooping her up off the floor and booping her nose.

"Help me out here, Helen," I said, looking over at her as she walked up, shaking her head.

"Girl, give it up. This is the first Mallick girl in five generations. She's going to be spoiled rotten."

"One of you needs to find yourself a girl," I said, trading Shane the food for my daughter, "and make some new babies for this family to fawn over."

"Hey she's two now," Hunter's dad said, nodding his head at me. "I think it's time for her to get a little brother or sister."

I laughed, rubbing a smudge of purple icing off her cheek. Someone had given her sweets before dinner. Again. There really was no talking to them. "Daddy?" she asked.

"He's coming from work," I said, putting her down and patting her bottom as she took off toward the closest of her uncles.

I stood back and watched my new family mull around. Helen was taking the food out of the to-go bags and piling it on the table. Shane and Eli were grabbing beers. Mark was talking to his father. And Ryan was tossing Becca up and down in the air above his head, making her shriek and giggle.

It was hard to believe that just over three years had passed since I was living in the city, alone and afraid to get too close to anyone. I was completely consumed by my past, cutting into my skin, and drinking myself silly every night. And that was okay. At the time, that seemed like the best I could get. And, coming from what I came from, it was pretty damn good.

Sometimes it's crazy how much can change when just one thing changes.

Hunter. Hunter came into my life and changed everything.

As if I had called him, he came in through the door, moving beside me and wrapping an arm around my waist. We stood there silently a long time, watching everyone.

Just over three years ago, Hunter was running like hell away from these people. And yet there we were: all together. One big, happy, crazy, dysfunctional family of loansharks, and phone sex operators, and tattoo artists.

"Daddy!" Becca yelled, trying to wiggle down out of Ryan's arms and he fumbled to catch her as she started to fall. That was my daughter, completely unconcerned with danger and consequences.

Next to me, Hunter stooped down and grabbed her, settling her on his hip and leaning back into me.

"Funny how things change, isn't it?" I asked him, laying my head on his shoulder.

Who would have thought that fucked up little Fiona Meyers would have a family and a husband and a perfect little baby? All those years that I had believed in my uselessness, my brokenness... all those years I punished myself for things that had been out of my control. All those years of pain and misery so deep I could fucking swim in it. All of that had somehow led me to this.

I still had my phone sex business. But I wasn't the one taking calls anymore. No, I had an office in town with little cubicles and I employed other women who needed a leg up in life. I trained them. I offered them the tricks of the trade. I paid them well. I helped them up get up in their feet because it would have been nice to have had that help when I was struggling on the streets; when I had no where to turn. Maybe it wasn't the kind of community service the bible and the church suggested we should do to help our neighbors, but it was doing good. It was giving back for all the amazing things I had gotten out of my life.

Hunter worked in his tattoo shop, kept busy with all the biker traffic and his own brothers. He was happy there, his little tattoo gun buzzing in his hands. He did one weekend a month of free tattoos to cover scars. It was a tribute to me and the tattoo he had given me to hide the "wicked" I had been living with for fourteen years. We had spent endless hours looking at images online, trying to find the right cover up. Eventually we had decided on a floral and vine design that wrapped around my body, dipping low down toward my groin then sneaking up toward my hipbones and around my lower back. It looked like panties. Like super fancy underwear.

I thought it had a fun sort of irony.

"I wanna see Pop Pop," Becca grumbled and Hunter put her down on the ground.

I watched her barrel away. Our little energizer bunny; always on the run.

"Hey, Fourteen," I said, wrapping my arms around him.

"Yeah, Sixteen?" he said, burying his face in the hair at my neck. We were good at that. We were so good at being in love it made me sick. Even after years. Even after a baby that sucked all of our energy. Even bone deep exhausted, we loved so deeply it was almost painful.

"You know that spare room of ours?" I started, smiling because he couldn't see me.

"Yeah?"

"I think it's time to get some new furniture for it."

"Okay..." he said, sounding confused.

"Yeah," I said, pulling back slightly so I could look in his face. "You have about... eight more months to build a nice nursery set."

He stared at me uncomprehending for a moment before breaking into a huge, dopey smile. "Oh yeah?"

"Yeah," I smiled back. I had known the next morning; like I had known with Becca. The morning after brought on a wave of nausea that could only be explained by one medical condition. I waited to tell him, just to make sure. Just in case. But five weeks in, there was no denying it. I was gonna be a big fat pregnant lady again.

Hunter leaned forward and kissed me until my toes tingled, then squeezed me tight, lifting me up off my feet. "That's great, Fee. You're amazing."

"Daddy is kissing Mommy," Becca declared, her baby voice high pitched and everyone turned to look.

"Damn straight," Charlie nodded, planting a kiss on Helen's cheek.

"Pop Pop said 'damn'," Becca yelled and everyone laughed.

It really was too much to ask in that family to have a kid that didn't repeat cuss words. If I could keep the word 'fuck' out of her mouth until she was at least fourteen, it would be a miracle.

"I think Mommy and Daddy have something they want to tell all of us," Helen announced, looking at me with knowing eyes. The woman was downright freaky with how she knew things sometimes. Maybe it was just because she herself had been pregnant five times. Maybe she picked up on how green I looked some mornings; on how my nose spread ever so slightly. She was the kind of person who would pick up on small things like that.

"Oh yeah?" Charlie asked, smiling. "Big news?"

I looked at Hunter and he nudged me. "You tell them," he whispered.

"I'm pregnant," I said loudly.

There was a short silence before the yelling began, making Becca jump and then clap at the commotion, not knowing what it was about, but excited nonetheless.

"See?" Charlie asked, slapping Ryan hard enough on the back of the neck to make him stumble two steps forward. "Grand babies," he yelled. He walked over to us, the scariest, most intimidating man I had ever met, with a huge happy grin on his face as he pulled me out of his son's arms and enveloped me in a bear hug, spinning me around.

"Babe," Helen called, stepping closer and putting a hand on his shoulder, "she's going to puke all over you if you keep doing that."

"Nonsense," he declared, but set me on my feet. "You had five boys and were never sick one time. Oh," he said, smiling fondly at Becca, "maybe that means we are getting another little girl."

I silently agreed with him. I thought it was another girl. But, I mean, you can never really know. Not for a couple more months anyway.

"My daughters are never going to be able to date, are they?" I asked, looking around at all the men they would have in their lives to love and protect them and feeling so incredibly grateful that my heart hurt. My daughters would have so much more than I did. They would never grow up thinking men were raging rivers. They would never have to worry about keeping their heads above water.

"Hell no," Shane said, scrunching up his face in disgust. "No one would ever be worthy."

"That's probably true," Hunter agreed, walking up behind me and putting his hands on my belly.

I realized right then, as I had many times before, that what I had was the life my mother had wanted for me. I had a good man. Actually, I had seven good men around me. I had the touch of someone who loved me. And it was rare and beautiful and godly. And I had my perfect daughter, my perfect future children. I had the chance to break the cycle.

"Love you, Fee," Hunter said against my ear.

"I love you too," I said, putting my hands on top of his. "Even though you stole my cactus." And he laughed, squeezing me tighter at our little inside joke.

xx

DON'T FORGET

If you enjoyed this book, go ahead and hop onto Goodreads or Amazon and tell me your favorite parts. You can also spread the word by recommending the book to friends or sending digital copies that can be received via kindle or kindle app on any device.

ALSO BY JESSICA GADZIALA

The Henchmen MC

Reign

Cash

Wolf

Repo

Duke

Renny

The Savages

Monster

Killer

Savior

--

DEBT

For A Good Time, Call...

Shane

FOR A GOOD TIME, CALL...

The Sex Surrogate

Dr. Chase Hudson

Dissent

Into The Green

What The Heart Needs

What The Heart Wants

What The Heart Finds

What The Heart Knows

The Stars Landing Deviant

Dark Mysteries

367 Days

Stuffed: A Thanksgiving Romance

Dark Secrets

Unwrapped

Ryan

ABOUT THE AUTHOR

Jessica Gadziala is a full-time writer, parrot enthusiast, and coffee drinker from New Jersey. She enjoys short rides to the book store, sad songs, and cold weather.

She is very active on Goodreads, Facebook, as well as her personal groups on those sites. Join in. She's friendly.

STALK HER

Connect with Jessica:

Facebook: https://www.facebook.com/JessicaGadziala/
Facebook Group: https://www.facebook.com/groups/314540025563403/

Goodreads: https://www.goodreads.com/author/show/13800950.Jessica_Gadziala
Goodreads Group: https://www.goodreads.com/group/show/177944-jessica-gadziala-books-and-bullsh

Twitter: @JessicaGadziala

JessicaGadziala.com

<3/ Jessica

FOR A GOOD TIME, CALL...